'Through the Woods'

by Troy Blackford

© 2012 by Troy Blackford

This 2nd Edition © 2013 by Troy Blackford

All Rights Reserved. No portion of this content may be reproduced, publically performed, or otherwise disseminated without the written permission of the author. Any resemblance of content contained within to persons or events is entirely coincidental.

Cover, layout, design © 2013 by Troy Blackford

http://www.troyblackford.com

Also by Troy Blackford:

First There Wasn't, Then There Was
Flotsam
Booster & Reeves: The Night of the Revenants
Strange Way Out
For Those With Eyes to See
Emergent Pattern
Through the Woods
Critical Incident

For Liske and Lianne
For believing in me
And for Smudgy and Rayne
For believing in them

Special Thanks to:

Antonios Poppos for Extreme Help
Dave Conrad (for De-rouging the terrorists)
& Kent Peterson (for Clarifying the Timeline)

ONE

After a winding two hour drive through the woods, Ben had arrived. "STAY OUT!" read the weather-beaten sign clinging to the gate. "By order of MINNESOTA STATE FORESTRY COMMISSION!" He shook his head, an excited smile playing on his face. An innocent hiker who opted to ignore that innocuous warning and straggled over the fence would, within minutes, have serious problems with folks possessing a bit more clout than had yet been granted to any state forestry commission.

Ben reached up and pressed a button on what looked like an ordinary garage door opener clipped to the driver side sun visor. The fence swung open with a clatter, and he pulled through. 'Second day on the job,' he thought, 'and I'm already working the secret gate like a pro.' He still had a ten mile drive ahead of him, and another gate check once he got closer in. He tried to relax: his own car was on file. If even half of the dark hints intimated to him upon his hiring about what would happen to an unknown occupant of an unregistered car driving onto Agency land were true, that was the only thing saving Ben's life right now.

"The Agency," he said, under his breath, as squirrels, disturbed by the car, leapt from branch to branch above.

He spoke the name in tones of reverence. Ben still couldn't believe that he had the job. To be hired after such a smooth application process, right out of school, into *the Agency*. His dream job. Almost too good to be true.

Everything after his hiring seemed to happen in a bubble of unreality. Not just from the sustained giddiness of nailing his best-case employment scenario, thought that of course played a role. A lot about the Agency was unreal. Ben's new employer worked in a very specialized area, one so bizarre that he might never grow used to it.

As far as the public knew, the state of Minnesota had dedicated this massive block of the Chippewa National Forest to the 'Colburn Forestry Preserve Project' since the early sixties. The government permitted no airplane to fly over it, no member of the public to enter it, and rigidly enforced all the restrictions common to a wildlife preserve, raising a fence of rules and regulations.

People had long since grown used to these stipulations. In the great forested region of upstate Minnesota, such state preserves were common. The public had lost all interest in the region. As such, they would have been shocked at all the enhanced security they would encounter if the more daring among them had tried getting in for a look around at all the pristine wilderness.

When it came to what really went on inside the Coburn Forestry Preserve Project, the need for secrecy had never been greater. Deep inside the expanse of trees, the Agency – perhaps the most guarded of all the secretive arms of the government – ran a sprawling research center exploring the frontiers of the impossible. At least six unbelievable projects were being run at any given time. The point of the Agency was to explore the limits of the unlikely. As such, the Agency's research laboratories were the least predictable place to work in the country.

Ben whistled to himself. When he knew with certainty that the Agency job would be his, he attempted to prepare himself mentally – as best he could, at least – for the kinds of national security secrets he would soon become privy to. Ultimately, all his efforts were in vain. The strange world of the National Unexpected Countermeasure & Preparedness Agency – NUCPA – made for the most shocking transition from student living to the working life anyone could imagine.

* * *

The higher ups had impressed upon Ben from the start that, as an entry-level employee, he would need to know very, *very* little about what went on at the facility. He over the following weeks he would, in fact, learn only the most rudimentary things about the handful of projects he might be working on at a given time. His work touched upon very sensitive national-security concerns, and the less Ben knew, he was assured, the better.

Even at the end of his first couple months, Ben had only worked directly on three projects, and possessed only the most basic grasp of what they entailed. The first had to do with a particular type of lens for a new kind of sensor – he once overheard one of the high-level scientists calling it 'hyperluxonic,' before being hushed by a co-worker. The other two, he knew even less about.

It was Ben's job to deal with the suppliers – either well-known companies doing occasional military work while operating under strict non-disclosure agreements, or completely unheard of outfits that existed only to supply classified technology to the government. Early on, Ben was tasked with obtaining parts for a mechanism employed by low-earth orbit satellites. What these satellites were for, he did not know. He was responsible only for components destined for the thruster mechanism – and even those came from a list given to him by someone higher up, who actually understood the stuff.

Ben may have been 'just a parts guy,' but that was as big of a role as the lower-level people ever played the NUCPA labs. Being part – even just a small, anonymous part – of something big, secretive, cutting-edge made Ben feel special, even if he didn't understand the ultimate result of his efforts. The pay was respectable, the work *interesting*, to say the least, despite not usually knowing exactly what it was he was doing.

Ben found his job to be every bit as engaging and rewarding as he had hoped, and as he pulled his battered Chevrolet Monte Carlo down into the natural-looking 'cave' that housed the lab's subterranean parking lot, ready for the first day of his second month of work, he looked forward to an orientation briefing. He had been told by his boss that he should expect to start work on a new project today.

All Ben knew in advance was that, unlike his previous posts, this one had something to do with genetics.

*   *   *

A different field of focus meant different sorts of work. The materials for this project would be coming from different suppliers, for one thing. Sharp and Samsung might make systems-on-a-chip and flexible OLED displays, but they didn't make gene sequencers, catalysts, sell *e. coli* stock, and so on. Ben felt excited to get his feet wet in supply chains for an entirely different industry, and see what kind of lingo he might start picking up.

He had even read the Wikipedia page on basic biology the night before in anticipation of his duties. Which was why, when he first began pouring over his notes, he was surprised to find that he would need to contract with local (the closest business of any kind was a full fifty-six miles from the lab, so the term 'local' was relative) pet stores, in order to obtain two gross of non-lab rats.

"Why the specification for 'non-lab' rats?" he asked his supervisor, a squat, brusque fellow named Rick Hathaway.

"Because," the burly man responded, his voice husky and his eyebrow furrowed, "ordering lab rats signals 'bio-research' to the bean-counters. That sort of thing needs to be cleared. Form after form of bio-ethics and genetic purity affidavits and certifications about stuff that doesn't matter for the work we're going to be doing. What they plan on testing won't need the kind of biological analysis that lab rats are commonly used for, so going through a normal supplier for normal lab rats would set off a chain of unnecessary paperwork that would slow us down and add a ton of extra costs to the project."

Ben's boss savored the confused look on Ben's face.

"It gets complicated, but basically if we use 'lab certified rats,' we have to jump through piles of paper hoops. But we don't *need* lab certified rats. We aren't *researching* the damn rats, and so if we go through a local supplier, we side-step all the form B.S. and get straight down to business."

Ben had to admire his boss's thinking, even if he couldn't follow the line of thought exactly. Ben was getting used to not understanding what exactly it was he was doing – it would be his *modus operandi* at the Agency for years to come, until he got into a position where he would actually know more about what went on here.

If he was ever that lucky.

"So if we're not researching them, why do we need them?" Ben asked, regretting his inquisitiveness a moment after he spoke.

"Cuz it's what you're gonna do, Ben." Hathaway said, forcing a smile. "Just like everything else around here: you do it 'cuz we're asking you to."

"Gotchya, boss," a sheepish Ben replied. "I knew better than to ask. Just slipped out."

"Good guy," his boss patted his shoulder. "You're doing fine. Takes some folks three solid months to learn not to ask questions."

As Hathaway scuttled out of Ben's cubical, the papers on Ben's desk rustled with the wind he created.

Okay, so they needed to get some rats in here. No issues there. Ben could handle that. Other things were a little more specific.

"Ocean fish? What the hell is an 'ocean fish?'" Ben asked himself.

He had been pouring over a long list of chemical compounds with names like phenylalanine and tyrosine, interspersed with awkward terms like 'ocean fish' and 'extruded goat protein,' before he realized he was looking at a list of separate ingredients. He googled a few of the terms together.

Top result: *Cat food*. What the hell?

Just as he began to scratch his chin, a window popped up on his screen.

'You're curious. That's bad. I thought we just talked about this?' read the instant message from his boss.

"*Dammit!*" Ben said under his breath. He was an idiot to forget his computer workstation was probably being monitored at all times.

He didn't know what else to say, so he just typed back: "One question: what the hell is 'ocean fish?'"

'LOL,' read the reply. Ben couldn't imagine Hathaway 'lolling.' 'It's what they call all the unknown shit they catch in their deep-sea nets that looks at all fleshy, so they can still use it for something. They sell it as pet food.'

'OK, I'm done with questions,' Ben replied.

'Doesn't matter so much what you say. We'll watch what you actually do, and base our opinion on that.'

The chat window closed. Ben breathed in sharply through his teeth.

He wasn't a kid anymore. He was sitting here in an office on a Top Secret government facility, possibly serving 'at the pleasure of the president' for all he knew, and if he wanted to know what the hell you got when you combined 'ocean fish' and 'Threonine' from here on out, he would have to wait to check until he got home.

*   *   *

"So this is some kind of... *theater*?"

Ben was having an increasingly hard time containing his questions. This time, however, his inquisitiveness was appropriate: *he* would be in charge of making sure this... whatever it was – was put together properly.

"Of a sort, of a sort."

Hathaway had sounded distracted to Ben all day long, and as they went over the final checklist of supplies for the day's work, this effect became more pronounced.

"God, I'll tell you: I'll be glad when this is all set up. These facility switchovers absolutely kill me."

"Safe to tell me what this was before?" Ben asked, looking around the massive, empty chamber.

"Some kind of echo thing for sound waves." His face wore a blank expression as Ben searched it for meaning. "Yeah, that's right kid. They don't even tell me everything."

Hathaway laughed. "I'm glad I seem important to you, because that's about all the goddamn sense of importance I got in life."

He pulled out his e-cigarette case and went through the motions of 'hiding' his puff. Ben thought that was hilarious.

"Anyway," Hathaway continued, trying to hide the light wisps of nicotine vapor as they came out with his syllables, "Yeah, it sort of *is* a theater. The plexi-people are going to be in here tomorrow and those grooves in the floor are going to be slotted with five-inch thick panels. See through, water resistant, *yadda, yadda*."

He whistled, shook his head, and took a slightly less concealed drag of his e-cig.

"Good *gawd*, the forms I have to fill out when they come in here with those *fragging* forklift things. God-effing-damn. Half the time they have to take the whole wall out to fit their equipment in. Then they just build it right up again. Damndest thing."

Ben felt on edge, full of butterflies. He had wanted this job at the Agency for pretty much one reason: he wanted to be *in* on that Top Secret stuff. He wanted to know: *what did we really know?* The ultra-secret, not-on-the-books 'Agency' was one of the few organizations in the government who had full access to everything.

All the 'known knowns,' sure. But all of the known *unknowns*, too. And, unlike almost any other arm of the government, the 'Agency' had as much info on the unknown-unknowns – or 'Code Ws' – as was, well, *known*. Ben had an elaborate fantasy that on his first day he would learn that the moon landing *was*, in fact, faked; that North Korea had been nothing more than a CIA experiment meant to expand the fear of the 'Red Menace'; possibly even that Brian Williams was a cyborg created to disseminate disinformation to the American public.

Nothing like that had happened – not at first. Fantasy had given way to reality. The imagined intrigue he had basked in upon getting his acceptance letter wasn't, however, entirely fanciful. It just took a while for the truth to begin to emerge through the cracks.

"Anyway," Hathaway went on. "Looks like we're all set here. You got those field sensor things rigged up?"

Ben checked his tablet.

"Yep. Says they're online *here*, anyway."

He pressed a few onscreen buttons and the nearer of the two sensors – a thing that looked like an elementary school photographer's lighting umbrella on picture day – flashed blue and proceeded to emit a series of loud cracking sounds. Ben rushed to press the button again, and the sound and lights ceased.

"Looks like an 'all clear' to me," said Hathaway, wiping his forehead with the back of his hand. "Pretty slick, Ben. I'd say that's a day's work."

Ben looked at the grooves in the floor, where crews would be installing the Plexiglas sheets.

"When are they going to put the barriers in?"

"In the night, in about five hours," a weary Hathaway responded. "I got to be here all night. Goddamn thing sucks." He looked off into the distance, then seemed to come back to himself. "You run along now. You got a long drive. Tomorrow's going to be a big day around here and I'm going to need your help. I'm already beat."

"Will I *ever* have a clue what's going on around here?" Ben asked, instantly regretting his repeatedly loose lips.

Hathaway just laughed.

"You naïve little bastard! I've been here fifteen years and I still don't know what's going on. Not knowing's 'an *Agency* thing.' That's what we like to say."

Ben smiled, shutting the door behind him as he left.

Two

'The Agency' was the organization's only permitted reference to itself, all that could be written, spoken, or electronically transmitted in unclassified communications. No external documents could mention its full name. Public records show that there *is* a federal branch named the 'National Unexpected Countermeasure & Preparedness Agency,' yet there was no indication that the facility contained in the depths of the 'Colburn Forestry Preserve' was connected to it in any way.

Some secrets aren't just soft secrets, but chillingly *hard* secrets. People's darkest fears run along the lines that there are strange things the government keeps under wraps because the 'public would be shocked.' Most believe that these things are secret because civilization would break down if it learned that, say, aliens exist.

The real reason these things are secret is less comforting.

* * *

Let's assume, for example, that a band of rogue terrorists have no idea that a certain type of sulfide can change the spin of every electron in a human being's brain, and, from a distance, instantly erase their minds. Not only do they not know how to perform this strange feat, these terrorists haven't got the slightest clue it might be possible

This is the second most ideal configuration of possibilities. Less optimal arrangements exist. Enemy factions could become aware of this effect before we did. Worse still, they could already have implemented their knowledge into a working mechanism.

The most desirable arrangement is one in which the opposition does not know this terrible, inexplicable thing is possible, but we have mastered it.

Seeking always to secure that most optimal configuration is the mission of the National Unexpected Countermeasure & Preparedness Agency.

*   *   *

"It isn't silly until we say it is" – that's the NUCPA motto. Unbeknownst to the world, some of the best scientists in the world, from the tops of every discipline you can imagine, had been toiling away under the Agency's auspices for decades: proving, disproving, cataloging, or confirming phenomenon ranging from the abstract to the absurd. What success they've had, and with which experiments, isn't entirely clear even to high ranking officials within the group itself.

Only one thing was clear to all involved: once you had clearance to get into the facility, you were effectively operating in a different world from the one occupied by the rest of humanity.

As Ben was about to find out, the NUCPA headquarters was a place where the unimaginable proved commonplace.

Three

"How's the amino acid balance on that?" Hathaway asked.

Ben scrolled through the spreadsheet on his tablet, but he wasn't really looking. He didn't have to. He knew full well that the balance was optimal to within one one-hundredth of a one-hundredth of a percent. That wasn't really why Hathaway was asking, and Ben knew it.

"Looks good, boss," Ben replied. "We're in good shape here."

"*We* are, sure," Hathaway twisted his torso, going through the motions of hiding his compulsive eCig drag. "*We're* goddamn fine. You're good at what you do."

He sat down hard on the revolving office chair and stared into his lap.

"But the fact is, what you and I do is fill racks and build walls. I'm worried about the researchers. Some of them don't know what they're even *trying* to do." He coughed out a clear haze of e-nicotine. "This… *this* is the tricky part," he said, rubbing between his eyes.

"Now that we've got the cat food ready, we finally get to the tricky part?" Ben asked.

He couldn't imagine what his boss felt so nervous about. Hathaway snorted dismissively.

"We'll see how you feel after you get your first *real* glimpse of 'Agency' life." He shook his head. "This stuff isn't secret because it makes it easier to sleep at night, son. I'll tell you that much."

* * *

The first thing Ben did upon arriving at work the next day was oversee the delivery of a peculiar shipment: ten 'fully-enclosed hog farm containment units.' Apparently, that was a thing. Minutes later, on schedule, two separate crews came to install the bulky things on the roof of the facility – one crew piecing the structures together, the other handling the electric wiring. A series of ten black, plastic tubes descended from these pens, which were then routed through piping into the plexi-glassed chamber inside. They looked, to Ben, like large versions of the pneumatic tubes at a bank drive-up window.

Ben tried to piece things together in his head. *Genetic testing. Homemade cat food. Non-lab rats. Five-inch thick Plexiglas sheets. Mega-hog farm enclosures.* Despite what he liked to think of as an imaginative nature, he couldn't come up with any element that linked these things.

* * *

"Hey-ya, Ben." Hathaway said, rubbing his palms together in a 'let's get to work' gesture.

Ben couldn't understand it. His boss, so nervous the night before, seemed pretty chipper for a chap who had just pulled an all-nighter.

"So, did the rat people come through yet, or what? Or *what*?" he asked, laughing.

Ben took an unconscious step backwards.

"We have uh… procured the required amount, in the rat regard, sir." Ben responded, still wary.

"Need some more damn coffee. Haven't had any since I ran out."

Hathaway reached compulsively for the e-cigarette case in his shirt pocket, saw Ben's bemused smile, dropped his hand.

"So, the rat folks worked out. Good."

Ben glossed over the awkward pause by running down his checklist.

"We have the dry mixes, representing each of the major protein groups, loaded into the dispersal system, with a verified balance of aminoes in every one. Meticulously checked by yours truly – in triplicate."

Hathaway bowed slightly.

"A credit to your nation, kid. Go on."

Ben took a deep breath and started ticking things off his fingers.

"Feed, check. The enclosures are set up and tested: fully operational and locked in automated mode." He gestured at the ceiling, and his finger traced a line down the walls as he spoke. "We have the delivery system in place, feeding into the auto-enclosures."

"A damn fine job you've done, champ. I told the honchos you'd be up for the task. This is where you and I take a break for a minute while the coats come in and double check everything a third and fourth time."

Ben's face crumpled in confusion.

"Coats?"

"Scientists, kid." Hathaway looked at him. "These folks in long white lab coats who go over everything with doodads to make sure it's up to spec. Your job is to get the stuff here. Mine is to make sure it's up to code. Then, the coats go in and make sure it's up to *spec*, whatever that means."

The burly man laughed.

"Then, they do whatever it is they're trying to do in the first place. Our job, important though it might be, is just the beginning. And we aren't really anything but help to the scientists, if that makes any sense."

Ben thought it did.

"That's why we never really know what's going on around here. Not *really*, I mean. We're just doing what we're told."

Hathaway nodded, slurping his e-cigarette.

"But kid: that's all anybody anywhere is ever doing. Don't let anyone ever tell you any different."

Ben wasn't sure he agreed, but he could see why Hathaway thought so.

"So what exactly are the, er… *coats* going to need from us once they get here?"

Hathaway shrugged, throwing up his hands.

"They tell ya that stuff when they show up. Sometimes you can even sort of tell what it's for."

He laughed for a moment, but then his face grew serious.

"I think something a bit weirder'll be going on in here than echoing sound waves, this time." He coughed wetly. "But that's just a gut feeling talking."

* * *

Ben and Hathaway rounded the corner of the outside wall, heading to the newly installed 'hog enclosures' on the roof. Ben gasped in surprise at the rapidity with which the scene had been altered. A metal scaffold, affixed to the side of the building and rising high above the small field surrounding the facility, had been erected – without Ben's knowledge – sometime in the last couple of hours. Crisscrossing stairways led up to a platform, where a second set of stairs gave access to the roof thirty feet above. There, the hog-farm enclosures sat, each feeding into one of the delivery chutes that lead back inside the lab.

"What the hell all that going to be? I didn't see forms for *any* of this!" Ben sounded agog.

He didn't think the stuff was going to be installed on the *roof*. He had got the sign-off for the enclosures, he realized, without ever having a clue as to *where* the things had been set up.

Hathaway laughed.

"It's a sort of nursery, from what I understand. Exciting, huh?"

A pair of crewmembers came down the stairway empty-handed while another pair walked up carrying girders and large pre-fab pieces between them, moving in a circulatory rhythm.

"Trust me: you'll get forms aplenty this afternoon. Once this gets built up, they'll need you to fill it with stuff."

"Can't wait to see the inventory requests for this one," Ben remarked. "Perhaps there will be a ball of yarn or two on there," he blurted.

Hathaway shot him a look.

"Keep running your mouth, kid," he said, keeping his voice playful, "and you might see a request for a new acquisitions and inventory guy in with your forms."

He pulled on his e-cig, not bothering to hide its blue flashing tip, and the familiar ritual seemed to lighten his mood.

"You got more theories than a guy running a UFO site, kid. Swear to *gawd*."

*   *   *

"OK, we're going to need you and *you,* yeah – sorry," said an older woman with long, yellow hair and wearing a white lab jacket that went down past her knees, briskly addressing a line of workers. "Yeah, if you could move that to the left of the red line. Great, thanks."

So, these were the 'coats?' Ben felt a sense of surreal excitement again for the first time in weeks.

Standing over his boss's shoulder, he viewed the proceedings. Amongst the so-called 'coats,' a fair-haired, middle-aged woman seemed to be taking the initiative. Endlessly manipulating her jet-black tablet's screen even as she spoke, she checked item after item off a list with each of the department heads. She turned from person to person, finally alighting on Hathaway.

"Did you get a full balance of aminoes in the feed material?" she asked him in the same pointed but restrained voice she had used to ask the others.

Intimidating scientist, thought Ben.

"In triplicate, twice," replied his boss. "You can count on our new guy: Ben."

He gestured Ben's way.

"I'll believe that when he's proven it; but, I am inclined to trust your opinion," she said, ticking something off a checklist. "And the rodents. Have they been procured?" she asked Hathaway.

"Yes, ma'am," Ben blurted out. "Non-lab certified, just like you wanted."

"This is Ben?" she asked, making eye contact only with Hathaway.

Hathaway nodded. Ben fought the urge to gulp. After a moment, however, the woman continued.

"Alright, check. We have the rodents."

"When are the deliveries coming on the subjects?" Hathaway asked.

"Tomorrow." She sighed. "Tomorrow, and tomorrow, and tomorrow. Always tomorrow. But I think this time there's a real chance they might actually have everything cleared. That's why I wanted to make sure we had everything in hand. On the, you know, off chance that they actually have everything done when they're supposed to."

Hathaway grinned at this.

"And how will we know if things are actually a green tomorrow?"

"Oh, you'll know," she said, checking off more items on her tablet as she spoke. "There'll be a fair amount of bustle if the delivery is on time. Should keep you and your new guy on your toes."

She smiled in a somehow hasty manner.

"See you tomorrow, with any luck."

She turned on her heels, and left.

"Who was that?" Ben asked, after the doors had whisked shut, putting them out of earshot of the other coats.

"Dr. Elmyra Pettinger," Hathaway said, in an artificially formal tone. His normal voice returned. "She's head coat on this project. She runs a lot of crap around here, from what I can tell."

His voice trailed off wistfully. "But then, what the hell do *I* know?" He laughed. "I'll tell you this much, though: there'll be no calling off sick tomorrow. Duty calls."

Four

Ben, in his short time on the job, had already processed his share of weird requests, and received his share of odd deliveries, but what he found waiting for him back on his desk seemed to take the cake. When he walked into the procurement office and entered his cubicle, he saw a box of two-dozen circular gold tags, packed with two dozen silver chains, along with a 'Dyna-Etch Engraving System,' sitting on his desk.

"Scientific as hell, eh?" he remarked aloud.

Ben pulled one of the tags out by the chain and let it dangle from his fingers; its shining surface reflected bursts of gold light around his cubical as the medallion spun. The effect was mesmerizing. Its twirl slowed, and for a moment the tag's blank surface reflected Ben's puzzled face back at him. He came back to himself.

"Love to see what they're going to etch on these."

They looked for all the world like the kind of nametags you would put around a housecat's neck. Ben felt increasingly certain that at least one detail of his suspicions about the experiment were correct.

But he still couldn't understand why: what kind of experiment were a group of governmental defense technology scientists gearing up to perform that required a bunch of cats?

* * *

"Bring that over here!" Pettinger bellowed in the imperious voice of a Norse Goddess come to life. "Drop it and I'll see to it you disappear from the face of the earth!"

Ben didn't doubt that Pettinger's threat carried as much weight as the team – hauling a large, metallic cylinder, the function of which Ben could scarcely guess at – she was addressing. Now that her pet project was front and center at the Agency, she was going to make sure it came off without a hitch.

So this is what Hathaway was talking about. When he had first met her, and she had been asking her checklist questions, Pettinger seemed catty yet distracted. Now that the team readied the experiment in earnest, she directed events with an explosive, commanding tone that brooked no disagreement. People quailed before her.

"No worries, ma'am," said the shortest of the men struggling to carry the implement, "we have this under control."

"You don't even know what it is!" replied Pettinger in a bark.

The man wilted. She obviously didn't want consolation, she wanted concrete results.

"Just don't drop it, and I'll have no worries."

Ben, out of the corner of his eye, watched Hathaway pull on the e-cig tucked in his baggy sleeves. Ben, who had never smoked in his life, started to think he could understand the appeal.

"When they get that all put in place, then it's my turn," Rick said to Ben, his voice morose.

"What do you have to do?" Ben asked.

Hathaway shuddered.

"Wire the damn things up. Hook 'em into the network. Benchmark 'em. Stress test them." Another slurp on the e-cig. "Compare the test with the simulated test, analyze any differences. If the discrepancy factor is above .05, *re*-wire, *re*-bench 'em. Hope to *gawd* that doesn't happen. I don't want to be up 'til four again."

He shook his head.

"Goddamn place." Hathaway turned towards Ben. "But this is going good. She sounds mad, but she's happier than a cat in a–" He cut himself off. "She's happy as a clam," he amended, "and don't let her attitude fool you. Pettinger lives for stuff like this."

He gestured at the room: teeming with workers, crawling with cables, and littered with elaborate apparatus. Hathaway continued.

"She just wants things the way she wants them." He turned to Ben. "It's not a diva thing. She wants accuracy. She and the coats call it 'rigor.' With Pettinger, it's not about her. It's about the science. If you keep that in mind when she's busting your ass, it won't get to you quite as bad."

Ben nodded. He could understand that. Exacting principles – precise measurements, concrete conditions – were a prerequisite to the gathering of empirical information.

Pettinger wheeled back and forth, giving commands to two different groups simultaneously.

"Set that over there–" she said, then spun around to address the other. "–and the blue wire goes into the third socket–" Another spin. "–and then link it in with the induction coupler." After another twist, she ended with "–and then the green connector runs into the parallel power rail like an ordinary Doppler array."

From a safe distance, Hathaway laughed.

23

"She's certainly something. But if you really want to see what makes her tick, try to send her on vacation. She hasn't once stayed gone for an entire leave. You and me, we go home at the end of the day. This is her life, right here."

Soon, the bustle was over and the crews retreated. The thick plexiglass walls now stood in place, heightening Ben's sense of standing in a giant theater. Sets of chute openings leered out of the far wall in pairs, like hollow, staring eyes. Sensor field generators stood in a scattered pattern on the other side of the wall like beige palm trees. They began to pulse weakly with a throbbing, bluish glow.

"Sure looks Top Secret, don't it?" Hathaway said, his tone wistful.

Ben nodded in awed agreement.

"They going to get to work on this tonight?"

Hathaway shook his head.

"Thought so yesterday, but there was a bit of a problem in the shipping of the… *erm*… subjects or whatever you want to call 'em."

Something about the way Hathaway pronounced the word 'subjects' sent a chill through Ben's heart.

"Nothing serious?" Ben asked, concern coloring his voice.

Hathaway scoffed.

"If it were, they wouldn't tell me. And if they did," he said, lowering his voice and dropping his gaze to meet Ben's stare head on, "I sure-as-shit wouldn't tell you, whippersnapper. Get back in there and file this stuff. I'm going to read a magazine."

Ben knew what that meant – he wouldn't see Hathaway for at least ten minutes, during which time he should steer clear of the second floor men's room.

"Sure thing, boss."

Ben went back to his desk to process forms, but his mind was pulled away by other thoughts. Cat food. Pet collars.

"Shipping problems with the subjects."

He sighed, pushed the thoughts out of his head, and continued with his paperwork.

* * *

"Medic! Is there a medic on site? *Hello?*"

Ben heard the voices drifting down the hallway, the sound growing louder. He pushed himself away from his desk and ran out from his cube and through a short hallway. Ben opened the lobby door and saw a pair of men standing with their backs to him: a tall, burly man, hissing in pain and being propped up by another – this one a slender, stooped man who looked like he was exerting all of his strength to help hold up his co-worker.

Ben stepped a little further into the lobby. The injured man's head turned towards Ben at the sound of the closing door. Ben saw that the entire right side of his head – from the forehead just above the eyebrow all the way down to his chin – was soaked in blood.

"What the hell?" Ben said, involuntarily.

Hathaway slammed a phone down.

"They're on their way," he said. He turned to address the injured man. "Can you talk?"

The bleeding man tried, but all that came out was a weak mumble. The fingers of his right hand scrabbled at his throat. He coughed thickly, and at last managed to take a wheezing breath.

"Kinda," he finally forced out in a weak voice.

He continued to fight for breath, his eyes wide with fear. The sight of his terrified eye – the naked white staring out from the darkened, blood-rimmed socket – made Ben's skin crawl.

"What the hell happened?" Hathaway asked.

"Got me," the bloody man said, an apologetic smile touching his mouth.

Two men in medic uniforms ran into the room and threw the man on a stretcher before Ben could even process their arrival. The injured man laughed weakly, accompanied by a sickening gurgle deep in his chest.

"The little bastard damn near got my fingers."

The man held up his left hand. Ben blinked in shock. It looked like it was encased in a shiny maroon glove. The worker wiggled his fingers and the tip of one digit bent at a sickening angle, like a broken dandelion stalk. Ben pulled his hand away from his mouth and realized he had thrown up in his palm.

"Jesus, get the kid out of here!" Hathaway bellowed as a security guard forcefully shoved Ben back down the hall and into his cube. "Jesus *gawddamn Christ*, people!"

"Just sit a spell, pardner," the guard said to Ben sympathetically, tossing him a box of Kleenex to wipe his mouth with. "You didn't do nothing wrong. Don't worry. Just procedure."

Ben nodded to show he understood. The guard left him there alone with his thoughts and his vomit. He dabbled the bile off his chin with a tissue.

Agency life.

His mind was locked on the image of the man's staring eye: white and green against a sea of red – helpless and wild with fear.

Five

It had been dark for so long that the slightest touch of light now entering the chamber seemed to blaze like a torch. His small eyes snapped reflexively shut, a small hiss of displeasure escaped his lips. Around him, many others did the same. All around him, tiny creatures stretched their paws, and twisted to avoid the sting of the light.

Six pairs of slitted eyes squeezed tightly shut as the door opened, widening the shaft of light.

"Hey, little guys!" said a pleasant, youthful sounding voice.

A silhouette came into view, and the irises in their feline eyes – yellow, green, grey, blue – expanded to clarify the dim image.

Framed by her outline, the woman's features were indistinct. She stepped out of the light and into the dark chamber. A grey cat, smallest amongst the litter, lifted his head and gave a cautious *yip*. Around him, his five brothers and sisters began to gather their bearings.

The group of cats were twelve weeks old – not yet grown completely into adulthood, but old enough to live on their own. They had just recently been taken from their home, where they had lived with their mother. Their new, sudden life in the small, dark room had lasted only a day or two.

One thing only stopped them from complete dissatisfaction at being trapped in the lightless chamber: *food*. Now the woman had come; their mouths watered. Soon, they would have what they wanted.

They had all been, to varying degrees, eagerly awaiting the return of their 'Nana,' and the provisions she would bring. When the woman entered the room, an odor struck their nostrils like an old, yet unknown friend. Anticipatory saliva ran down their tongues. The general agitation intensified. The tiny bodies went from milling about to darting about in eager expectation. The small grey cat, along with two of the others, ran to her and began pawing at her pant legs.

"Oh, you good little guys!" she said, reaching down to stroke their heads. "Good, *good* littles."

She laughed, and spilled a handful of crunchy treats on the floor. The small chamber thrummed with excitement now, the swarms of small cats eagerly snatching up the food. Rita 'Nana' Jessup laughed at their high-pitched, anxious sounds when she slid three big, empty food bowls closer. She started filling them, to a chorus of excited yelps.

The tiniest cat – the grey one – strolled over to the dish, his tail flipping to the right as he looked up at her inquisitively.

"Go ahead," she said, smiling. "You can have it. It's for all of you."

His brothers and sisters had all made their way over to the bowls, but the small, grey one simply stood there, his head cocked, staring at her. Rita sighed to herself. From the way he looked at her, she felt like he almost seemed to know what was happening, what she would have to tell them.

She bent down and stroked his head.

"But you couldn't know that, could you?" She said aloud. "You're just a cute little kitty-cat."

The grey kitten stood on his back feet, balancing with his forelegs stretched out amusingly before him, and twisted his neck as she scratched him. He basked in her attention for a long moment before dropping back on all fours and looking at her again in that curious way.

"It *is* like he knows," she said, bemused.

She made a quick decision and sank down into the one, heavily-scratched chair in the room.

"No sense pretending, I guess." She sighed heavily. "This is going to be our last little dinner time, babies."

She fought to keep her voice steady. Nobody could hear her, but Rita still felt she had to maintain some standard of decorum.

"You guys don't know what you've meant to me these last few days, and it kills me to say it, but you're going to have to go away soon."

The other cats kept crunching down the dry food she had brought, but the gray one stepped closer. She looked down through misty eyes and reached her hand out to him. He lifted one paw and put it on her index finger, staring into her eyes.

Rita fought tears.

"I'm going to miss you, little guy," she said, blinking. "You're a funny little guy, you know. You're special."

He hopped up onto her lap and meowed sharply, rubbing his head on her shoulder. She wrapped her arm around him.

"You *all* are." She took a deep breath. "Oh, why the hell not?"

She started muttering to herself. After a moment's seeming indecision, she quickly excused herself from the room.

"Be right back, babies," she said as she eased the door closed.

It was only a few moments before she returned, carrying her purse and still muttering.

"Look, there are rules and then there are *rules*, right?"

She sounded like she was trying to convince somebody who wasn't there.

The young cats, however, needed no convincing. They could smell what she had in her purse before she had even made it halfway down the hall. Some could even see the thing, in their own way: like a dimly remembered idea dancing into the back of their minds.

The grey cat could actually *hear* it – not close, but far away, like hearing something down a cavernous corridor. Not it's sounds, but the sound of its presence, of its nature. The others could only sense what it was it this moment. The grey cat could hear what it used to be.

Splashes in silent water.

He was pulled out of his revelation when Rita began to talk.

"I mean, I'd like to see them explain why this particular regulation is such a high-risk matter," Rita continued.

She pulled something wrapped in greasy newspaper out of her bag.

"This isn't exactly Bay of Pigs-level stuff we're talking about here."

She flung the opened newspaper to the floor. Fleshy hunks of salmon lay glistening in the dim light.

"*Grrrleeeeeow!*" came a harsh feline cry, and a gray and yellow cat – the most peculiarly colored of the litter – rushed the newspaper, taking a wide-footed stance over the salmon.

His upper lip pulled back, and he began hissing at an incredible volume – a sound that seemed almost obscenely loud coming from his relatively small body.

"*Sheesh*, little buddy," 'Nana' laughed. "*Some*body likes fishies! You share with your brothers and sisters, now."

The cat in question, standing out as improbably large amongst his littermates, did not look particularly inclined to share. He dipped his head, sank his fangs into the pulpy fishmeat, and ripped away a chunk of flesh, his eyes glittering with carnivorous relish. By now, the other cats had begun to tentatively surround the salmon, but their focus was on the other two pieces. The first cat had 'claimed' the largest piece for his own.

"Go on, go ahead!" 'Nana' urged the grey cat. "It's for you, too. I like you most of all. If you didn't have any, I'd feel bad."

He looked at her a moment before hoping off her lap and joining his siblings. The reaction of the grey and yellow cat to the sudden encroachment of the smaller, grey one in his newspaper territory was instantaneous – his ears flattened to his head, his tail rose, and his spit flew as he hissed: a wicked, grating sound like chains dragged across jail cell bars.

"Now, you *stop* that!" 'Nana' urged. "You've got to learn to share."

She prodded the big kitten gently with her right foot, backing him away from his smaller brother. Reflexively, the snarling cat twisted and clamped his mouth onto her big toe.

"*Ouch!*" she cried, shaking her foot to loosen him.

His jaws remained locked on her toe, and his tiny body swung through the air with her foot. If anything, his grip tightened.

"*Bad* kitty! You're very naughty!"

A litany of such cries poured out of Nana's mouth, as close to spouting obscenities Rita Jessup had come in decades, despite her very real agony. Even her best efforts couldn't pry the cat off her foot.

Unnoticed by Nana, the small, grey cat had walked up to her left foot and fixed his gaze on his brother's tail. The yellow-streaked cat, swinging through the air with jerks of Rita's leg, suddenly dropped onto his back with a growl, his paws splayed. Instantly, he flipped back onto all fours again, looking furious but subdued.

The grey cat rubbed up on Nana's leg once more. She was more focused on stanching the flow of blood from her wounded toe.

"Go ahead, eat quick now. I have to throw all this away when you're done. I'll be in for it if they find out I went against feeding guidelines."

She shook her head as she gathered all the greasy newspapers, the bleeding gash on her toe apparently forgotten.

"Most ridiculous thing I've ever heard. I've been working for our little wing of this man's army since back when nobody said 'sexist!' if you called the army that, and I've seen them tell every type of person what they can and can't do. But cats?"

She shook her head and sighed.

"When the Department of Defense starts telling *cats* what they can and can't eat, well… that's when you know you're getting close to retirement."

She laughed a final time, stroked each of the cats heads in turn – except for the big, mean one.

"Well, you little lovelies have brought a lot of joy into this silly old lady's last few days as a working stiff, I'll tell you that."

Once more, the grey cat was at her feet. She reached down, picked him up, and held him in her hands, right in front of her face.

"*You!* I'll miss you most of all," she said, trying to maintain her composure.

He extended his two front paws towards her face, and rubbed her nose with the smooth black pads there.

"You cute little jerk, I wish I could take you home with me! Fish I might be able to keep secret. Stealing one of the *subjects* – well, even *I'm* not that crazy!"

He left his paw on her nose for a second before she decided it was time to leave, and set him down.

"Take care now, littles," she said, trying to hide her tears as she shut the door.

Hiding them from who, she could not say.

Six

"How could this happen?"

Hathaway paced in great huffing gasps. His face was red.

"I thought we had... I thought we had goddamn *safeguards!*"

He pounded his desk each time he passed it. A heavy moment passed before anybody dared speak. Wilson, one of the medical crew, spoke up first.

"We did blood analysis on all six subjects, and came up negative. But when we ran the fecal analysis..."

He trailed off.

Hathaway stopped pacing, spun, fixed Wilson in his gaze.

"Yes, yes?"

"Well, the proteins that came up were positive for-"

Hathaway gestured with his e-cigarette case in a 'Go *on*, dammit!' motion.

"Yes, well, tested positive for Phosphatidylserine exposure," Wilson explained carefully, slowing around the difficult word's corners, "along with those polycyclic aromatic hydrocarbons that we were supposed to screen for-"

"*Dammit*, people! Leak in the chain! Break in the chain! Broken goddamn *link!*"

Hathaway pounded his desk three times in rapid succession.

"This is supposed to be the American goddamn *government!*"

He took three deep breaths through his nose and began pulling on his e-cig like he was trying to drink the thickest milkshake known to man in a single gulp. The red color of his face deepened three shades in five seconds, before he finally released his breath.

"But *Golding*. What I want to know is *how is Golding?* Is he going to make it?"

Wilson replied in an even tone.

"He's fine. He will have a lifelong numbness in the tip of his left ring finger, but that hardly–"

"He left handed?" Hathaway asked, taking another drag.

Wilson shook his head.

"Good," Hathaway said, coughing. "Good, good, good. I've had a tip of a left ring finger my whole goddamn life, guys. Don't remember a single good time we've ever had together." He shook his head, taking another quick pull. "Okay, so things aren't as bad as I thought."

He ran a hand through his shock of hair.

"I'm not going to sit around while people get maimed on my watch, though. We need to track down exactly when and where that protein was introd–"

Another man in the room spoke up.

"We've already got that narrowed down. It comes down to Rita at Central."

Hathaway crumpled upon hearing the name.

"Goddammit, people! I wanted to bring the hammer down. Poor old thing's last day is what, *tomorrow*?"

Hathaway thumped his desk twice in rage. Then, a look of apprehension filled his eyes. His face brightened.

"I know. We can't throw the book at her, but send her a picture of Golding before they cleaned all the blood off, if you have one." He shook his head. "That would be giving away classified information. No good. Damn. Would have been perfect."

Hathaway turned to Ben.

"Don't ever make that mistake, bud. You're new, but she's not. Rita Jessup has been at the central office of the Agency since before my Dad watched porn, and she should know better."

He put a hand on Ben's shoulder, wagged a sobering finger in his face.

"Don't ever make the mistake of thinking there aren't good reasons why we ask that you do things the way we want you to do them. She made that mistake, and you saw what happened."

Ben's mind reeled. What had this Rita Jessup done, exactly? Something, evidently, that had seemed innocuous to her, but somehow resulted in Golding's injury. His attack. Attack by what, though?

'Tested positive for Phosphatidylserine exposure?' That didn't explain anything. What did that even mean? Beyond that, *who* tested positive?

Golding? Rita Jessup? That didn't seem right. Besides, what did that stuff even mean? Ben filed 'polycyclic aromatic hydrocarbons' away in his mental 'To Google Later' folder.

In the meantime: what had Golding said when they brought him in?

"Got me."

But *what* 'got him,' and how? After the scene in this room, Ben was less sure than ever that he wanted to find out.

*   *   *

Fresh animal protein? Ben had snuck off into the bathroom, entered a stall, and performed a voice search on his smartphone for 'polycyclic aromatic hydrocarbons,' since he couldn't spell the term he had heard Wilson use. He winced as he realized he was on the Agency WiFi network: there were no 4G towers out here in the protected zone, for some reason. Oh well, too late to do anything about that.

The search results came back: these represented chemical compounds that appeared in animal meat. What the hell could that mean?

Ben was more confused than ever. *Who* had tested positive for these molecules? The idea that it might be Golding or Jessup made no sense – almost everybody eats meat.

The only answer Ben could come up with unnerved him. Who could they have been talking about *but* the 'subjects?' Why else would molecular traces of fresh meat be a red flag?

Ben scratched his head as the stall door swung shut behind him. Stepping up to the sink, he stared his reflection with reddened, weary eyes. He looked like he had been awake for two days straight. He splashed cold water on his face, watched it run down his cheeks and splash onto the porcelain.

His mind continued probing for answers. Why would it be weird even for the *cats*? What could they possibly be studying here where it was a life or death matter whether a cat did or did not eat food that contained fresh animal protein? He thought back to the careful preparation and balancing of proteins and amino acids in the dry cat food he had been putting together.

Life or death.

Ben remembered Golding's searching eye, wheeling in its socket. He remembered the wheezing, remorseful explanation: "*Got me.*" What had 'got him?'

None of it made any rational sense.

Ben supposed that getting used to not being able to understand his work might well take the rest of his career.

*   *   *

"They're *here*," Hathaway said, drawing out the last word.

He looked more refreshed than he had for weeks.

"Who's here?" Ben said, already pretty sure that he knew.

Hathaway held his hands up to his head, pointing his index finger upward to mimic ears.

"*Rowwwwww!*" he cried in a sharp parody of a feline voice.

Despite the jocular tone, something about his boss's pantomime made Ben feel uneasy. He didn't know what to say. Hathaway noticed his trepidation.

"Aww, come on, kid. It's nothing to be worried about. I can take you up there and show you, if you want."

Ben nodded and they stepped out the office doors, heading down the corridor to the main entrance. Hathaway tugged on his e-cigarette tube as he walked, gesturing with it when he wasn't sucking on it.

"There haven't been any more incidents since Golding, but I'm not going to go around talking about it like I'm some kind of expert."

"What the hell happened to Golding? I mean I realize things here are on a 'need to know' basis, but at what point do the people *on the project* need to know… I dunno… *anything* about what's going on?"

Ben had a hard time keeping the fear out of his voice, and he felt embarrassed.

"Alright, alright," Hathaway said, pushing the double doors open and heading outside. "But you've got to understand, none of this would have happened if no one in the goddamn chain had broken *procedure*. *That's* why we have procedure, bucko. For a *reason*. You take that to heart early, you'll never have problems."

They rounded the corner, and paused at the foot of the closest of the pair of stairways leading to the scaffolding above.

"What happened? Someone somewhere along the chain thought one of our procedural items didn't matter. They thought it sounded whimsical, and figured they could ignore it. I *guarantee* you that they thought 'What harm could it do?' before they did it."

Hathaway gestured to Ben to start climbing the metal staircase leading up to the roof. He spoke as they ascended.

"That kind of thinking might fly at a regular government job – there's plenty of those. But this is the Agency, not the goddamn National Teddy Bear Bureau. If we say *anything* is part of procedure, you need take that as meaning 'Follow this to the letter,' or you'll be putting yourself and others in serious jeopardy.'"

"Understood," replied Ben.

They had almost reached the top of the scaffold steps. Hathaway tugged on Ben's sleeve, bade him to stop.

"You're about to see one of the most heavily guarded secrets in the country. In the world."

Ben's curiosity was piqued, the sight of Golding's blood-slicked face temporarily forgotten. They climbed to the top and strode across the platform, where seven enclosures had been erected.

"One of them didn't make it. Died really early on," Hathaway said as they arrived at the closest enclosure. It was empty. "Poor little guy. We never got the memo – we're just infrastructure."

Ben peered into the empty cage, where two empty dishes sat in a corner. They walked on to the next enclosure. When they appeared, a small, black cat inside spun around to face them.

It was what Ben had expected, but still struck him as bizarre. He had heard, he supposed, of using cats for experimental research before. Somehow, this didn't feel like that sort of experiment.

The cat mewled with delight – perhaps excited that some other being had come into her area. The young cat had only recently been separated from her siblings, and the slender thing seemed to long for contact with anybody, as long as they were warm and kind.

Ben, unthinkingly, stuck his finger in through the mesh to stroke the feline's pink, wet nose. Hathaway smacked his arm away. The kitten gave a sharp bark of displeasure.

"Don't do that, boy!" Hathaway said, a look of shock on his face. "Dear *gawd*, how much talk about procedure do you have to hear before a damn word of it gets in those ears?" He shook his head, clearing his thoughts. "OK, well – I guess I'm technically breaking procedure by taking you up here, and you weren't ever briefed on proper protocol…"

He trailed off.

"Just don't do that, I guess," he added.

Ben was mystified.

"Why not? Is that what happened to Golding?"

He leaned down, peering into the cage. The young cat dropped to the ground, rolled onto her back, and began waggling her feet in the air.

"Jeez *gawd*, but she's a cutie," Hathaway said admiringly before addressing Ben's question. "But, yeah. That's what makes it so creepy." He shuddered. "I've seen a lot of weird technology in my years at the Agency, and I've seen a few creepy genetic things but…"

He trailed off.

They walked past a few more enclosures. Calico cats, tortoiseshell cats. Ben didn't know how it was possible for all of these different-looking cats to be littermates. He realized he knew precious little about feline phylogeny.

Hathaway continued, picking up where he had left off.

"I seen a lot of things on this job, but before now I've never seen stuff that got me believing in ghosts." He took a deep drag of his e-cigarette. "They can play around with all the lasers and satellites and food that doesn't spoil and speakers that can kill a man and all that type of shit all they want, but messing around with things like this: it gives an old-fashioned guy like me the willies."

They passed the next enclosure. The small, grey cat inside was already pressed against the cage walls, as though waiting for them. Both Ben and Hathaway flinched, startled by the cat's expectant gaze. The cat's green eyes stared at them calmly, as though the two were already familiar to him.

"Jumping *Jesus,* you scared me!" Hathaway said, laughing away his embarrassment.

The cat pivoted its head slightly, staring Hathaway down.

"What a funny little guy *you* are."

Ben returned the feline's gaze, and felt a powerful sense of familiarity, like sitting down to have a heartfelt chat with an old friend. Like looking into someone's eyes, and knowing they are truly listening to you. Ben didn't understand how a cat could evoke such feelings.

"Hey there, fella," he said, lamely.

He resisted the urge to poke his finger in through the mesh, his arm still smarting from being whacked for his prior transgression. The cat returned the gaze, steady and unwavering. Soon, and with apparent reluctance, Hathaway moved on.

They passed two more enclosures, each containing a new cat, before arriving at the final one. Inside luxuriated a large cat, sleeping on his haunches. If Ben had seen the cat in a photograph rather than in person, he would have written off the striking patterns of vivid color as nothing more than a Photoshopped effect: the stark yellow and light grey bands in the fur seemed too vibrant, their mixture too improbable.

"Fat little bastard," Hathaway said, e-cig tube clenched in his jaws.

The cat's left eyelid shot open like a pulled window blind. The right eye, however, remained closed. Hathaway jumped back, hand shooting up to his neck.

"What?" Ben said.

Hathaway glanced over at Ben with a harried, blank expression. He slowly and deliberately lowered his hand to his side, furtively wiping it on the pant leg of his black slacks. Hathaway chuckled, but kept backing away.

"Damn thing spooked me, is all. Come on, let's go."

Ben nodded, and they began to descend the scaffolding stairs. Ben still didn't feel any closer to understanding what was going on here, and said as much.

Hathaway coughed, a burbling chestful of phlegm underscoring his wheezing breath.

"Doubt even Pettinger is close to understanding what's going on here. Though, I must say, I damn well hope I'm wrong."

They went back into the office. Ben filled his coffee mug in the break room while Hathaway topped off the water in his thermos.

"So, when does Pettinger start work?" Ben asked, idly.

Hathaway shrugged.

"We only know what we need to know. Now that the infrastructure is in place, we're going to find our involvement dwindling on a day to day basis. But, 'cuz all this is on-site and operational now, when they do need us, they're gonna really need us to jump – so be prepared for that."

Ben nodded as Hathaway bade him farewell and exited the break room. As he left, Ben noted a shaving cut running down the side of his boss's neck. Something he hadn't noticed before.

He puzzled over this observation for a moment, but when he sat back down at his desk (where he promptly spilled a few drops of coffee and hastily mopped it up with a handful of Kleenex) he saw that he had six new unread e-mails, and his mind was pulled away to other topics before he ever connected Hathaway's 'shaving cut' with the quick backwards step the man had taken on the roof.

SEVEN

This place *sucked*. The large, yellow-and-grey-furred cat was sure of that. The harshest hiss his angry throat could muster wouldn't do his displeasure justice. Even the memory of the ridiculous human's bloodstained face screaming in terror did little to lighten the cat's mood.

He had been forced to make a number of adjustments over the last twenty-four hours, none of them to his liking. However dull it may have been back in the nursery, at least he had been with his brothers and sisters. The yellow and grey cat didn't like them much: it was more a question of heat economy than a matter of who he did and did not like.

Even by those low standards, however, he found writhing around with a bunch of runts he could easily smack and claw for amusement to be infinitely more engaging than sitting alone on a smooth, cold surface, assaulted with the odors of a world that sat just out of reach, while he stared at precisely nothing.

That's why, when someone finally passed by his cage door, he lashed out. He had been asleep, but still the noxious human thoughts seeped into his mind, invading his dreams. He realized quickly that this lumbering oaf was useless except as a target for sport. The man's mind was weak, pathetic in comparison to his own.

So disgusted at the thing's presence was the cat, that he lashed out without a moment's hesitation. The big cat found it amusing, the way the big man jumped back. The way his flesh tore under the cat's mental claws. However, the instantaneous pang of hunger his effort had prompted dulled the enjoyment somewhat.

That bit of fish that 'Nana' woman had given him had been delicious, filling him up with a level of mental energy he wasn't aware he could contain – but between attacking Golding and nearly dismembering the man's hand, and cutting the neck of this latest meddler, the cat had grown tired, and empty.

He hungered for more.

It was all around him, too. The forest that spread around his rooftop cage on all sides thrummed with the buzz of life: sounds, smells, the occasional sights he was able to catch. Often these glimpses had to be gleaned from the minds of the other cats or humans in the area, rather than coming firsthand from his own physical eyes. The cat hissed in rage at being imprisoned in a sea of life, this small island of lifelessness his only world.

The sunlight played on the leaves of the trees, sending wavering shadows dancing across the grass. Squirrels flickered through trees, voles crawled through the earth at the bases of trees. Birds danced in the trees above and wheeled through the sky with innate grace.

The yellow and grey cat wanted to squeeze their eyeballs into juice.

Everywhere around him, the birds sang in their cloying voices, warbling away with their fleshy tongues: so full of life and vibrance that the cat could almost taste them. Their tiny bird minds – utterly incongruous with the cat's predatory, mammalian view of the world – filled him with disgust. To him, their thoughts sounded like clicks and pops on a skipping record, a record he couldn't stop. However great his irritation, he couldn't rid himself of the annoyance of that constant clattering.

The rodents scurrying on the woodland floor, the squirrels racing up the forest's trees, even the very trees themselves drinking deep from the depths of the earth – each of these made a sound in the cat's mind, and each of these other, foreign minds had its own clear pattern, purpose, and shape. To the cat's mind, however, their purposes all seemed empty.

From what he could tell, nothing out there was worthy of his respect. It all seemed so maddeningly pointless to him – none of these chirping, bleeping creatures seemed to have the peculiar spark of life that he felt burning inside himself. The same radiant energy and burn to control, to dominate, to own.

The angry yellow and grey cat had seen precious little in his short life that had aroused his awe or appreciation, save for his own strength, mind, and claws. In such of the wide world as he had yet seen, there had been nothing he had so far encountered that had inspired *fear*.

He wasn't, as many youthful creatures are, simply untutored in the ways of pain and struggle. His confidence and sense of ease came from a deeper, darker place. He actually *felt* the assurance that others merely seek to convince themselves they feel.

The cat's eyes flicked to the right and caught the movement of an insect bounding through the bars and into his cage. A grasshopper had flown up here, and for whatever misguided reason proceeded to jump right into his pen. A second later, it was speared through on the end of a long, curved claw.

Its angular legs twitched powerfully in its sudden desperation. The cat fixed the squirming bug with his gaze, lowering his snout to more closely examine it. Round, black, insectile eyes reflected the cat's fangs as his mouth gaped to encompass the floundering thing.

A crackling flurry of colorful bursts and sonic pops filled the cat's head like mental fireworks. He shut his eyes with pleasure as the grotesque life fluids of the insect gushed into his mouth and splashed onto his tongue. The mental clicks and pops of the birds and squirrels sharpened and grew louder, resolving from a dull hum into a thrumming buzz of life.

That snack was better than nothing, but the big yellow and grey cat wanted more. He reached out with his mind, probing the nearby trees until he found what he was looking for. Following the path traced by his mental ears, he glanced up at an overhanging branch and saw a slight tremble in some of its leaves. A moment later, a thick green caterpillar fell from the limb and smacked the facility roof, landing on the other side of the enclosure gate, about six feet from the cat's reach.

The creature writhed weakly, in a state of shock after its fall. Its small, tinny mental voice sounded, to the cat's special ears, like someone shaking a bag of rocks. The message was clear. The caterpillar was hurt.

The cat trained his mind on the green, squirming thing, and slowly it began to move towards him. Its pulpy body, aflame with pain, slid along against its will. The cat squinted, exerting himself fully, and the thing tumbled and rolled across the flat roof, like a horizontal version of a slow-motion video of a doll tumbling end over end down a set of stairs.

The instant it was within the grasp of his claws, the cat's arm shot out to catch the spongy green creature. A sound like shrieking ice burned through the cat's mind for a moment as he sucked the gloopy organs out of the pitiful thing.

No butterfly here.

The cat belched, and decided to take a nap. If his experiment lashing out with the energy gleaned from the the contraband fish had taught him anything, it was that he shouldn't go wasting his strength.

Eight

Ever since he, along with his brothers and sisters, had been left behind by their 'Nana,' a restless emptiness possessed the small grey cat. No other being he had met had been so radiant with unqualified generosity, so warm and so considerate towards him, as Rita Jessup. The others all treated him coldly, clinically. But not her.

And now she was gone.

After being taken away from the dark room, they separated him from his littermates, introducing him to isolation for the first time in his life. And then, he had come here. Wherever this was. The only thing the grey cat knew for sure was that this tiny cage under an expansive sky was the farthest thing from a darkened room he had yet seen.

He was with his siblings, but not together with them. From their one-directional vantage points in the pens, none of them could see each other. They could *feel* each other though, quite plainly: musical mental voices, each mind complementing and completing the whole. Despite the mental link, their new physical separation left them feeling cut off and alone.

The grey cat put his head on his two front paws and lazily blinked out at the day through the bars of his enclosure. His mind wandered back to all the times he had huddled with his brothers and sisters, and taken their closeness for granted. Looking out from his tiny rooftop cage, surrounded by trees and cloaked in cloudless sky, he thought of the empty, dark rooms in which they had spent their lives so far, and realized that – though they had now been separated from each other – up until arriving here, they had, in a different sense, been alone together: a group of siblings barred from a wider world.

This new, green world surrounding him was full to the brim with life, but the grey cat was painfully aware that the life out there existed free of constraints or bonds. Even in their vulnerabilities, the plants and creatures that filled this wood were *free*. Free to be consumed by a predator, or to fall to their accidental doom, perhaps. But their lives had an essential *dignity* – an element of personal freedom – that his current life, in this four-by-six foot enclosure, couldn't match.

He lay flat on the floor, his head on his paws, and watched the sun climb in the sky. He couldn't see its thoughts – the great burning thing in the sky was the only living thing the grey cat had ever encountered that gave off no sense of mind. The cat couldn't understand how that could be – even rocks spoke to him, on a long, slow timetable the cat seldom had the patience for. Yet the sun, the most vibrant and full thing that there was, was as silent as a corpse.

The cat supposed that the sun had some special role in the world, and perhaps its mind was somehow above his own. The thought gave him a feeling of satisfaction. As the sun climbed the sky, the grey cat appreciated its freedom, and wondered what it could see, from its high spot.

Into the midst of these thoughts barged a mental sense of an oncoming presence: an approaching pair of people. Their thoughts started off low and quiet, like the soft sound of a water faucet drifting faintly from down a hallway. As the pair of humans climbed the stairs, the shape of their minds became clearer, and the color of their thoughts deepened in richness.

The shorter, older looking one had a mind swimming with memories of days long past, and a heart that pretended to feel bored with the world, but was really still in love with it. The man, for whatever reason, guarded this love like a secret, hiding it behind a wall of brashness and flippancy. Though the grey cat thought he seemed like a good person, the fellow didn't remind him very much of Rita Jessup.

The other one was more of a mystery.

This other gave the impression of being younger. He seemed eager, excited, but also almost scared – unsure of himself or what might happen. None of the weariness of the other, older person in this mind, only a sort of trepidation that colored everything, making the mundane romantic and the merely uncertain vexing. There was a *restlessness* to this other mind that the grey cat could identify with… but also a withering insecurity the cat couldn't understand.

There was something else, too, in this one, though the grey cat understood it least of all: a kind of fog between the cat and the young man's mind: the mental equivalent of hazy waves and mirages coming off a hot road. Something was obscuring the overall vision, like a dirty sheet or a filthy window. Something from outside the man, but still inside it. The cat could still see his thoughts, but it took some effort. The feeling was unusual for the cat, who had never before needed to exert himself to see the minds of others.

The cat felt certain that these two people now approaching his cage held the key to the mystery of his life: *what was going on?* In his anxiety to get a better look at the two approaching humans, he leapt across his cage, and leaned against the cage door. Soon, the pair appeared around the corner. He stared at them eagerly.

"Jumping *Jesus*, you scared me!" yipped the closer of the two men, the older one. The cat playfully wondered if he had added some excitement to the man's supposedly dull life by startling him, and wagged his tail.

"What a funny little guy *you* are," the man said, a broad smile on his face.

The two humans bent down to peer into his cage. The grey cat wagged his tail, keeping himself pressed to the fence. He could see the younger human fighting against the urge to reach in and pet him, and wondered what was holding him back.

The sea of conflicting motivations that came from the young man's mind seemed helplessly confusing to his feline sensibility. The concept of protocol meant little to a cat. Still, despite his regret at the nice seeming pair of people not playing with him, and his complete lack of comprehension of the very human reasons why they restrained themselves from petting him – protocol, procedure, process – the young cat did somehow understand that they wanted to.

He rolled onto his back, wagged his paws, and yawned. The grey cat felt a glow from the two humans reach out to him, and he soaked himself in the warm waves emanating from the pair.

"Hey, little fella," said the younger one.

The grey cat gave a meow of approval and flipped back onto his four feet. The feelings streaming from these two people were sincere and appreciative, and the cat beamed these feelings right back with his strange energy. The two smiled at him for a protracted moment before shaking their heads clear and passing by his cage door with a last wave of their hands.

The small grey cat stretched his paws back out in front of him, his ears lying flat against his head as he stretched himself out. The two people had certainly seemed nice, and after their visit he felt a renewed appreciation for the song of the birds, and the sound of the beetles, and the slow dark thoughts of the trees as their roots grew deep, seeking water in places no cat would ever think to go looking.

It had been a nice day, the grey cat thought, smiling at the sun as it started sinking into the trees. He may be trapped in this small space, no nearer to answers than he was before, but he had begun to feel like he just might be a part of the wide world that stretched into the distance as far as his gifted eyes could see.

His lids started to slide close for a peaceful nap, when he was jolted awake by a discordant, jangling pang of hostility coming from several cages over.

"*What?*" came the harried voice of the younger person. The concerned cat felt the fear radiating off the two like steam from a kettle.

"Just spooked me, that's all," said the other.

The cat couldn't tell what these quite tell what these human sounds meant, but the tone behind them was as clear to his feline ears as the intention behind a cat's hiss or a purr were to any sane person. He saw the two of them back up trepidatiously from the furthest enclosure before they wheeled around on their long legs and headed to the descending staircases.

The steaming, radiating menace billowing from the furthest cage started to fill the entire rooftop with its hateful energy. The grey cat backed into his metal cave, ears lowering. The fog of the yellow and grey cat's hate wafted by, red and thick and sickening. The furthest tendrils of the mental stench stretched into long, vaporous fingers that reached out to squeeze the two departing humans before they could disappear down the stairs. The smoky constitution weakened and faded moments too soon, and the two vanished just before the vaporous energy clouds did.

The atmosphere on the rooftop began to clear. The grey cat shuddered. His big brother – the grey and yellow cat in the furthest enclosure – had obviously run out of energy and grown tired. What might happen, next time, if this brother of his *didn't* get worn out? What could his strange, spiteful sibling do if he really put his mind to it?

The grey cat curled into a ball, and contemplated his family. They all held a sleeping power that rested below their surfaces, each special in their own way. When Rita let them feast on the contraband fish, the living energy of the animal did something special to them.

The cats began to fill with that energy, faint though it was: the fish in question had been dead for days. It took fresh, living meat to really charge them up. But the chunks of fish were the first real flesh the cats had tasted in their short lives, and it had done something to them.

The littermates had all begun to charge with their strange energy. Each among them possessed a strange skill, yet so far, none of the grey cat's other littermates had demonstrated a glimmer of a possibility that they were capable of anything remotely like what their largest, strangest-colored brother had already done.

As the young cats had ripped away at that fish, their awareness deepened rapidly, the life force inside transferring into their psychic reservoirs. The grey cat, though the smallest of the litter, proved no different. His mental clarity grew and soon, after swallowing down bite after bite of the salmon, his vision sharpened enough to feel the cold, dead mind of the water animal staring back at him, as it were, as he ate.

The sensation unnerved him.

The more of the fish he consumed, the more the grey cat felt his connection to his siblings strengthening. His brothers' and sisters' voices had always been present in the back of his mind, ever since they had possessed minds to speak of, stretching back to the weeks before their births. It wasn't until that first meal of actual meat – not dry dusty, crunchy, grain-based cat food, but real animal flesh – that the minds of the other cats became, to his mental sight, bright beacons in a darkened room.

He saw that one of his sisters had a tremendous sleeping power that would need to be fed an enormous amount of living energy to realize. He tried to peer into her mind, to uncover the nature of her gift, but he felt blown back from her secrets as though by a tremendous wind. Another brother – black and white with brown spots on his snout – had a whimsical streak reflected in his odd ability to mimic sounds of creatures, people, and things. Not just their vocalizations, but any sort of sound.

His abilities, like the grey cat's own, didn't require energy from the living to function, though it *did* make the effect much, much stronger. Unlike the grey cat, his feline mimic brother was daunted by his surroundings. If any of his siblings needed the grey cat's help, it would be the black and white brother.

And, from the top of the roof, he reflected that if any of his siblings required *watching*, it would be the one at the edge of the roof now. The one who had tried to kill one of the humans moving the cats to their new home.

* * *

Everything had been going fine with the transfer – the relief coming from the human moving crew was clear even to a cat. The grey cat could peer inside their minds and literally *see* their initial concern about carrying pet totes filled with top secret government genetic research subjects, but that feeling was too complicated and human for the cat to grasp. Now that the four workers moving the cats from the truck to their enclosures on the roof felt safe, the grey cat had begun to feel safe himself.

That's when it had happened.

Still filled of energy from the illicit fish snuck to them as a parting meal by their well-meaning 'Nana,' the yellow and grey cat hadn't been dormant. He had merely been waiting for his moment to strike. The grey cat could feel the gathering of his brother's coiling energy, but by the time he moved to mentally intercept the psychic blast, it was too late – the cat's fury had already been loosed.

The grey cat pressed up against his tote wall to get a better look. He saw the tips of one man's fingers suddenly bend off kilter, as though hacked at with a giant, invisible knife. The man began to scream, and a gash slid open on his face, gushing blood as it widened from just beneath one eye socket to the space above his mouth.

The grey cat, without thinking, sent out a sort of mental shield, but it was too late. The dark energy of the yellow cat had already dissipated. There was nothing he could do to help the man.

"Medic! *Medic!*" one of the other four began to shout, dragging the wounded man inside.

That was the first sign the grey cat had that his biggest brother might be a problem that would need dealing with.

NINE

"This is *far* more variation than I was expecting," Pettinger said, pacing. "*Far* more!"

"Is that… bad?" Hathaway asked, standing to the side and gripping a piece of paper in one hand more tightly than necessary.

Pettinger was the only person Ben had ever seen who had that effect on Hathaway. The senior scientist on the project burst into laughter.

"No, it isn't *bad*," she said, beaming a huge grin at him. "This means there is far more potential in this line of research than we thought! The original genetic variation isn't just some fixed state, it's a literal biological *doorway* into a further line of – apparently – *very* differentiated skills and abilities. And, I'm sorry, but…"

Here Pettinger lowered her tone and spoke conspiratorially. Ben strained his ears to hear.

"I'm very sorry, and what happened to Golding was awful and a tragic breach of protocol and in that sense an utter *failure*…"

Ben could hear where this was going, and thought her attempt to give lip service to the basic bit of human morality where you aren't supposed to be happy about a colleague's disfigurement was… acrobatic, if not fully satisfying.

"...it was, in another, very *real* sense, a sort of successful 'beta test,' if you will. A 'statement of capabilities.' And in that sense I think it actually went rather spectacularly well."

Even Pettinger had realized the embarrassing mess her words had gotten her into, and her sudden agitation had prompted her to usual eloquence to break down. Ben didn't think Hathaway agreed, though his boss nodded gravely. Ben noted his teeth were clenched.

"At any rate," Pettinger went on, having recovered her composure, "we need to get to work. Can we enter the viewing theater for the first of the tracked evals? Is everything *definitely* operational?"

Hathaway nodded vigorously, looking desperate to assure Pettinger everything was in hand.

"All operational. Everything's up to spec or better."

Pettinger rubbed her palms together.

"Then let's get to work on the initial evaluations. This is going to be some remarkable stuff."

She gathered a few of her things, and hit the intercom button to call for the other scientists.

Ben stood back, uncertain if he was intended to come along to witness the evaluations or if he was expected to stay behind, always stay behind. A second later, his doubt was removed.

"Come along, kid," Hathaway barked, pulling a last drag from his e-cigarette before entering the lab, where he would have to refrain from even stealth puffs. "We aren't going to wait all day."

*   *   *

"The what?" Ben asked. It had been a while since he had handled it. "Oh, the *Dyna-Etch* or whatever it was called?"

"Bingo, muchacho!" Hathaway said.

"I'll go get it! And all the tags?"

"Well," Pettinger sighed. "We have an extra tag, it turns out. We had seven, but only six from the litter survived. There was a runt who died after only a few days."

Her expression changed, her voice becoming nostalgic and far away. Ben had never seen or heard the imposing Pettinger in this mood before.

"He seemed fine when they were packing them to ship to Central. Reports said he kept bopping his head with all his brothers and sisters to the point where they were pushing him away."

She shook her head, and Ben fancied her could see the glint of tears forming. He was astounded.

"Don't really know what happened. They say it was like a stroke or something like that. It was very peculiar. I've read the reports and they were very inconclusive." Her voice became speculative. "Usually, runts die of a lack of nutrition. You know, fighting over their mother's milk. But obviously we didn't let that happen."

She shook her head again, harder this time.

"At any rate, they were only a few days old."

"So…" Hathaway said in an accusing tone, as though Pettinger's story had wasted her own time, "he should only grab *six* of the gold tags?"

She looked at him disdainfully.

"Yes, I suppose that is what I mean."

She pushed her glasses up on her nose, and put her hands behind her back as she stared Hathaway down.

"I'll go get them as fast as I can!" Ben said, eager to diffuse the situation, and ran out of the room.

He quickly returned, relieved to see that the tension seemed to have passed.

"Excellent!" Pettinger said, taking the Dyna-Etch machine and looking it over. "I see, fits in here…"

She grabbed a blank nametag and slid it into the corresponding slot on the etching machine.

"I *see*." She looked up. "This will be excellent. *Thank* you."

The other three scientists filtered into the room, each holding a digital tablet and wearing their signature white coats.

"Who are we starting on?" asked a tall man with dark hair.

"We're just going to go through them one by one and give them their names and tags right after the assessment," Pettinger explained. "They're going to be hard as hell to tell apart without names."

After a brief fiddling with the controls, Ben watched as a kitten slid down the first tube like a child at a waterpark.

"*Row!*" they heard in a tinny, amplified voice over the speakers as the tiny thing reached the cushioned bottom on the other side of the thick Plexiglas.

"Subject: One," spoke a computer generated voice. "Gender: Male."

Ben felt a wave of creepiness wash over him, not knowing for sure what all this was about but beginning to have sinking suspicions.

"Alright," Pettinger said. "Release a rat."

Hathaway turned to Ben to explain.

"You remember how we had you put together the best possible, most balanced dry cat food for 'em? That's what you Googled up that first week when you thought you could do whatever you wanted, remember?" He laughed. "Well, this is the real deal: actual fresh meat. Big difference, for these cats. When they got this in their diet, these guys and gals got... a little extra going on. Particularly when it's *live* meat."

"We'll see just how much 'extra' *this* one has after he eats this rat," Pettinger commented.

Sure enough, the cat was a bundle of ancient feline instincts, whatever strange new gene might be active inside him, and the moment the scurrying, whiskery brown rat began to waddle through the enclosure, the cat was upon him. The small, black and white juvenile cat hadn't seemed in the slightest bit threatening or menacing a moment before, but the instant his hunting instinct kicked in, the feline's entire aspect changed.

He became a hunter, fangs and claws emerging from his cute, furry paws and fuzzy muzzle to expose the true nature of the beast. The rat's pitiful moans sharpened, and soon quelled, as his neck snapped in the cat's vigorously shaking jaws. The slurping, ripping sound of the cat's feast turned Ben's stomach, but for some reason he couldn't look away. The moment seemed almost perfectly poised in time.

For some reason, Ben had the feeling that the walls were falling away. The sounds of the birds, and the wind, and the chirping of insects seemed to be drifting inside, even to this sound-proofed chamber. He could almost feel the wind on his face, and he reached up to brush a buzzing insect away before realizing that there *was* no insect. Then how could he hear it?

"Is this picking up on the audio?" Pettinger said, excitement trembling in her voice.

The dark haired scientist beamed back at her, pointing at the dancing waveform on the audio monitor.

"Absolutely," he mouthed.

"Perfect," said Pettinger, quietly.

She put her finger to her mouth, deep in thought. She then took the Dyna-Etch system and tapped its keys with her thumbs. The machine dutifully etched her input onto the tag.

It read: 'DECIBEL.'

"I think he's safe to collar up now. We had a good evaluation."

The cat walked up to the Plexiglas, meowing at the people on the other side.

"Perfect," said Pettinger's clear voice over the sound system, but her lips had not moved and she had not been piped into the speakers.

"That's extraordinary!" exclaimed one of the scientists whom Ben had not yet met.

"Extraordinary," came a strange echo over the sound system.

The cat stood on his hind legs, putting his foot pads on the Plexiglas, and meowed again.

"Extra-fect, *chee, chee,* Decibel, *chee chee chee!*"

The sound was eerie, and it took Ben a moment to recognize the '*chee*' as the sound of a squirrel, scolding from his arboreal vantage point. *Dear God,* thought Ben. This cat could clearly make any sound it wanted to. The sound of birds intensified.

"How are you going to put a collar on him?" asked Ben.

Pettinger smiled, and nodded to Hathaway, who pressed a few buttons on one of the panels. A bluish gas began to hiss out of the floor in five rows of nozzles spaced at three foot intervals. The cat meowed woefully before falling limp on his side. Within moments, the spraying ceased and fans were engaged. Ben watched in astonishment as the blue-tinted miasma of sedative gas in the chamber behind the transparent wall rapidly thinned, and two workers in biohazard suits rushed in.

One of the pair scooped Decibel up and into something resembling a large, circular cat bed. The other hazmat-suited worker came along with what looked like a giant vacuum cleaner nozzle. Ben began to realize what he was looking at. The circular cat bed would act as a platform to drive the cat back upwards through the same tube it had descended from.

Sure enough, the cat was loaded like a bullet into the chute, the nozzle was temporarily clamped on via special latches and slots built into the tubes, and then Pettinger at the control panel fired the apparatus upwards. Ben joined the others, all crowded around the screen showing the rooftop enclosure belonging to the cat now named 'Decibel.'

The team tensed as the cat shot upwards towards the enclosure, and then gave a soft, relieved sigh in unison when he was slowly and safely deposited in his chamber. The cat bed platform used to shoot Decibel through the chute dropped away, the hatch closed behind it. A smooth transfer.

"Excellent!" shouted Pettinger in triumph as Hathaway gave her a high-five.

The squat man turned about, clasping Ben by the shoulder.

"Just so you know, so much of your work went into making what you just saw possible. I want you to know that. Even if you don't and can't know most about most of these projects, this is one of those times you can see what the seemingly mundane little jobs we give you here add up to. And you've been a huge help."

Ben was too busy feeling happy and proud to be aware of it, but he was grinning.

Ten

The experiment was far from over. After Decibel came the next cat.

"Subject: two," said the robotic voce, sounding lifelessly indifferent to the potential of these cats. Down the chute came another mewling test subject, this one a tortoiseshell cat – speckled and dark. Another rat was released.

One of the scientists with Pettinger – a shorter woman with straight, shoulder-length hair and, Ben hated to admit noticing, a pleasant-looking pair of pants – popped a roll of fruity candy out of her pocket, and Ben instantly thought of Hathaway's e-cigarette addiction.

Her thumb expertly flipped the candy out of its cylindrical wrapper. She grabbed it in mid-air, and popped it into her mouth like a pair of aspirin. Ben was so focused on watching her eat the red candy that he was startled by Pettinger's initial whoop.

"Dear *gawd!*" Hathaway drawled as necks snapped to look.

"Holy *crap!*" Ben cried in alarm as he watched the rat, pawing at the smooth floor in desperation, being slowly sucked backwards towards the cat as though caught in a river current.

Ben could hear the thing's feet squeaking on the floor as it tried to slow its inexorable progress, but it was like the cat's open jaws were a vacuum cleaner, and the struggling rat nothing more than a dust bunny. Its final squeals of alarm and confusion ended abruptly as the cat snapped its neck.

"Release another!" Pettinger cried, mashing the button herself.

Soon, two rats scurried into the room, quick to hug the wall when they noticed the prowling feline in the middle of the chamber.

"Just watch!" Pettinger said, to no one in particular.

The mood in the room was tense. Everybody held their breath until the first of the rats began to lift off the ground, then gasped as one when it flew through the air like a pitched baseball. The thing landed, bones broken, in an amorphous, twitching pile of rat in front of the evidently very pleased cat. Her sinuous feline tail flicked this way and that as she leaned down to snack on the now-exposed innards of the recently-dead rat.

"Do you think letting out *two* of those things was a good idea? How much energy to do you suppose that cat is going to have after eating *three* whole ra–" Hathaway began.

"*Shut up!*" Pettinger hissed.

Her mistake had been made, and she seemed more interested in finding out the results than being lectured on the potential dangers.

The third rat, for the moment, looked to be safe from harm, though it didn't seem to feel that way. Scrambling to find some kind of escape, scurrying from here to there and testing the boundaries at every turn, the furtive thing was desperate to get out of the chamber before the preternatural cat turned her attention on him. No exit, however, was forthcoming, and the rat had no choice but to go back over potential escapes it had already ruled out.

In the background, the beautiful, mottle-coated cat feasted on the glistening meat of the second rat – the first rat's body long since disappeared down the cat's throat.

"I don't know if she'll even go to go for that third rat," the tall, dark-haired scientist asked. Ben felt stupid for not knowing his name by this point, but the 'Agency' was not a nametag kind of a place.

"Wait for it," Pettinger said, sounding confident that something would happen.

Within moments, the tail of the third rat rose sharply into the air. Soon, its search for an exit was cutoff. The rat's front feet scrabbled for purchase as its back legs rose off the ground. The frightened rat desperately strove to grab onto any kind of handhold, anything to prevent being sucked away into the ravenous mouth of the cat.

For her part, the cat did not seem particularly invested one way or the other. Her body language, rather, seemed to suggest that if the rat wanted to die, *fine* – if not, *whatever*. Somehow, that apparent apathy made the inexorable pulling apart of the rat, limb by limb, all the more horrible to watch.

The rodent managed to grab onto the tiny slits in one of the air vents – slots just barely large enough to fit its tiny claws into – and it now struggled to hold on. Inside the chamber, no wind rippled, no papers rustled. Nothing stirred whatsoever, save for the satisfied looking cat calmly licking its paws, and the clinging rat flapping like a flag in a windstorm.

"Magnify it!" Pettinger said, again working the controls herself as the image of the rat appeared, repeated in ultra-high resolution four times across the sixty-inch displays in the control room.

"Are those its *fingers?*" Ben cried in astonishment as tiny, fleshy digits flew backwards through the air, striking the cat's tongue like snowflakes.

The irresistible suction of the cat's mouth had produced such pressure on the poor thing's fingers that the metal vents had severed the rat's miniscule right hand fingers. Soon, the doomed creature's left arm bent disgustingly, the bone inside snapping with the strain. One pearly-white bone shard stuck out of its arm like a dagger. It squealed one last cry of agonized protest and flew backwards, looking like a passenger sucked out of an open airliner door at twenty-thousand feet.

The team gasped as, inside the jaws of the cat, the rodent splattered apart into a bloody mist. It was as though the cat's mouth was a black hole – and the crimson bloodspray of the disappearing rodent was some massive interstellar object disintegrating at the event horizon.

"*Meow,*" commented the tortoiseshell, a faint glimmer seeming to sparkle over her glossy coat, as she serenely licked her paws.

"To say merely '*Holy shit*' would be to damn with faint praise," said Hathaway in a subdued voice.

*   *   *

Once the newly-named 'Vortex' was back safely in her pen, the team readied the third cat. The strained sense of unreality in the room deepened. After a brief delay – when it looked like nothing of note would happen – the cat earned her name 'Charlotte' by spinning a near-instantaneous web around the released rat, a tough netting from which it could not escape. The cat then easily finished off its prey.

There was debate of breaking off for lunch after the third cat – but there were only three more. The team decided to keep going.

Ben recognized the fourth cat sliding down the tube – it was the small, grey cat from the roof. Unlike the other cats, this one didn't look the slightest bit confused by his surroundings. He looked only sad and subdued. Ben felt his heart going out to the cat as it stared down at its own paws forlornly, uttering a small and dejected *'row'* before falling silent.

"Poor little bugger is lonely, or something," Hathaway said in a quiet, introspective voice.

"Well," Pettinger said, releasing the next rat, "let's see if a quick meal will perk him up."

The cat's head shot up when the rat cleared the door of its enclosure, but when the cat saw what had caused the noise, its gaze dulled and the hopefulness in its eyes dimmed once more. It placed its head back on its paws. Evidentially, the grey cat was not hungry, or playful. Its hunting instincts had not been aroused by the sight of the rodent, or by its smell, or even by its darting, mammal motions.

"*Row!*" the cat again insisted, the emotional state behind its vocalization evident even to the humans, across the gulf of species.

"Poor little guy!" Hathaway said, clearly feeling more sympathy for the cat's loneliness than he had yet displayed for the rat's sufferings.

As though he could hear Hathaway's voice through the thick Plexiglas wall, the grey cat turned his head and fixed him in his gaze. Slowly, the cat gathered his legs beneath him and rose, approaching the glass gingerly. He lowered his head, took a step towards Hathaway, and repeated himself:

"*Row.*"

"Aww, hey little guy!" Hathaway said, bending down to tap on the glass.

The change that had come over the man amazed Ben. There was no sign of the rough dude who stole hits from his e-cigarette when he thought no one was looking, and who told ribald jokes when he was sure they were – instead, Hathaway had been replaced by a man-sized toddler filled with delight at the fact that a small animal found him as entrancing as he found it.

Tap, tap, tap.

"You're a kee-*yute* little guy, ain'tchya? *Ainchya!*"

Hathaway giggled as though he were being held down and tickled. Ben smiled, despite himself. Everybody but Hathaway remained completely silent, holding their breath, as he continued to talk babytalk through the glass.

"Good widdle buddy, eh? Iddint he a good buddy? Good *bud*-dy! Good widdle *bud*-dy!"

Finally, Pettinger broke the silence.

"Uh, *a-hem*," she began, clearing her throat.

Hathaway stood up straight as a ramrod, as though electrocuted.

"Goddamn little guy doesn't seem to want to eat!" Hathaway blurted out, as though caught with a hand in the cookie jar and looking for excuses.

Ben bit his tongue – laughing at his boss was the sort of thing you were supposed to stop yourself from doing, even if his boss's boss was also laughing.

"Yes, I can see that," Pettinger said, her own smile looking slightly cruel as the uncomfortable Hathaway hemmed and hawed. "Hmm, I wonder what the explanation for *that* is," she said thoughtfully, glancing at her screens. "We'll do a repeat tomorrow and see what we come up with. Stress can throw off a lot of physiological factors, that's for sure."

Ben blinked at the small, grey cat as it pushed its head against the glass, trying to get Hathaway's attention. The chastised Hathaway would have none of it, however, and continued to pretend he didn't notice the cat, now at his feet, cavorting on the other side of the glass.

"What are you naming him?" asked the taller scientist.

"Just a second, Jeff," Pettinger said, squinting down at the Dyna-Etch machine. "Been forever since I spelled this. Let's see, e, i, i. I'm pretty sure this is right?"

She dangled the gold tag down on the end of its silver chain. The tag read: 'Leviticus.'

"How do you figure that one?" Hathaway asked.

"Isn't that the one that goes 'Don't bear a grudge or seek revenge?'" she said tentatively, suddenly concerned she had gotten something wrong. "'Love thy neighbor as thyself?' Something like that?"

Ben laughed. "Yeah, it is." He caught his breath before going on. "It also says not to have sex with your neighbor's cattle, which I think we can all agree on."

They laughed.

"He sure doesn't seem to bear a grudge against those rats," Pettinger said thoughtfully.

"Well," Hathaway said, once again distracted by the cat, "I think it's a suitably interesting name for an interesting little cat."

"What's so interesting about *that* cat?" Jeff asked, crossing his arms. The feeling of automatic dislike for the man Ben had initially felt renewed itself. "I mean, compared to the others, this one is just about the worst one yet."

An offended look creased Hathaway's forehead. "Say what you want, but this is a decent cat. He might not be as good of a murderous experiment as the other cats," recrimination coloring his voice, "but he's the best damn *cat* out of the bunch."

Hathaway said this in a tone that almost demanded the others to challenge him. Pettinger didn't seem interested in arguing over which cat was the best.

"Well, that makes him the least notable for our experiment," she said flatly. "*Next.*"

The chamber began to fill with gas. Leviticus's eyes widened for a moment before fluttering closed.

"*Row,*" he said a final time, before the workers slid him back into his capsule and sent him back up to his enclosure. In a moment, the newly-named Leviticus was gone.

Eleven

Pettinger yawned as the fifth cat descended their tube.

"After that Leviticus, with only two to go, *anything* would impress me now."

Ben's gaze slid from Pettinger to Hathaway, and he didn't know whether to laugh at or sympathize with Hathaway's hurt look.

"Hey, now," the older man shot back gruffly, but he didn't add anything further.

"Alright," Jeff said, nodding towards the brown, slightly mottled cat that was now *'row'*-ing away on the other side of Plexiglas barrier. "What have we got here?"

Pettinger sighed and depressed what Ben had come to think of as the 'Rat Release Button,' her body language communicating disinterest. Though Pettinger was heavily invested in this project, Ben had to imagine her love of dinner and cigarettes – coupled with her lack of further expectations for the night's final subjects – was starting to outweigh her more professional concerns. As Ben tried to figure Pettinger out, a rat scurried out into the chamber, its fur as brown as the cat's. The thing ran desperately for a moment before freezing dead in its tracks.

The team watched. Pettinger perked up.

The rat hadn't just stopped running – it was completely immobile. Not completely, Ben noticed – its whiskers were still twitching fearfully, yet the remainder of its body seemed plastered to the ground. After a moment, the rat seemed to vibrate gently.

"Jeezus *gawd*, look at that!" Hathaway exclaimed.

Ben felt almost frantic – he didn't see what Hathaway was talking about. Everybody was gasping but him, dammit! What was it? He looked and looked until he finally saw what was happening, and then he gasped, too. It was so obvious, yet just far enough outside normal experience that he hadn't been able to process it.

The rat was losing its color. A curving, wavy horizon slid ever upwards across the rat's body, clearly delineating the point at which all color was leeched from the rat. Its brown fur turned white as a sheet, its brown fingers becoming the color of bone.

The only thing remotely comparable Ben had ever seen had been in a cartoon, and even there it had been surreal and unsettling. When the strange bleaching reached the rat's head, the frantic motion of its whiskers ceased. It became a lifeless statue of a rat.

The cat walked by the colorless carcass, and to the team's shock the frozen thing blew away in a cloud of dust.

"*'Holy crap sandwich'* is the official vote on that one," Hathaway said, his voice tinged with nervousness.

"What's stopping kitty from doing that same thing to any of us?" Ben asked, a hint of anxiety creeping into his voice. "Five inches of clear Plexiglas? I have a feeling that's not how it works. I mean, I *could* be wrong. But, you can understand my concern, right?"

"Calm down," Pettinger said, holding up her hand. "Calm *down*, okay?"

"*Meow*," remarked the cat on the other side of the glass, as if to underscore this point.

"Jeff, start the evac right away," she said to her team.

Soon, the bluish gas was visibly streaming into the room. The cat gave a few small, agitated sounds of disapproval before succumbing to unconsciousness and falling on her side. Ben gave a sigh of relief. It was then that he noticed Hathaway's leather shoes.

"Holy shit!" cried Hathaway, who had seen them at the same moment.

His black leather shoes had been turned bleach white from the soles up almost to the ankle. He kicked one off unselfconsciously, and ripped his still-dark sock off. His foot underneath, though very pale and pasty, seemed to be fine.

"Everything okay?" asked the short-haired woman with the glasses and roll of candy, a young scientist named Nayeli Reed.

Hathaway nodded vigorously, rattled but relieved.

"Tried to give me two-tone shoes or something. I'm going to expense a new pair, Dr. Pettinger, and you are *damn well* going to approve it!"

She laughed.

"I can just see 'Approval for replacement shoes' becoming a huge explanation in the audit, but if that's what you want, you've got it. You almost lost your feet!"

Ben, leaning against the closest wall in shock, had blended into the background during this fiasco. During the exchange, something suddenly clicked for him.

"All these weird abilities the cats have, you're hoping they can be used for–"

Pettinger replied calmly.

"We're hoping there are defensive capabilities to be gleaned from these developments. And, secondarily, any other kind of purpose."

Ben shook his head in disbelief for a moment before remembering his setting. 'Defensive, and then any other sort.' Those priorities were, of course, normal for the 'Agency,' but Ben thought it a strange perspective to take on creatures as unique and challenging to human understanding as these cats.

"That's what you signed up for, bub," Hathaway said, a harsh strain of bitterness in his voice Ben had never heard before. Hathaway turned to Pettinger. "And *you*. You're supposed to be *smarter* than that. Just rattling out redacted facts like you wouldn't be in Leavenworth for life if I told the right people about it – *bah!*"

Pettinger's two scientists began backing away uncomfortably when Hathaway started raising his voice, but they quickly ran out of room to retreat, backing up against the consoles. Hathaway saw them out of the corner of his eye and made a grunting sound before downing his coffee in a massive gulp.

Ben eyed his boss, whose Adam's apple bobbed up and down as he drank. *What was going on?* Ben flinched as Hathaway suddenly smashed his coffee mug to the floor and wheeled around to confront the two scientists.

"And *you!* Cowards! Look at you, hiding in the corner like a bunch of sissies! At least the kid didn't plan up this whole crazy thing! He's scared of what you guys are doing, you up-your-own-ass bunch of hypocritical dipsticks!"

Ben was shocked at Hathaway's vehemence. It was as though a switch had been flipped, turning him from a cantankerous but largely pleasant individual into a violent, condescending maniac, all in a matter of moments.

"*Release the hounds!*" cried Hathaway. "That's what you want, right? You wanna test them all, don't you? Release number six! Release number six why don't you? *Next!*"

He pounded the button on the console before anyone realized what he was doing, triggering the mechanism before he could be stopped.

"Number six is a real *bitchkitty*, boys and girls," Hathaway said, starting to cackle.

Ben gasped in astonishment at the sight of foam speckles forming at the corners of Hathaway's mouth.

"Rick, I think that's quite enough," Pettinger said, starting to gather her wits, scattered by Hathaway's outburst.

"Oh, no. Not yet! We have to test, and prod, and poke the limits - maybe there's some kind of capability we can use!"

He laughed as the cat landed on the chamber floor. The young cat was huge, colored strangely in a mix of yellow and grey, and looked - if it were possible - at least *twice* as furious as Hathaway.

"Look! The poor little thing is *hungry*," Hathaway said, going to the rat release.

"Rick, isn't this the one who... the one that Golding..." Jeff stammered, but it was too late.

Not one, not two, but three furtive rats scurried into the chamber. The cat was on them at once.

"Rick, what are you *doing?*" Pettinger squealed in alarmed agitation as rat limbs flew against the Plexiglas barrier.

Hathaway laughed louder, mashing the rat release button over and over again. Soon, no fewer than twenty rats were scurrying around on the other side of the glass. Jeff had begun to struggle with Hathaway. As they spun, Ben caught a glimpse of Hathaway's eyes – his huge black pupils seemed to whirl in their sockets.

Nayeli screamed, and Ben spun to see what had happened. One by one, the rats were crumpling inside the chamber like empty paper cups with the air sucked out of them, shriveling into dark, dusty cores within seconds. The cat shuddered and juddered as strange blue bolts of energy flew from the extinguished rats to his open mouth. Dark steam began to ooze from the charred rat remains.

Hathaway – with Jeff hanging off him, trying to pull him away – continued to mash the button. Still more rats flooded into the chamber, only to instantly shrivel away like snowballs thrown into a furnace. Ben gasped aloud as a red-faced Hathaway spun around and drove his fist into Jeff's face. The taller, wirier man crumpled to the floor.

Pettinger, meanwhile, had been frantically working at a separate panel, and soon her shoulders slumped in relief – she had deactivated the rat release mechanism. Soon, Hathaway himself collapsed face down, having seemingly fainted. Ben screamed in horror when he saw Hathaway's left leg rise violently into the air behind him, an unseen force tugging him bodily off the ground.

Nayeli bellowed in fear as she too rose through the air and slammed into the Plexiglas with a sickeningly wet *smack*, a gurgling gasp escaping her lips as the impact drove all the air out of her. Her arms and legs, at first splayed out like a backseat window-cling, went limp and dangled lifelessly as the invisible force pulled her body away from the clear wall and then drove her back into it, like the banging of a massive human gavel. Jeff, still woozy from the battering he had taken from the crazed Hathaway, reached up and tried to catch her leg to stop her flight, but was only pulled along with her. There was a sickening *pop* as his arm joint was yanked from its socket, and his body twisted unnaturally with the dislocation, Nayeli's heaving body tugging him along.

The cat inside the chamber didn't even seem to be standing on firm ground now. Rather, he appeared to float in a strange green mist a few inches from the ground. Around him, more rats burst apart like light bulbs shot with a pellet gun. He yawned, throwing back his jaws and exposing rows of razor sharp teeth.

He rose into the air: one foot, two feet, three, and then the green energy of the mist in which he floated seemed to coalesce in his mouth with a burst of light. He dropped to the floor, landing athletically on all fours. If anything, the cat looked bored.

Hathaway tried to sit up, a massive red cut on his forehead oozing blood.

"What happened?" he mumbled.

Nayeli and Jeff were piled in a jumbled heap of limbs in front of the window, Ben crouched over them to help, with Pettinger alone still standing. She fiddled with a panel, and cursed as the menu screen refused to roll over to the next set of options.

"Come *on*!" she said as the cat hissed, fixing his yellow-green gaze on her hunched form.

Her long hair began to pull back from her head. She ignored it, focusing on the panel. Ben, operating on instinct, ran over to try to stop whatever was pulling at her hair, and felt a slashing force catch him across the chest. He took a step back, his hand automatically flying up to his chest where he had been hit. Ben stared at his hand in amazement: it was splattered lightly with blood.

"You bastard!" Pettinger growled.

She had finally activated the sleeping gas, but the cat had given her hair one last, vicious *yank* before it succumbed to the anesthetic. Tufts of her golden hair fluttered around her reddened, terrified face. She fanned them away, and shrieked upon noticing smoke issuing from one of the tufts. Her hair had begun to smolder. With as much dignity as possible, she dumped her lukewarm coffee on her sizzling hair to make sure she was out.

Meanwhile, Ben, still bleeding from the gash on his chest, ran back over to help up the stunned Jeff and Nayeli. Jeff moaned as he popped his shoulder back into place.

"Last time *I* try to help anybody," he grumbled.

Hathaway staggered to his feet, gingerly feeling the cut on his head. The technicians in hazmat suits on the other side of the panel were already scooping this last cat back into his capsule, readying him to be fired like a bank deposit back up the tube and into his holding pen.

"Everyone okay?" Hathaway asked, his voice full of concern.

Ben blinked incredulously. Hathaway didn't seem to remember his strange outburst: how he had released at least twenty rats into the pen, screamed at all of them, and began beating his co-workers before passing out. Jeff vocalized Ben's thoughts.

"Rick, do you even remember what *happened*?"

Hathaway's bloodied face scrunched up in thought. After a moment, he spoke in a dazed and tentative voice.

"Damn thing got us!"

His words and tone eerily echoed Golding's.

Pettinger – already rattled – looked even more stunned.

"Hathaway, you went *crazy* there for a minute. You were freaking out! You released like two dozen rats to that thing. You don't even *remember?*"

Hathaway shook his head, looking frantic and puzzled.

"That cat's *dangerous,*" Nayeli blurted out.

Jeff sighed.

"We'll have to review the recordings on this, for sure. But if we were looking for anything, *this* is it."

It was Ben's turn to blurt things out.

"You can't honestly advocate *using* this sort of thing to fight *wars,* can you?"

He instantly regretted vocalizing his thoughts.

Jeff responded vehemently.

"Of course I don't *advocate* it! I'll tell you what I *do* advocate." Jeff got right in Ben's face, passionately defending the Agency's morals. "I *do* advocate keeping Boston and Cincinnati and Los Angles and New York and even Minneapolis safe from a terror cell of Al Qaeda cats, and the only way we can do that is if we know what we're dealing with."

He took a deep breath, shaking his head.

"I'm sorry, but I *guarantee* you that the people who want to kill us aren't going to have as firm of a moral compass as you do, Ben." Jeff took another deep breath. "You've got to understand: it's not people who think like you that make the world dangerous, Ben – and I'm sorry, but nice people like you can't keep yourselves safe from murderous lunatics worth a *damn.* It's a proven fact."

Hathaway was hunched over one of the screens, reviewing the tapes of him screaming at Jeff, releasing the rats, and all the rest. He shook his head, wanting to put distance between what he was seeing on screen and what he accepted as 'reality.'

"I don't remember *any* of this. *Any* of it."

"*That* cat is dangerous," Nayeli repeated. "First, Jessup gave him that fish, and he got Golding. We've proven that in the hemo-crit analysis. But what did he eat *this* time?"

"Isn't it obvious?" Jeff said. "Like twenty rats."

"*Before* the rats," Nayeli responded. "He had enough energy to affect Hathaway before he ate rat one."

Jeff rubbed his aching head.

"We have full video feed of the pens, right?"

Nayeli nodded.

"I know what I'm doing for homework tonight," he said. "I'll review at least his camera for the last twenty-four hours. Hope to *god* there's something there, because if he can just *do* things like this…"

Hathaway smiled nervously at Jeff.

"Glad you're taking this so well." He pointed at himself on the monitor, punching Jeff in the face. "Looks like I just tried to beat the shit out of you!"

Jeff shook his head, a slightly bemused smile on his face.

"I know even a royal scrote like you wouldn't just start wailing on me – at work, anyway."

Ben started feeling uncomfortable with the increasing jockiness of the two men's banter, and turned his attention to Pettinger. He noticed that she was fiddling with the Dyna-Etch machine.

"What are you naming *this* one?"

Pettinger looked up.

"I'm naming him after the worst thing in the world. My oldest grandson was just telling me all about it last weekend."

She frowned in concentration as her thumbs worked the keys.

"I hope I'm spelling it right."

She pulled out the nametag and dangled it from the chain in front of them.

'DEINONYCHUS' read the tag.

"Dine-oinkus?" Hathaway said, flabbergasted.

Jeff elbowed him.

"It's probably 'Dean-on-eichus,'" he said.

Pettinger shook her head. "You're both wrong. It's 'Dine-ON-uh-kus.'"

Everybody in the room repeated the name.

"Deinonychus," Ben said. "Sounds like a kind of dinosaur. What does it mean?"

Pettinger nodded, smiling darkly before answering.

"Give that man a cookie. It *is* a kind of dinosaur: the worst kind. Its name means 'Terrible Claw.'"

To the battered and bloody crew who had just witnessed the newly-christened Deinonychus in action, that sounded just about right.

TWELVE

There was no real reason why Deinonychus should be so much less attuned to the thoughts of others than his smaller brother Leviticus. He simply chose not to care about others. On top of this apathy of others, the big cat was *infinitely* more self-regarding.

Deinonychus never paid enough attention to the mental input coming from others to notice it for what it was. What sounded, to Leviticus, like complex symphonies of thought, perception, experience, and emotion woven together and into each other struck the psychic ears belonging to Deinonychus as nothing more than irritating buzzing sounds – grinding and grating and cloying in his ears even as they shared information. He could still sense small bits of knowledge in those noises: was the creature hungry? In pain? Excited? Sick?

If the sounds had been *merely* irritating, they would have driven Deinonychus to constant anger. They were, however, sometimes useful. As it was, he had learned to live with them, though he never explored them the way his grey brother did. And if things ever got too loud inside his head, Deinonychus just found whatever was making the mental sound and slowly put it out of the misery he intended to inflict upon it.

He never realized, as Leviticus effortlessly had, that these were the sounds from the *insides* of the other creatures' minds. They were just bits of stuff to him, the ones that were not immediately useful to him be seeming no better than candy wrappers blowing around in the wind. If they communicated something useful, it was in the same manner that the smell a skunk makes tells you when it's frightened.

When the sound of the caterpillar's mind had first reached Deinonychus, his first reaction had been irritation. What began as mere irritation at a tiny scrabbling sound had resulted in a delicious meal. Once the cat finished off the caterpillar that had been bothering him, he moved quickly on to every grub in the tree hanging over the roof.

Then, right when he was getting the hang of his trick – luring the tiny little things with his mind and then catching them in his mental jaws – he had noticed an *opening*. Somewhere, down below, was a mind with a space in it – a space just waiting for Deinonychus to step into. He couldn't take *total* control of this mind – not yet, not with the limited energy he had gleaned from these disgusting, crawling prey. But he could, he sensed, affect it just enough to topple its delicate balance.

Deinonychus had only to give the boulder of this human's thoughts a stout enough shove, and it would go tumbling down the hill of sanity, wrecking everything in its path. The cat sensed that something about the man was poised just on the brink, and Deinonychus didn't take more than a second's thought before acting on his instinct, viciously plucking at the strings of Hathaway's mind.

The feeling was satisfying, and the trick seemed to work. He felt the man's thoughts quiver and gyrate, broken like the calm surface of a lake disrupted by a thrown rock. This was fun!

A moment later, as he was getting used to the new sensation, the ground went out from his feet.

*   *   *

His bleary eyelids fluttered open in the experimental theater, but his first reaction wasn't fear or confusion. His first thought was *whiskers*, and a second later he had a pawful of them. His mind had been pulled by the scurrying motions of a group of rats, and Deinonychus sank his teeth deep into the neck tissue of the closest before he even knew he was reacting, or what he was reacting to.

Instantly, the burst of warm blood against his pink tongue flowered into a wave of energy, expanding inside him like a mushroom cloud. More rodent voices came crowding into his mind, and he was on them at once, tearing into the minds and bodies with a combination of physical and telekinetic claws that sent streaks of blood and chunks of rat flying. He still did not really notice the group of humans on the other side of the Plexiglas divider, though their voices and frightened thoughts were clamoring around his mind.

Deinonychus thought only of the rats, and of the burning life inside them that seemed almost desperate to escape and fill him, to *serve* him. He rose from the floor, floating in a sickly glowing mist that forming out of the writhing vapors that issued from the bodies of the rats. His eyes flickered green as Hathaway dropped face down to the floor. That's when the cat noticed the humans for the first time, and he instantly thought them better sport than the rats.

Why, they were *bendy!* Deinonychus wasn't used to toying with prey that didn't break. He remembered the gleeful surprise that had accompanied finding he could use the bits of energy from that fish the woman had given him to cut his first human – Golding, though the cat didn't know or care what the thing had called itself.

The cat only appreciated that the tall, awkward thing would bleed when scratched. Deinonychus had been inexperienced then, and operating off a meager snack of rotting, slimy fish. Barely chordates, barely aware, barely fresh. A low form of life, already dead by another's hand. A disgusting, fishy vessel nearly empty of living energy.

Now Deinonychus had taken his fill of living blood, the blood of a mammal – an animal much closer to him in nature. His insides pulsed with the light of its energy like a thundercloud flickering with the threat of lightning. He turned this energy on the humans on the other side of the glass and they, now his playthings, began to dance and twitch.

He could just *slam* them wherever he wanted! Nayeli rammed the Plexiglas so many times that her forehead began to squeak a bloody streak across the barrier. Deinonychus liked the sound of that. Then the tall, gangly one who always frowned had tried to help her, and the cat heard his arm *plop* right out of its joint. Deinonychus liked that sound, too.

There were a few people on the other side of the sheet, but Deinonychus found that some were easier to focus on than others. Jeff and Nayeli, in particular, seemed to stand out to him, glowing a little more brightly and giving off louder (and, to the cat, more irritating) sounds than the rest. Once Hathaway, who's mind had been the doorway the cat used to get his fill of rats, had passed out, they took the brunt of his attack.

The woman with the light hair and tall, straight bearing in the corner, messing with glowing banks of people things, seemed dim, almost transparent. The exultantly destructive cat halfheartedly pulled at her hair even as he slammed the others into the glass. She was too hard to focus on.

One person, however, didn't even ping Deinonychus's radar. Even as Ben ran over to help Pettinger, when his darting movement and interfering action should have made him especially apparent to the cat, Deinonychus could hear or see nothing. It wasn't quite as though Ben weren't there at all – but like he wasn't *alive*.

Not the same way the sun seemed to lack a mind – brightly burning in the sky, declaring its silent presence to all in spite of its mental silence. Ben was like a desk, or a chair, or flashlight. Deinonychus could see him, but he didn't register as a creature.

The others were all crumpled on the floor now, and Pettinger started to stand out more and more to the cat. What was she doing? A stream of frantic clicking sounds poured from her mind and he got the general impression of her intention – trying to *stop him*. She was going to make awful smells come, and then he would sleep.

He did not want to sleep.

He hissed, and concentrated all of his energy on Pettinger's still hazy form. Her hair began to smoke and curl. Deinonychus snarled, throwing more of his energy into the act.

In this time, Ben had come up behind Pettinger, reached his hands up to her hair to help, and Deinonychus had noticed *nothing*. Just as the cat sent a vicious burst of energy her way, he felt it *snap* back, bouncing off some unexpected object like a bird flying into a pane of glass.

The effect was similar to a furious drunk stubbing his toe – Deinonychus lurched out senselessly to counteract the unexpected force. Digital screens sparked and hissed. But it was too late – even as Ben stared, blinking in disbelief, at the bloody clawmarks on his chest and hand, Deinonychus could feel the curling tendrils of gas overtaking him. The sleep was coming. The burning smell had begun to overwhelm him. It was over.

Deinonychus had… fainted?

Deinonychus didn't know what fainting was. A lot of cats don't. To a feral cat, fainting is something you do right before you bleed to death, and to a housecat, fainting is pretty much how you spend three-quarters of the day. Deinonychus only knew that, at the precise moment that everything he could smell and see and hear seemed to go fuzzy, and tilt sideways, his sensitive feline nose was *assaulted* by a caustic, burning smell. Then the now-fuzzy world went dark and silent, and he had awoken back in his chamber.

But Deinonychus had learned two very important things – he had learned how easy humans were to hurt, and he had learned how much he loved to hurt them.

Thirteen

It was early, the sky still grey, but tendrils of gold had begun to seep in. Ben and Hathaway sat alone in the Agency cafeteria, drinking coffee. They needed the caffeine to wake themselves up, but they didn't really want to be awake, so they drank their cups slowly. It was Friday, the day after the 'incident,' and they had both had a long week.

"So what do you suppose they'll do with them?' Ben asked.

Hathaway shook his head.

"Not sure. You know, it isn't really these particular *cats* that we are studying, as much as it's the genes that enable them to demonstrate the sorts of things they've been doing." He cleared his throat. "As far as my understanding goes, the best of these will go on to be used for some kind of genetic stock for the next batch, until we can really isolate the exact genes that switch these abilities on."

Ben nodded, a sort of emptiness descending on him. He should have suspected something like that.

"What are they going to do with any that seem like duds?"

Hathaway's glance shot up.

"You mean like Leviticus?" He scowled. "They'll probably sequence the genes anyway. In fact, I'm sure of it – they'll look for differences between the effective siblings and the… *dud* as you put it. That will help them isolate it even faster, I imagine."

He shook his head.

"But I'm telling you, we don't understand what's happening here. We don't understand what these cats can do. The coats act like they know what's going on, but *you* saw what happened in there. Nobody knows what's going on."

He pounded the table, sending a spume of coffee droplets from his paper cup into the air.

"They send a bunch of rats out into a room, measure the way the cats hunt 'em, and catalog the anomalous behavior the cat exhibits afterwards. Straightforward, right? Except we don't know what the hell we're measuring. How do we know Leviticus doesn't have some weird power that doesn't manifest itself as physically or violently as the powers Vortex or Deinonychus have? I mean even Charlotte and Decibel can do *physical* things – that Decibel can eat rats and turn that energy into sounds is about as intangible as a physical effect can be, am I right?"

Ben nodded, vacillating between taking another sip of coffee or setting the cup down. He took another sip.

"So the coats get these cats in here. We're paid for out of the defense budget, so even if they accidentally see that these cats cure cancer or magically increase orphan literacy rates or whatever positive effect you could think of, that would be of tertiary importance to a cat that could, say, give a foreign head of state an embolism. I mean they'll *study* it and pass it on to the right agency who will actually continue to study it, but the red tape a thing has to go through to crossover from defense to simple research is hellacious."

He shook his head at memories of past paperwork.

"The crossover projects, we call 'em, might as well not have been discovered for five years after we find them, because we aren't 'authorized' to work on non-defense stuff. You know how all this bureaucracy stuff works – after all, you got *hired* here. What I'm trying to say is, if these cats can do anything helpful *besides* destroy stuff, even if we did catch on to it – which it's hard to imagine we could do when all we are testing them for is to see how destructive they are – we would be in a very poor position to get that turned into something useful in a reasonable timeframe."

Ben had been trying to figure out where Hathaway was going with all of this throughout the conversation, but by this point he felt certain that there was some subtext to what he was saying that Hathaway wanted him to pick up on. Ben just wasn't seeing it.

"What do you mean?" Ben finally asked.

Hathaway sighed.

"I guess I just find myself wondering, over the last day or so, whether we should even be trying to learn more about this. If there's no possible positive outcome, what's the point?"

It was Ben's turn to shake his head.

"Treasonous thinking."

He saw a hurt and frightened look pass across Hathaway's face.

"At least that's what they'd say." Ben quickly added.

Ben had grown used to Hathaway calling others treasonous over minor offenses, and he felt awkward using Hathaway's own term against him. Hathaway nodded understandingly.

"I know, I can't believe myself, either." He laughed, rubbing his temples. "I haven't felt quite right ever since that little incident yesterday." His eyes widened. "I mean, did I really clock Jeff in the face like that?" He shook his right hand gingerly. "Sure as hell *feels* like I did." He laughed. "But I don't damn well *remember* it, so where's the fun in that?"

Ben just looked thoughtful. It seemed to him that something more serious ought to be happening. Ben couldn't understand why they didn't regard the 'Hathaway Incident' as a more major breach of protocol. He knew that Jeff was reviewing the security footage and inspecting the enclosures – but what could that show? These cats were damn near magical. Ben was about to express his misgivings when a high, piercing squeal ripped through his skull. Hathaway's' paper cup dropped to the table, his mouth falling open.

"What the hell is that?" Ben asked over the shrill noise.

Red lights on the walls had begun flashing. A recording of a crisp, calm female voice began to say "Please make your way in an orderly fashion to the nearest marked emergency exit. These can be found at the northwest and southeast sides of each facility arm. To ensure maximum safety, please proceed calmly and stay alert for future updates. Please make your way in an orderly fashion to the nearest…"

Ben felt a strong hand taking him by the arm, and let himself be tugged. It was Hathaway, who had pulled a ridiculously bright-orange emergency vest out of a red box on the wall and carried it looped over one arm.

"Fifteen goddamn years, this is the *third* time those alarms have ever gone off," he said through clenched teeth.

Ben's feet were catching up with him, and now he wasn't being yanked along as much as he was taking three strides for every one of Hathaway's – looking like a tiny dog trying gamely to keep up with its master. Hathaway continued muttering as they approached the stairs.

"Dear God, this better not be anything like the *last* time," he said, wrapping his meaty hands around the door handle. It didn't move. "*Christ!*" he shouted.

"Locked?" Ben asked, incredulous.

"*...in an orderly fashion to the nearest marked emergency exit,*" the loop of voice repeated before shattering apart into crackling static.

"Hello? Is this thing on? *Hello?*"

Jeff's voice came out of the speakers. Hathaway and Ben froze and cocked their heads in unison, like dogs who had just heard their master's voice played on a phonograph.

"Look, guys: if you can hear me, *don't go to the emergency exits!* Please, *stay inside!* Wherever you are – do *not* go outside. Do *not* get near the windows. Things on the... uh..."

His voice sounded manic. He gave a hysterical laugh before continuing.

"Let's just say that things on the roof are a little *strained* right now."

Ben turned to Hathaway, about to ask him something, and gasped when he saw Rick standing by the window. He was *opening* it.

"What are you doing?" Ben screamed, running over.

Hathaway's arm pumped as he spun the rotating handle that opened the window. As Ben stepped closer to it, he could see that something darkened the sky, blotting out the sun like storm clouds. He couldn't make out what it was because Hathaway's stocky body was blocking his view.

"*Rick!*" Ben yelled as the window swung open.

Dozens of squalling crows began to pour through the cracked window into the room like water rushing into a submarine. Feathers filled the air. Blobs of red and blue seemed to pulse through the black cloud, and Ben realized that the mix included cardinals, blue jays, sparrows – anything that could claim a Tyrannosaur as an ancestor and lived in the 'Colburn Forestry Preserve Project' was currently inundating the cafeteria.

Ben hadn't realized how utterly alien avian wildlife could be to his mammalian sensibilities until he found himself subsumed by a living cloud of squalling, desperate birds. The mass of flighted creatures beat their wings furiously, seething and screeching as one inchoate entity. Hathaway still stood by the window, though he was difficult to see through the feathers.

When Ben finally made him out through the dense cloud of birds, he was aghast. Hathaway stood only steps from the window, with his head limp and his arms dangling, battered by the onrush of beaks, pinions, and wings. Ben would have guessed that his boss was having a stroke, if it weren't for the eerie similarities between this situation and what had happened the day prior.

Ben, bracing himself against the onslaught of feathers, tried to reach down and grab Hathaway around his knees, to pull him backward. Hathaway was a hefty man, however, and difficult to budge. Just as Ben began to despair, Hathaway seemed to suddenly snap to attention. Flailing his arms, he fell backwards, stumbling over Ben and crushing the smaller, younger man to the floor. Ben spat out feathers.

"Jeezus motherfuckload on a *gawddamn crisp*!" Hathaway screamed.

The older man sounded terrified, but definitely like himself once more. He sprang into action, never faltering in the face of all those birds. Crawling on his stomach to the island in the middle of the cafeteria, Hathaway ripped the fire extinguisher off the wall and tore the safety tag out. Ben heard a sharp *hiss* as a chemical cloud erupted in the cafeteria space. Birds screamed harsh cries, some dropping to the ground – reduced to mad flopping in their desperate attempts to get the extinguisher's concoction off their plumage.

Hathaway kicked himself up onto his feet and gave Ben a hand. Birds still battered them from every angle, but the fire extinguisher had opened up a space where the onslaught of wings was lessened, and the two Agency employees ran through it.

"What the blue hell do we do now? *Eh?*" Hathaway laughed at himself. "*Ha.* Why ask: *that*, or *anything* else? Fuck if *you* know, *fuck* if I know."

He laughed again, spittle flying in gobs from his lips as he spoke, prompting Ben to step back without thinking, almost out of the safe zone. Hathaway spoke on.

"Knowledge rots, and straight lines go on for a very long *ever and ever*. And people who say so are so very clever, until the people who say everything's forever curved come in and sever their ties to this *line* bit of word…. *then* they're absurd!"

Birds pelted them both as Hathaway cackled out this doggerel. Ben's stomach sank. Hathaway seemed to be cutting in and out - sane one moment and babbling the next.

"*Go!*" Ben geared up, growled, and then rammed his boss in the shoulder.

The bulky Hathaway revived, resuming his mad dash down the hallway as though he had never been interrupted. Amid the rush of wings, Ben grabbed another fire extinguisher and pulled its tag out with his teeth. As he prepared to let the pressurized contents fly, he felt a raven take his short-cropped hair in its pinions.

Squealing in outrage and pain, Ben gripped the metal cylinder of the extinguisher like a block and lifted it high above his own head, intending to smash it down with as much force as possible and looking like a crazy Moses going off balance trying to smash the tablets.

He swung, and a dull *thunk* signaled the raven's last breath. Its body bounced off the wall and rolled along the floor. There were still dozens of other birds in the air. Ben tried to grasp the extinguisher's metal body in his sweaty hands, to keep ahold of it, but he lost his grip and the canister clunked to the tile behind him.

"*Dammit!*"

Hathaway wheeled around, and the look burning in his eyes terrified Ben. It was as though the man had been split into two men – Ben's boss, and a lunatic. Even as Ben saw recognition in Hathaway's eyes, the senseless humming that had overridden the man's sanity drowned it out with is manic insistence that seemed to cry only '*I see you!*' in a shrill, relentless voice.

His boss reached up to grab him, and in a moment of absolute clarity Ben knew that the crazed thing that had taken hold of Hathaway's mind meant to break his neck.

As the man's fingers tensed on his shoulders, Ben heard wet, animal sounds coming from Hathaway's throat. There was a war being fought behind those wild, whirring eyes – a war between man and beast. The fingers around his neck tightened, as cold as crab claws and as hard as horns.

Ben, unable to do anything else in his frightened paralysis, resorted to screaming, certain he would soon be strangled.

"*Dee bop,*" Hathaway said, as if to confirm his essential non-humanity, an elongating length of drool descending from his mouth.

Ben felt himself dropping to the floor under the pressure of Hathaway's hands, felt his knees bending and giving way beneath him. Time itself seemed to slow, and he could see the seething mass of birds seem to clarify and resolve themselves, like images solidifying on a loading webpage. A blur of red became a cardinal – its feathers crisply visible, its tiny, folded set of feet tucked neatly beneath it. The background 'chatter' of the birds had become a thousand tiny streams, each filled with its own sound that did not blend or mix with the others, but hung together with the others in a shining, interwoven whole.

Ben could see a sweat droplet flying from his arm, tracing it as it flew inch by inch through the air.

The floor was rushing up now, and Ben braced himself for impact. An instant later, he reasoned, his senseless boss would be upon him, driving his full weight down on him and grinding Ben into the floor. Ben didn't have time to roll out from underneath.

Time was running short, slow-mo or not. In fact, Ben was surprised that he hadn't hit the floor *yet* – even at this pace, it should have happened by now. He blinked twice in complete disbelief when he saw the door he and Hathaway had been standing near go flying upwards, past him. Everything was gone now, except for Hathaway, and Ben's own arms.

Hathaway's frizzy hair seemed to be hanging from his head at impossible angles. Everything had vanished, and Ben had the stomach-lurching sensation of descending twenty stories in an elevator in the space of a moment. Ben couldn't make sense of what his senses were telling him for a moment, before he realized that the pair of them were *still falling*.

Hathaway must have triggered some kind of emergency chute. Ben, now that his mind had adjusted, could feel the metal walls sliding past him.

"*Ben?*" Hathaway shouted, sounding like a man who had just woken up in the dark to discover that something is chewing his leg.

"I'm right he–" Ben began, but Hathaway's heavy – and apparently steel-toed – boot chose that moment to catch him in the temple, and after a brief spray of bright sparks, Ben's world fell dark and silent.

Fourteen

There was a dull sort of burning – too muffled to be considered an ache, but not dull enough to be oblivion.

"Is he ok?" Sounded like Pettinger.

There was a suffuse yet dilute red color to the universe that, in other circumstances, might have seemed something like light – to Ben, the effect was like seeing the airplane warning lights of a cell phone tower through the haze of a blizzard. He didn't like the red, *or* the voices, and wanted them all to go away.

"I feel bad as hell for the way I clocked him like that," said another voice.

Ben groaned. He could tell the voice belonged to Hathaway. Until the encroachment of the red light and the voices, Ben could convince himself that he wasn't actually a person, and that *here* wasn't really a place. Now it was increasingly obvious that he was a person in pain, and that *here* was a real – and, at the moment, very sucky – place.

"What were you even *doing*?"

It was Nayeli. Ben groaned again – he felt how a baby must feel when it realizes that it was going to *have* to go along with its mother's wishes and be born; that it can't just hide out in placental purgatory forever. Hathaway's response, when it came, sounded wounded.

"Gosh, I don't know! Once those birds got in, it all went to hell in a hay basket."

"*That's* what we're trying to find out, Rick."

Pettinger again. Ben didn't groan at the sound this time, but merely tensed his lips. His headache was getting better. Pettinger continued.

"*How* did they get in? Did you see?"

Hathaway sounded put out.

"Well, not *exactly*. I mean, by the time I noticed the birds, they were already–"

Ben sat up like a reactivated robot in a kid's television show, spat some blood, and spoke.

"You crazy fucker, you went and *opened* the window."

* * *

There were a few choruses of "Ben!" and "You're alright!" before what he said sunk in.

"Wait – you're saying *I* did it?"

Hathaway was a pitiable mix of outrage and terror: outrage that anyone would ever accuse him of doing something so horrible, and terror because, now that he had heard it from someone else's mouth, he realized in his heart it must be true.

Pettinger shook her head, looking like someone who walked into their three-year-old's room and found it destroyed with permanent marker.

"We underestimated this entire project."

Her voice had a resigned tone that chilled Ben.

"Where's Jeff?" he asked, not wanting to hear the answer.

Pettinger turned to him, and Ben saw a hallow listlessness in her eyes that scared him even more.

"Oh, you know. The roof. He's probably still there." Her voice sounded 'checked-out.'

Ben looked around, shaking his head.

"Where are *we*, for that matter?"

Ben thought it looked like a shed. Four stone block walls rose into the dim heights above. No ceiling was visible, and the chamber around him was sparse. Rimmed with lockers, it contained a central table, a top-opening freezer slung low alongside a small cutting board stacked with portable oven burners, and an open space in the corner for laying out the four cots that were stacked there in rectangular cases, ready for assembly.

"What does it look like, kid?" Pettinger sounded irritated and impatient, but not upset. "It's an emergency goddamn bunker."

She sounded completely unlike the buttoned-up scientist persona she usually displayed. In fact, Ben noted, Pettinger was starting to talk like Hathaway.

Hathaway grunted, too upset to laugh but too amused at Pettinger's changed tone to not react.

"That's right, 'kid.' This 'goddamn bunker' is here for emergencies, and we went through the chute together there at the end."

Ben finally understood part of what happened. But not the part where Hathaway flung the window open, stood there limp-handed and slack-necked as birds buffeted his body, and stated "Knowledge rots, and straight lines go on for a very long *ever and ever and ever…*"

Ben finally understood how he had gotten where he was now, far underground in one of the Agency's emergency bunkers, but didn't understand how Hathaway could have had the presence of mind to enact a sane plan like 'get to the emergency chute' – not when his eyes had been whirling so madly, with his mouth twitching and spittle spraying as he said '*Dee bop*' in a cold, lifeless voice.

"We might as well come out and say it," Ben said, wary but resolute. "They seem to be able to get to Hathaway and… cross out his wires or something. He seems to be their easiest gateway."

"Gateway? *What are you saying?*"

Hathaway was furious and indignant.

"Relax, Rick," Pettinger said. "Calm yourself. Can't you see that it must be true? It's not your fault. Nobody is blaming you. It's just…." She trailed off.

Hathaway, wheeling from face to face, looked furious, but didn't persist in arguing.

Nayeli spoke up.

"All that's as may be. The question is: what can we do about it?"

They all fell silent as they pondered this. Ben, first to break the silence, sounded certain about their duty.

"Jeff is on the roof. We can't leave him up there."

There was a mutual gasp.

"Ben, I don't know if you understand that alarm that sounded just a bit back. That's a *serious* breach. There's a chance that this experiment has compromised containment for other Agency projects. Do you understand?"

Ben's racing mind didn't immediately grasp the implications.

"So we might be getting cats up in the other buildings? Cats over-running everything?"

That sounded bad enough to him.

"Well, *yes*," Pettinger sounded perplexed and exasperated. "But the real problem is that the things from the other labs can now get *out*. Do you even understand what the 'Agency' does here?"

She was talking down to him, and Ben felt like he deserved it.

"Think about it for a moment: ours is only one of dozens of experiments on this site. The security for *all* of them may be compromised."

The reality of this hit Ben like a prizefighter's right hook.

"Then we've *got* to get out there. We've got to find Jeff, figure out what's happening, and stop it."

Ben's voice and posture left no doubt – he was resolute and certain.

"Ben, what the hell?" Nayeli sounded stunned. "We can't do *anything!* Who do you think we are: the crew of the starship Enterprise?"

Hathaway, after a hacking cough and a deep drag on his e-cigarette, added his two cents.

"Yeah, kid. You were obviously raised on a steady diet of Ninja Turtles defeating the robot menace with laser cannons made out of stuff they found dumpster diving in a neat half hour every Saturday morning, but this is real life. We're just people."

Ben was barely listening. He was looking through the lockers, already strapping an automatic rifle onto his back. He hefted a case of revolvers out onto the central table, flipped it open, and grabbed one, sticking it into his waistband.

"Where is the door out of this place?"

"You have to climb," Nayeli said, in a detached, unreal voice. "There."

She halfheartedly pointed at metal ladder rails sticking out of the stone walls. Ben nodded, strode to the ladder, and started climbing before anyone could express surprise.

"You better come with me, people," Ben said over his shoulder as he worked his way upwards. "You guys are the ones who came up with this."

Hathaway, Nayeli, and Pettinger frowned at each other for a loaded moment before grabbing revolvers of their own and starting up the ladder after Ben.

As they neared the chute at the top, the cries of the birds grew louder.

Fifteen

Jeff hadn't started out thinking that his daily tour of the cats' enclosures – a procedure he had come to think of as 'inspecting the troops' – would be significantly different to prior day's rounds. Though the intense 'incident' in the testing chamber the day before had primed him for the idea that the unexpected *was* possible, he wasn't so cynical to assume that the cataclysmic was *inevitable*.

Now, stuffed into the empty cage for safety as a maelstrom of feathers and fur raged around him, Jeff swore to himself that he would never be so forgiving in his assumptions.

* * *

It had begun innocently enough. The cats seemed to be doing as well as ever – though Charlotte had got something bound up in her cage that hadn't been authorized or distributed to her. A cursory inspection showed it to be a squirrel – wrapped up in webbing like a dwarf in *The Hobbit,* its half-eaten head sticking grotesquely out of its thready prison. So they *were* getting contraband food, Jeff thought.

That was no good.

While he was up here, he was going to check the video feed, and see exactly how Charlotte had trapped the squirrel. Did she lure it over, and then catch it in the web? Did she weave a web in a tree, from a distance, and then pull the squirrel to her cage with her mind? So many unanswered questions.

Chief among them was this: how was number six (the cat in the seventh cage, the cat with the wretchedly unpronounceable and even more insidiously un-*spellable* name: Deinonychus) getting food? Jeff had no doubt that he was. It was number six who had unleashed the fury, number six who seemed to be bursting with energy. *How?*

They had to find out soon. If the live testing continued to be so dangerous and unpredictable, they would likely have to euthanize the cats, and then test only the genes of the cats who exhibited the strongest 'anomalies.' Though that would still be productive, Jeff thought testing the genes alone would take at least twice as long as the living tests. They already had genetic material from all of them – enough for cloning or splicing or whatever needed to be done. If they were too dangerous to keep alive, the genetic markers that made them special and useful could at least be studied, used, and hopefully perfected.

If these cats had anything useful to teach them while alive, Jeff reasoned, they better do it soon – before they had to be put down.

He didn't know it, but that was the moment Jeff made his mistake.

If only he hadn't thought that last bit – 'had to be put down' – so *vividly*.

*   *   *

Two green, feline eyes snapped open in the dark. Set in his light grey face, they seemed to burn like alien torches. Leviticus was awake.

He had just had the worst dream he could ever remember having – all the worse because it was a *people* dream. Leviticus didn't think of them quite as 'people,' of course. Though he had never really known a life without them – from the first warm bottle he had been fed by Nana Jessup to this latest insanity of chutes and gasses – the tall, talkative ones had always seemed like something different.

The world of creatures – birds, squirrels, the other cats – there was a unity to their voices, a *solidarity*, which made sense.

The humans, with their complex sounds and even more complicated feelings, were like the sun – they stood alone. Unlike the sun, he could hear them. That wasn't the problem. The problem was stuffing his mental ears *against* the din of their minds, their voices, and their (to Leviticus) meaningless struggles. The world seemed full of their reeking presence.

Yet there was something else there, and Leviticus could feel it. The cat had some kind of kinship with them, as surely as the moon shared its light with the sun. Leviticus could look out at the birds and the worms and see that they understood the tall ones far less than he did. He could look at the towering (but oh-so-thin) humans and sense a connection – ancient, dimly understood perhaps, but real.

Hadn't glowing eyes like his peered through the darkness at forms like theirs as firelight flickered and limbs flailed since either of their kinds had lived? Hadn't creatures like him fed on the vermin that plagued the cities of these incomprehensible manfolk since the two-legged giants possessed the wit to erect them? Silent recognition of this long legacy had flowed like water between his eyes and the eyes of the largest of the humans – the one who had seemed to warm to Leviticus most quickly.

The weight of the long relationship between cat and man was evident, though neither he nor Hathaway had been around to see its start, and with luck neither of them would be present to see its end. That kinship was ingrained on both feline and human through long association, and it left an emptiness in Leviticus's mind that had called out to be filled. He knew not with what until she had said it. The woman with the light hair had held up a sparkling, golden thing, upon which were carved tiny squiggles that the grey cat could not understand.

Then she had said the sound that hid inside the carved lines and curves: '*Leviticus.*'

The shapes her lips and tongue and throat impressed onto the air took the form of sound, and it was a sound Leviticus had heard fluttering in the back of his mind, unuttered, since his inception. He *flocked* to that sound, surrounded it, was filled by it. It *became* him.

He looked upon the woman who had bestowed this gift upon him, his eyes finding her surprisingly beautiful. She had given him a part of himself, something he had always needed and never been able to find on his own.

She had given him his name.

It was then that Leviticus realized the relationship between humans and domesticated cats, and realized what the tall ones really were. They were the Namers, and so he ever after thought of them. While humans and cats went together – had *grown* together some time in the distant past, like a tree growing through a fence until the two were inseparable – they weren't of quite the same stuff, and they would always be on opposite sides of an enormous gulf – separated by a wall of otherness.

*   *   *

That's why, upon awaking from such a *human* dream, Leviticus felt utterly disoriented. One word hung in his mind, looming like a dark cloud over his thoughts – *paperwork*. The word meant as much to him as the NASDAQ does to a duck, but its lingering presence in his mind filled him with a sense of disquiet. The dream had been a chaotic, abstract swirling maelstrom of sounds and ideas that all struck him as unfamiliar and alien.

It had begun with splashing bands of dark and light streaking across his vision, tiny little rectangular stripes that began to make up a sort of grid. Little dark and light rectangles in unnaturally symmetrical rows. What looked like a bloodsucking insect's spikey proboscis dipped down into the bands, not sucking up liquid but *injecting* it, like a mother mosquito injecting numbing poison before going to work. Light bands became dark, the clear proboscis withdrew, slid down, and then slipped inside another rectangle before injecting its dark venom.

The light-and-dark pattern of bands began to pull away, to shrink, as the cross-hatching of light became ever finer and increasingly more dazzling. Sounds began to weave around the black and white rectangles, sinuous and winding sounds that slid and slipped – like the tubular stinger – in and out of the boxes.

'Cytosine.' 'Mitosis.' 'Aminoes.' 'Thiamine.'

The pipette dipping in and out of the containers wove like the needle of a sewing machine, spreading its genetic markers throughout the tray – but to Leviticus it was the nest of some incomprehensible insect colony, its dark eggs endlessly patient for their time of hatching.

A cat has no concept of genetics – if you require proof of this, leave twenty of them in a building and check back in a few months. Leviticus could not understand the stream of thoughts he was receiving from Jeff, but he grasped the *size* of the thoughts. What he saw next, he understood even better.

It was his family – his siblings. All six of the survivors appeared now, shuffling their way across what was now a vast field of black and white rectangles. The lost brother – the one who *would* have been in that empty seventh cage – was of course gone, but all the others were there. Even the big one.

'Deinonychus' spoke a voice in his head, and he knew his brother's name. So the Namers had given them *each* a gift.

Leviticus could see them all now – Decibel, Charlotte, Vortex – and the sound and pattern of the vibrations that made up their new names danced around them all.

But the one, the big one. *Deinonychus*. Leviticus could see that he wasn't like the others. He wasn't even like the sun.

Deinonychus was some kind of accident, some kind of fluke. Deinonychus was like a rainstorm during an earthquake that births a volcano, spewing out so much dust that the light of the sun is choked – a statistically unlikely disaster, but one that is irrefutably devastating once set in motion. Deinonychus, to put it plainly, was a thing that should not be, and yet was.

Leviticus, for his part, did not see his brother as an abomination. The meek grey cat may not have had *much* in common with his less temperamental, larger brother – but they were sons of the same mother and the power that blazed in Deinonychus's chest slumbered in Leviticus's heart, waiting to blaze forth in full fire should it be kindled. Whatever power had coiled itself inside his brother's carnivorous cells, ready to explode into fury at the touch of warm blood, also slept inside Leviticus, gathering itself.

Leviticus knew something else with certainty: Deinonychus was fully aware of the power that slept in Leviticus. Leviticus could feel him desiring it. Leviticus knew his brother was covetous of what slumbered inside him, and anxious that he have the power for himself. What Leviticus didn't know was what could be done about it, or how he could protect himself. But that wasn't the most important thing at the moment, not by a longshot.

Because those bugs from his nightmare – the bugs with the long stingers – were already drinking from the cats. Leviticus felt very sure of this: he had seen it in Jeff's mind. The stingers took the blood from the cats and then *did something* to it, or *with* it, that was very dangerous. Leviticus meowled in displeasure. These thoughts were all so very *human*, they were impossible to understand.

What was the danger?

Then Jeff thought the thought that unlocked the mystery to Leviticus.

"If we're going to get anything useful out of these guys, I hope we do it soon, before they get put down."

Accompanying the word 'useful' was a mental image of a desert landscape, covered in tents. Leviticus watched this human illusion form and dissipate behind his eyelids – saw his brother slinking over a sand dune and into the midst of the tents, before the tents began to catch fire. Tents exploded as another and then another and another Deinonychus scrambled over the hillsides, dozens and then hundreds of yellow and grey striped terrors flying up out of the sand itself and dropping down from the sky.

Thousands of identical copies of his terrifying brother burst out from the flaming tents – a chorus of hisses and gnashing fangs accompanying the appearance of what now looked like a massive cloud of cats rolling over the landscape. A gargantuan wave of yellow-grey streaks began to wash across the earth like a flood, rising high above the dunes and blotting out the sun. Tongues of flame licked out of that towering wall of woven fur and claws like lightning bolts, and a crimson haze filled the air of the valley.

The mass of cats, a tempestuous sea of fangs and razor talons, began to shift and change, melting together into an indistinguishable blob of hate and rage. Leviticus stared helplessly as the power and terror of his horrifying brother became a raw force, divorced from beast or nature, devouring in its own name. His fear turned to absolute desperation – something close to unwillingness to live to see any more of the vision – as he witnessed the sea of unformed power turning into a thousand repeated forms – not of cats – but of angry, uniformed *men*.

Armed Namers, each casting out flames and fangs from their minds, ravaging the landscape.

In the distance, skyscrapers fell and ports swelled with tsunami waves. Installations exploded and munitions vaporized. In a thousand human ways that Leviticus couldn't quite understand, but could nonetheless vaguely *feel,* these Namers who had stripped the vast, sleeping power from his brother and put it inside themselves wreaked absolute havoc on the world around them. Perhaps their human minds – inflamed by the raw sense of insoluble, unstoppable power though they were – held some semblance of a rational justification for their destruction.

The cat, however, felt heat waves of pure, righteous hatred boiling through those advancing lines of Namer soldiers, blasting the world around them into desolation with their minds. They needed no reason beyond the raw surge of power and dominance they felt as they stomped and stamped out anything that stood before them. They were a force infinitely more destructive than his infinitely destructive brother, Deinonychus.

Deinonychus might kill a nest of rats until he had had his fill, or murder a forest of birds for nothing more than amusement or contempt. But Deinonychus's hatred was of a less specific, less *directed* nature. Deinonychus might happen to eat every rat in the world, but he would never start using his tremendous power to systematically wipe out every rodent in the world because the 'rodent world view' didn't 'accord' with the 'feline perspective.'

If he did kill them all, it would be mere coincidence – doing so might *happen* to amuse him on any given day.

That was the difference between the raw destructive power of Deinonychus remaining inside him rather than inside the Namers – where they wanted it. The Namers almost certainly *would* start applying their systematic, unnatural ways to the already terrible force. In the cat's vision, the uniformed stain of identical Namers seemed to spread across the land, and Leviticus's viewpoint rose and rose through the air until he saw something he didn't understand – a vast circle, looking almost like the sun, upon which blue and green and brown mingled in spots and swirls. Upon this globe, the stain of Namers spread like a mold, burning and crumbling everything.

The blue turned brown, the green turned black.

Leviticus felt stinging arms of heat envelop him, and he squeezed his eyes tightly shut for a moment before realizing all this was just illusion – a vision broadcast from Jeff's mind. With a sharp bark of surprise, his cat's eyes snapped open. Leviticus had realized in that instant exactly what the cats were being studied for.

He had seen, in that moment, exactly how the Namers could use the cats to spread their destruction – even if the cats themselves didn't wish to go along with their plans. The Namers had some way of taking their blood, and then removing the parts they needed from it. *That's* what the insect with the stinger was for.

And Leviticus saw something else – something that was worse than everything else he had learned so far combined. Deinonychus was looking back at him with his mental eyes. Deinonychus had somehow overheard all these thoughts in Leviticus's head.

Deinonychus *knew*. He knew that Leviticus had realized he was after him, and more importantly, Deinonychus now knew that the Namers (whom he hadn't really worried about before) were after *him*.

In this way, as Jeff was finishing the last of his rounds, his casual thoughts passed through the mind of Leviticus and happened to accidentally jolt Deinonychus awake, plunging the woods into the middle of a nightmare.

Sixteen

As soon as Leviticus saw what his terrible brother meant to do, he knew that he had to step in. Without his help, Deinonychus would soon lay this entire place to waste in his rage. Beyond that, however, Leviticus could sense all too clearly his brother's intentions: they radiated off him like heat off a stove. If Leviticus couldn't stop his brother now, before he really got started, it was very likely that nothing ever would.

Leviticus, feeling the situation out with his mind, pitied the poor Namer whom Deinonychus kept using to accomplish his goals. The man clearly had something wrong with his breathing – he constantly inhaled some kind of putrid chemical that clouded his lungs and formed a layer of mental mildew on this thoughts. This was why Deinonychus found it so easy to slip into the cracks of the man's mind – not exactly taking complete control of his body, but willing him to do things he knew better than to do.

Leviticus knew something his brother didn't – and he rejoiced in the knowledge, and kept it hidden in his mind as best he could. One of the Namers – the youngest, it seemed to Leviticus – was different in another way. His mind had something overlaying it, as well, but it was very different from the scuzzy lung-gunk of the shorter Namer.

It was a kind of *fuzziness*, a sort of mirage-like transparency. Leviticus couldn't understand it, but he could see into this Namer's mind and see where this haze originated: a small red bottle of orange capsules. Leviticus didn't understand things as alien and human as 'prescriptions,' and so couldn't understand that these orange pills were anticonvulsant medication. That, or why a certain type of medication should protect the human's nervous system from his brother's psychic prodding, wouldn't have made sense to the cat anyway.

All that mattered to Leviticus was the mental refuge it offered the young Namer. While Leviticus, with his greater power and compassion for things outside himself, could detect this person and their mind, he could sense that his rage-filled, self-involved brother could *not*. Especially enraged as he was now at the thought of being killed by these Namers, Deinonychus was completely unable see through the haze that these pills created.

To Deinonychus, the young Namer with the prescription bottle in his computer bag was effectively invisible. This encouraged Leviticus. He didn't know if he would be able to stop his brother on his own, and every bit of help he could get would be of immeasurable value.

Sadly, his siblings weren't going to be of much assistance there. They were lovely brothers and sisters – if they hadn't been forced into this strange situation with the Namers and made to deal with the ravenous ambition of their genocidal brother, they could have had a happy life together. Unlike Deinonychus and Leviticus, however, their siblings had a more simplistic outlook on things.

Leviticus could identify, at least slightly, with the world of the Namers, despite the great wall which existed between their species. He understood that, regardless of the differences between them, they were of one substance. When Leviticus looked out of his rooftop cage, gazing into the forest, watching the birds hopping in the trees and the people coming and going from their jobs, he could sense the overall unity which bound them all together – wild nature and human society, with himself somewhere between. Though a high wall lay between him and the people, or between the birds and the squirrels, he knew that if you dug deeply enough, that wall disappeared. It *ended* somewhere underground, and if you got to that point, all which could be seen was truly one.

Deinonychus, on the other hand, felt that *he* was one and all. He did not wish to burrow down beneath barriers to search for common unity. He wanted to tower *over* that wall, to look down on everything, and proclaim it inferior. His mind was so soiled with the delusion of his own superiority that he saw everything on the face of the planet as a disgusting, contemptible stain which must be either consumed or destroyed.

No other purpose existed to him – to destroy, to defeat, to consume, to *un*-create. If Deinonychus could not take the power of something by theft – theft of its life, theft of its blood – then he would destroy the thing through the decimation of its shape, through the theft of its very *form*. If he could not consume it and steal its power, Deinonychus would flatten it into oblivion until nothing else remained save himself.

Deinonychus didn't see unity in the world outside himself. The disdainful cat had set his sights on a very different kind of unity: the homogenization of all around him through destruction or consumption. Once *all* had become *him*, he would be content. Until then, he would be angry… and hungry.

* * *

Once Deinonychus had launched into his plan, Leviticus saw he didn't have much time. All the wildlife in the area began surging towards the cats – driven to them like lemmings by the wild power of Deinonychus's mind so he could consume them for the power inside their blood. Birds, squirrels, and raccoons stampeded towards the forest clearing even as the low, slithering things worked their way inwards in a vast, tightening circle, with Deinonychus at the center.

This was bad enough – Leviticus's furious brother would soon have all the power he could wish for. Leviticus, however, sensed a darker, more unexpected problem.

There were several buildings situated in the forest clearing, with two particularly large ones. Upon one of these the cats' cages sat. Probing outwards, he could feel from the minds of the Namers that a distant, smaller structure in the physical plant contained nothing but vials, refractors, processors, sequencers. Things which were alien to Leviticus, but apparently harmless. The large building which lay between that structure and this one, however, was different.

Leviticus had a vague sense of things that violated any natural order. Things that were alive, yet were not animals, and not Namers. Leviticus didn't know what they were, and every attempt to get a read on their minds further confused him. It was like a toddler trying to grasp the thoughts of a spider, or a mosquito trying to understand the workings of a Swiss watch. Leviticus's mind simply bounced off the things, like light hitting a mirror. All the cat knew for sure: these quasi-beasts were huge.

That wasn't the only problem: far from it. There were machines and devices in this middle facility that – while unintelligible to the cat – clearly made the Namers inside the building nervous. Leviticus couldn't understand all of the biohazard signs and symbols overwritten over the doors and chambers within the building (seen from afar, through the eyes of the people within, like the remembrance of a dream in the first moment of waking), but their curling, barbed look communicated something of the danger they were meant to convey.

Lightning bolt designs warding off a burning death through electrocution, twisted spirals warning of sickness through infection or radiation, exclamation points like daggers accentuating messages of danger. Leviticus couldn't grasp the central thrust of all this menace, unable to pick it up clearly from the minds of the nervous people within. It was too complex, too *human*.

But then something happened.

The tiniest mind touched upon Leviticus's – like a light breeze on an elephant – and his mental ears perked up. Small ripples of awareness radiated outwards through the cat's consciousness, and he tuned all of his attention in on it. It was a small, winged thing – nothing like a bird, and certainly nothing like a cat. At first, Leviticus wondered how its infinitesimal thoughts had even managed to catch his notice, but he then saw that the small thing was filled with terror. Something unnatural was happening to it.

Leviticus spread his mind around the room, and felt more terror swelling: the fear of Namers. They wore white coats, like the ones worn by most of the Namers he had seen, though the cat did not recognize the faces of these people in the far building. One thing was clear, however. Their protective barriers had been breached in the onslaught loosed by Deinonychus.

Their fail-safes had failed to keep them safe. Things were happening which should not be happening, but beyond that, things were less clear. The cat struggled to piece together what might be going on. Leviticus turned his attention back to the small winged creature. It was some kind of insect – but Leviticus saw with a start that he had been wrong about the thing's size. It wasn't as small as he had at first thought. It wasn't, as he had first thought, smaller than his paw. It was actually about the size of a bird.

This realization surprised Leviticus. He had been so *sure* that the creature had been a small thing. He usually didn't make mistakes of that nature – he either saw dimly, or clearly, but seldom *inaccurately*. Next, his jaw dropped open like a startled Namer. The thing wasn't as big as a crow: it was bigger than *he* was. Leviticus gave a grunt of confusion.

His attention was ripped away from the mind of the moth as the terror of the Namers in the room began to crescendo. The cat peered out through their eyes, and at once understood his mistake. He hadn't been *wrong* about the size of the creature – the creature was *expanding*. Growing at a hideous rate. Soon, he could see only decompression chambers, hatches, doorways and hallways. The Namers were fleeing. The creature was becoming bigger by the second.

It was the size of a large dog now, and Leviticus saw the monstrosity fly into a laminar flow hood overhanging the experiment and escape outside through an air duct. The thing wriggled and squelched through the opening outside just as it grew too engorged and bulbous to fit through any longer. Now, reveling in its freedom even as it struggled to understand what was happening to it, the cow-sized thing swooped and zoomed, slowly coming to grips with its changing size and momentum.

Leviticus could see this wasn't the last of the dangers that would come from this far building. He had to do something more than listen and watch intently. The events unfolding there would distract him from dealing with his brother, and they would slow down the Namers' efforts to put things right. The enormity of the situation began to truly dawn on Leviticus for the first time, and the young grey cat felt his responsibility weighing heavily on him.

Leviticus's power to affect the outside world was weak compared to the others. His gift had to do with the *inside* world of the mind. He was different from his siblings in another way:

he refused to eat more than he had to in order to sustain his body. His link to the minds of others was too strong, and their fear of his claws and fangs too sharp and awful, for him to relish hunting the way his siblings did. Though the power inside him would grow strong at a glut of blood like those of his brothers and sisters, he did not yearn to feed it as they did.

Using such powers as he had available to him, Leviticus would have to make his attempt the best he could. He had only one shot at this. Shivering in the expectation of the effort and pain to come, he lowered himself onto his haunches and sent a bolt of energy flying from the pit of his mind towards the metal hinges which kept him imprisoned. It worked – the cage door blew out completely, flying ten feet away from his enclosure. Leviticus was now free to leave.

But he did not fly out to action. He did not stir. Leviticus lay on the floor of his now-opened cage, sprawled out and unconscious from his exertion – a small rivulet of blood oozing from his mouth, snaking across the cement rooftop towards his brother's open mouth in another cage, crawling against its will like the worms slouching along the forest floor below.

Seventeen

The flung-open exit hatch clattered to the ground, and Ben crawled out of the narrow, chute-like opening. His eyes, exposed only to the soft red glow of the emergency lights for some time, winced shut as daylight seared his vision. After blinking gingerly, he realized he had come up inside a shed, with only the narrowest shaft of sun piercing through a narrow slit in the brick wall. He kept blinking as his eyes adjusted. He got to his feet, dusted his palms off on his pants, and helped Nayeli out of the sewer-like hole next, followed by Hathaway and finally Pettinger.

The high whine of the emergency klaxon had died down while they were below, leaving the woods draped in eerie silence. It made Ben uneasy. As Ben looked around, Hathaway drew his attention to a row of shelving. There, amidst what looked like landscaping tools and extension cords, Ben could make out the red glow of three walkie-talkie lights lined up on a charger. Hathaway threw him one. Pettinger took the other.

"I don't have anything to say to anyone, anyway," a nervous Nayeli stammered. "I just want help."

"Hello, *over?*" Hathaway said tentatively. "Anyone there?"

"Aren't you supposed to say '*over*' each time?" Pettinger asked, her brow furrowed.

Her ability to distract herself with insignificant minutiae, no matter the circumstances, never ceased to amaze – and irritate – Ben. Hathaway looked disgusted.

"Come off it, Myra," Hathaway said, his voice dripping with reflexive contempt. A line had just been crossed. Ben could sense - in the strained silence that followed - that Rick Hathaway had never called Dr. Elmyra Pettinger by her first name at any point in their lives. In less strained circumstances, the quick-tempered Pettinger would surely have had a few choice rejoinders. As it was, she just stammered out her agreement.

"Doesn't matter anyway," she said sullenly, winding her arm back to toss her talkie against the concrete floor in frustration. "Nobody is on the other end of these things."

Ben caught her arm, flabbergasted.

"*We* might need that to talk to each other!"

Her eyes widened in understanding, and she looked ashamed. Ben let go of her wrist and stepped back. He took a deep breath.

"Look, we need a few things if we are going to go forward here. One of them is clarity on our purpose. I think we can provide that."

The others stared at Ben like he had started speaking in fluent Esperanto. He continued, seemingly unaware of his colleague's surprise.

"Doctors Reed and Pettinger: you are going to stay here, remain in wireless contact, and, if necessary, retreat back below to the shelter." He plucked the walkie from Hathaway's hands and handed it to Jeff. "Mr. Hathaway and I are going to find Jeff."

Ben sighed and turned to look at Rick, a guilty, self-conscious expression at having volunteered his boss for a life-or-death assignment on his face.

"If you're up for it, that is, sir," he added meekly.

Hathaway just grinned. "Don't need to make excuses for me. I'm scared shitless, kid." The older man laughed, checking the safety on his revolver. "Hopefully, where we're going, we won't need any."

Ben looked at him incredulously. "Guns?"

Ben couldn't imagine being naïve enough to think they wouldn't need guns.

Now it was Hathaway's turn to look shocked.

"Guns? *Hell*, kid. I meant shit."

* * *

Chroma – the cat who could sap living beings of their color and essence and reduce them into a wisp of dust – had made a very bad mistake. She, like Leviticus, had sensed the gargantuan non-animals in the 'B' facility with her mind. Foolishly, she had judged them a good meal for her power.

Her abilities, like those of most of the cats, were special, and her method of feasting and extracting energy was unique among her litter. Though most of the other cats couldn't have drawn the energy they needed from the blood of these curious, not-quite-animal *blips* on her mental radar, Chroma sensed instinctively that *she* could.

Once the madness started breaking out – and most of the imprisoned cats, desperate for their fill of flesh, had blasted out of their cages – Chroma slunk her way over to the 'B' facility, taking a very different path from her siblings. On her way, she found plenty of ordinary meals, of course – anybody with the courage to walk through the courtyard during the bird onslaught might have wondered why there were isolated bursts of ash falling amidst the rush of birds, like bursts of lukewarm snowflakes – but she had set her mind on taking out whatever lurked inside that mysterious building.

Getting in hadn't been very hard for her – so many people were rushing to get out that most doors were wide open. In the mad scramble to escape, it is perhaps understandable that nobody noticed Dr. Richard Santikos freeze in place during the stampede. Nobody was really standing around looking at each other, or they surely would have noticed his dark shock of curly hair rapidly turning white, his olive complexion paling to something resembling fresh mozzarella, before his entire body collapsed to the ground and dispersed like the contents of a carton of sugar flung at a brick wall.

Chroma noticed, however, and her eyes gleamed a pale, sparkling purple for an instant as the energy she freed from within the respected physicist surged through her feline veins. Nobody stopped her, or even noticed her compact, slinking form as she glided through the passageways. The stampeding people weren't exactly staring down at their feet. Chroma managed to make her way into the most sensitive parts of the facility with relative ease.

Those… whatever-they-were… were *here* somewhere. She could feel the massive power inside her intended prey calling to her like the chimes of a distant dinner bell. She passed through corridor after corridor, and finally came face to face with the things she had been looking for. And now that she could see them, she wondered for the first time if she had no made a mistake in coming here.

The pair of non-creatures were inside some kind of holding pen – one that looked a lot, she thought in her feline fashion, like the one she had been forced into back in the other building. No matter – the barriers meant nothing to her. She would start sucking the life out of these two bizarre non-animals as soon as she got a good look at them. In a few moments, there would be nothing left to see.

The two things were bigger than any living thing she had ever seen – each as big as six Namers bound together. The semi-animals possessed a lovely pair of pelts – thick brown and silver fur covered their bodies. Their massive faces looked pleasant enough in their current calm state, but Chroma had no doubt their mouths could curl into appalling snarls if the mood took them.

That was what puzzled Chroma most about these things – they didn't seem to have moods. No minds to speak of. They didn't seem to possess anything remotely resembling intelligence or agency. That made no sense to the cat. Even the bugs crawling in the dirt gave off little glows of thought.

These two massive things – looking as much like mammals as anything Chroma had ever seen – were like dead bulbs. They *weren't* dead, however. They clearly breathed, and they gave off just enough sense of life for the cats to detect. Life, but no mind. Power, but no personality. All in all, these two things were unlike anything else she had ever seen.

That was a big part of why Chroma wanted them. If she could take in their energy, she felt she would gain some of that difference, some of that specialness. And now that she had taken stock of her prey, the time to do it had come.

The strange collars on their necks meant nothing to the cat. She could see that these bands wrapped around the two lumbering giants were Namer things, and like the Namers' clothes or the bird's indigestible beaks, they would turn to dust like everything else. Also failing to make an impression on the cat's focused mind was the 'Containment Breached' sign pulsing in deep red above her head. A little bit of flickering light didn't make the incomprehensible squiggles of the Namers any more coherent to her feline mind.

She readied herself to sap the two grizzly bears of their life energy, and then sprung her mental jaws. The sensation was the psychic equivalent of taking a deep bite into a metal bar. Her phantasmagoric teeth snapped inside her mind. She cried out in pain, and the twin Grizzlies roused themselves as suddenly as though an un-pause button had been pressed. They began to lumber towards her, their collars beginning to blink as their lips curled into exactly the snarls Chroma had imagined.

The barrier to their containment unit split like cellophane as the bears ambled closer, and Chroma knew she was about to learn the lesson she had taught all of her prey: what it was like for your entire life to be reduced down to a handful of painful final moments as all that you were became energy for something hungry, something that does not want you to live.

Eighteen

"So what do you know about these other projects?" Ben asked Hathaway out of the side of his mouth as they slunk through the undergrowth.

He feared he knew the answer. Hathaway suppressed a cough, only half-surprising Ben by continuing to pull on his e-cigarette even as he fought for his breath, and confirmed Ben's suspicions.

"All I know is that everything on site is on the same payroll, and all the bills go to the pointy building on the east coast that the terrorists keep trying to use as a landing strip. That answer your question?"

What Hathaway was trying so delicately to say was that everything going on at the Agency was certain to be dangerous, likely to be a matter of national security, and ran every risk of being absolutely unbelievable – but it was all too confidential for any one person at the facility to have an overall picture of the situation. The thought did not comfort Ben.

He looked around, quickly placing their location as south of the 'A' building. The tunnel system that ran underneath the facilities must be *enormous*. Right now, the pair were headed for the north side of the building, where they could climb the scaffolding to reach Jeff on the roof. Ben saw the distance they had to cover, though not vast, looked and felt eerily silent.

The air was thick with drifting feathers, and small clumps of them floated around the grass like snowflakes. The birds they had come from, however, appeared to have thinned out. Tension hummed in the air like an electric field. The sense that thrums in the eye of a hurricane, of things delicately poised on the edge of destruction, permeated everything.

They came to the edge of the woods, and looked across the clearing on the south side of the lot, a space used as a fire corridor between the woods and the building. There, a few large crows flopped listlessly on their sides in dying spasms, but the field otherwise contained nothing but grass and bird corpses. Many of them charred.

Ben and Hathaway prepared themselves to run for the scaffold, and dropped down into a starting position. As far as they could tell, their best bet for safety was speed. Ben put all of his weight onto his front foot, ready to spring, when a horribly loud crackling sound filled the glade.

"-ello? Ben? Ben? Rick? Can –ou –ear us?"

The voice cut in and out, but there was no mistaking Pettinger's concerned voice, even through the static. Ben and Hathaway cursed quietly as Ben grasped for his walkie's volume knob. The crackling box leapt in his hand like a struggling fish before he managed to hold it steady, nearly ripping the knob off in his desperation to lower the volume of its speaker.

"Christ!" Hathaway hissed.

"*Guys! Don't run across the south lot!*"

Ben's eyes locked onto Hathaway's. They had been less than a second away from doing just that.

"What is it?" Ben said steadily into the receiver, keeping his voice deliberately even, adrenaline surging inside him.

"*There's… there's something there,*" Pettinger answered, sounding unsure of how to continue.

Hathaway spun, looking past the tree he stood by, and squinted into the field.

"*What?*" he said, irritated. "I don't see anythi-"

"*Holy fuck*," Ben said, almost dropping the receiver.

He tapped Rick's shoulder, pointed upwards - past the first few rows of windows. Hathaway's gaze swept up slowly: not wanting to see, not able to look away. He made a small moan of despair.

The thing he saw was a thing that should not have been.

"There's *no way* Jeff is still up there!" Hathaway said. Ben could hear the backpedaling in his words. "There's just no way. He wouldn't want us to throw our lives awa-"

He cried in alarm and pain as Ben caught him on the shoulder with the butt of his gun. Not hard enough to cause real damage, but hard enough to snap Hathaway out of his blubbering. When the older man looked at Ben's face, he did not see the face of a fresh-faced young kid hoping to impress his boss.

He saw a stern, weary face expressing the one emotion that had the power to goad Hathaway into action: *disappointment*. Rick Hathaway may be an irritable bastard with a nicotine problem, but he wasn't going to stand around and let the kid look at him like that.

He sighed, took a resigned drag on his e-cigarette, and clapped Ben on the shoulder.

"Alright. Point taken." Hathaway shook his head. "I really don't get you, kid."

Ben wasn't listening. He had a plan. After another moment's thought, he turned to Rick.

"You think you can get to the lot side?"

Rick looked out at the southern clearing, followed the woods that wrapped around with his eyes.

"Well, I can sure as hell *try*."

Ben nodded. "How good of a shot are you?"

Rick made an involuntary scoffing sound.

"Better the bigger the target is," he conceded.

Ben smiled tensely.

"Well, you're in luck today. I'm going to create a diversion, right here. I'm going to climb this tree and distract it. Once I have its attention, that's when I'm going to need you to go to work."

Rick thought that he could understand what was expected of him.

"And what will *you* be doing?"

Ben smiled broadly.

"If my plan works out the way I expect, I'll already be done by then."

Hathaway appraised Ben with an inscrutable eye for a moment before vanishing into the woods – muttering that he better leave before he realized how stupid their 'plan' was.

Ben sighed deeply, gearing himself up to go, and took one last look at the thing clinging to the top stories of the building. It wasn't that the massive creature looked all that dangerous. It wasn't fear Ben felt as much as sheer atavistic revulsion.

The thing up there was far, *far* from him on the family tree. Everything about its feathery lightness was fundamentally *wrong* at this massive scale. The alien movement of its massive forelimbs rubbing together seemed to tie knots in Ben's mind with its *wrongness*.

Watching it fold its dozen-foot wingspan behind it, Ben felt sure that this abomination was merely a byproduct of one of the other secretive projects, not the actual project itself. Somewhere in the facility, a security panel was breeched, some kind of radiation had been released, and this monster had been accidentally created and loosed. That was the only explanation he could think of. There was no way that government scientists were researching this thing, itself.

As he climbed, he saw the trembling, silky stalks of its antennae sway in the light breeze. Ben almost laughed as a thought struck him: if moths of this size were common, mothwing dresses would be considered the height of fashion. The ethereal, glimmering quality of the shimmering, fur-like covering of the giant insect made the vision before him harder to accept.

Feathery bits of moth down rained from its shivering wings like a snowfall, and Ben shuddered as he realized that not all of the drifting 'feathers' they had seen out here had come from birds. Bark bit into his hands as he pulled himself still higher. Tree branches scraped at his face, and he blinked them out of the way. His mind was far away, crawling through his sixth grade biology class. His thoughts were on starlight, and proprioception.

If you had asked him in a social setting if he would be willing to risk his life on a dimly remembered biology lesson from more than half his life ago, Ben would have said 'no.' He probably wouldn't have even wagered a beer on it. Now that it was his only hope – not to mention the only hope for Jeff and Rick – he actually felt he had a pretty good shot.

Ben's plan wouldn't have had the slightest chance in hell of working if it weren't for his 'talisman.' As he wedged himself in position near the top of the tree and grabbed his wallet out of his back pocket, his racing thoughts had a chance to catch up with him. He pulled out the shard-like fragment, and held its light weight in his hand. The sense that he had just thrown his life away foolishly was very hard to ignore.

The small, bluish-silver shard looked something like a massive, jagged guitar pick. Ben stared down at that shard – a fragment of a recordable CD made eight years before, carefully split into four roughly equal bits by the self-described rock band – a group of young friends with a dream – who had recorded it. He saw himself reflected in its shining surface, and felt despair rising like bile in his throat.

How could something so small affect something so big?

Ben held the CD-R fragment up in front of him, like Frodo confronting Shelob. Only, in the stories, Frodo had been given ancient captured starlight by an infinitely powerful Elven queen. Ben had only a cheap chunk of obsolete plastic that had more value as a nostalgic memento than anything else. No magic incantations, the thing had been imbued only with binary patterns constituting amateur recordings of his poorly-tuned high school band's 'jams.'

He jittered the shard in his hand, and his heart leapt up in his throat as he saw a bright band of reflected light cut across the brown, red, and purple plumage of the school bus-sized moth. His sense that he had a fighting chance returned, his brow furrowed, and he bit his lip in concentration. If he was going to die trying this, he was going to really try it.

The thing's huge red eyes were an easy target, and Ben didn't have to wait long to see if his perturbations had any effect. The sickening, surprisingly birdlike cry the thing loosed as Ben's CD-R stabbed its eyes with sharp sunlight echoed around the glade like an exploded mine. Ben shuddered, repulsed. The thing was never meant to have such a loud, powerful, deep voice. The wounded screech of the gargantuan moth was so alien, Ben had to fight the urge to drop to the ground and start burrowing.

He swept its unblinking red eyes with the jagged bands of light a few more times, trying to limit his motion. He wasn't trying to blind the thing, after all. He was relying the aspect of insect biology that had most impressed itself upon poets and songwriters over the years: that moths have an intrinsic 'draw' towards light that falls on their eyes, a system of navigation that evolved during the millions of years where burning hot, thin glass bulbs filled with halogen being bombarded with electrons were statistically less common than stars and sunlight. Recently, mankind had upset that balance, and rendered their long-held system of navigation more perilous to the order Lepidoptera.

Ben hoped to take advantage of this quality of moths, but as he passed his light band over its eyes a third and fourth time, he started to wonder about some things. How could he assure himself that the moth wouldn't start flying this way, then see the sun and fly off? How could he ensure that the CD-R remained the brightest thing the moth could see?

As the moth set its wings rippling, its six, stalk-like legs fidgeting as it prepared to take off, Ben realized he wasn't brimming with ideas in that area. The thing's wings fluttered, and Ben braced himself for the creature to approach. He had seen moths wheeling around a streetlight before, and he didn't expect the school bus-sized thing to move slowly.

Why had he waited so long to start the second part of his plan? He cursed as he clamped the CD-R fragment in his teeth and started fishing in his pocket for his cell phone. One thought passed through his mind in a loop as he pulled his phone out: this wasn't going to work.

He strove to properly aim the light band projected by the CD shard between his teeth as he fought to get his phone's battery compartment off. Too hard. The phone's back cover wouldn't come off fast enough. The moth started to veer to the eastern woods.

"Shit!" Ben cried in unthinking despair, and then gasped as he felt the CD shard slip from his teeth.

Reflexively, he ducked and bit down hard, miraculously managing to re-catch the bit of plastic in his mouth, but cutting his lip in the process.

With sweat rolling down his forehead and into his eyes, Ben jerked his head to the side, catching the moth squarely in its insectile 'face' with the light band once more. Just as quickly, its course swerved back towards Ben. He laughed in manic spasms as he tucked his now back-coverless cell phone – a fashionable new Samsung Parabola – into his breast pocket. The moth was bearing down on him like a runaway train.

The next step in his plan became clear in Ben's mind, and he realized he was about to die.

Ben had been so focused on the immediate next step at every point throughout his plan that he had never really thought about the ultimate end. Now that the tricky conclusion was all he had to contend with, and he could think about it with a clear and rational perspective, he realized his entire 'plan' was doomed to failure from the start.

It would require him to be a deadeye marksman, an expert stuntman, and a master of timing. It would require him to leap through the air like a flying squirrel with the accuracy of a Swiss watch, magically disrupt the laws of physics in multiple directions at once, and, on top of it, to possess the ability to slow time down by four-hundred percent. If he could handle all *that*, he might have a shot at pulling off what he needed to do. Otherwise, no dice.

The alien head of the moth rushed at him like a massive battering ram, the wind of its huge wings gusting all around

Ben, and he felt all the uncertainty fall away like a curtain. He had no choice but to try, so try he would. In one sinuous movement, he flung the phone towards the sky, plunged himself off the tree like a diver, and, aiming with what he hoped was intense precision, fired three shots up into the air.

The explicit and severe warnings printed on cell phone batteries, he was pleased to find, were absolutely valid. As the ground rushed to meet him, the air above Ben exploded into a caustic, chemical *woosh* of flames and fumes that clung to the moth's furry body like burning napalm. With a loudly percussive sound, the fire consumed the unnatural beast like dry kindling. The bulky thing's dying cries sent the branches shaking and leaves fluttering.

Ben hit the ground and rolled, covering his face against cutting twigs. Pain gripped him, lashing a hundred tiny cuts and small bruises into his skin, but he thought he would be alright. The fall, however, was the least of his worries for the moment. He covered his ears and screamed in unreasoning terror as flaming bundles of moth down rained upon him.

A rush of foul-smelling wind engulfed him, and he was reminded of the sick *whump* of ignition when one burns away a tick and the gasses inside the blood-sucking insect ignite. Bits of smoldering moth flesh rained all around him, fluttering down like tattered flags. He beat at his hair with his hands, feeling the sting of fire on his scalp. Viscous, fleshy moth goo splattered his shirt. The sight of it – so much of it – turned his stomach.

Ben pushed himself up on his knees, and a stiff, horny severed moth limb kicked him in the side of his head with the final lurching spasm of its death throes. The limb's sharp, beak-like tip lashed a cut into the flesh of his temple, and Ben cried out in pain and horror. It was too much, too gruesomely alien. He launched himself across the forest floor, revulsion beating at his mind like an angry father. His rational thoughts were buried beneath a rubble pile of fear.

The great, hulking carapace of the moth disintegrated, the final remnants burning away even as Ben watched. The four remaining, hook-like legs snapped open and shut like scissor-blades, the fire spreading throughout its body twisting the corpse in contorted spasms. Iridescently shimmering moth flesh, burning away, continued to fall all around him. Ben put the back of his hand to his mouth and coughed from deep in his stomach as he strove to reclaim his composure.

His walkie-talkie burst into staticky chatter, making him jump in alarm.

"*Great Gawd, Ben! Are you okay? Ben?*"

Ben gave up the struggle, coughed a mouthful of bile out onto the ground, and held down 'Send.'

"If I remember the plan correctly," Ben said evenly, "you were supposed to start shooting at some point."

A litany of static, beeps, and astonished relief poured out of his walkie-talkie as Pettinger, Hathaway, and Nayeli all tried talking at once. Ben just shook his head, a disbelieving smile plastered on his face, and held the walkie-talkie at arm's length as he began looking through the flaming wreck of the moth.

"*I was gonna start shooting, but I didn't know if I would hit you or not, kid!*"

Hathaway sounded guilt-stricken. Ben laughed.

"It's okay. We saved bullets this way."

Pettinger's voice came back on the air.

"*But what did you do, Ben? What was your plan?*"

Hathaway instantly grunted accordance.

"*Hell yeah, kid. What was that you used?*"

Ben bent over, brushed a bit of charred moth-leg aside, and picked up the shard of his old high school bands' CD – an album they had, for reasons he couldn't remember, titled 'Unbroken Edge' – looking at it like he was seeing it for the first time. A bemused smile pulled at the ends of his mouth.

"Just a crazy dream a silly kid used to have," he said, placing the CD fragment back in his wallet. "I can finally tell my mom she was wrong."

He laughed again.

Something *had* come of his high school band, after all.

"Look, I'm on my way to the eastern edge, Rick." Being repeatedly called 'kid' had loosened his tongue towards his boss. "Dr. Pettinger?"

Her voice came back nearly instantaneously.

"*Yes?*"

"I'm going to be sending you an expense report for a new cell phone. Mine got broken." He paused for effect. "See if you can't fast track the approval on that."

Nineteen

Hathaway clasped Ben's shoulders in his meaty hands. The two of them met up about fifteen feet inside the woodland encircling the artificially cleared-out glade. After a brief yet exuberant re-introduction, their survival instincts kicked back in, and they sobered up.

"The scaffolding's clear now, kid," Hathaway said. A look of doubt crossed his face. "Well, clear of anything we can *see*."

Ben shivered.

"That's a start. Have you heard anything new from Jeff?"

Hathaway shook his head. "No, but I think he stopped talking into the PA when he noticed our pal Buggy up there."

Ben nodded.

"We didn't hear him *screaming*, so that's a good thing." He turned to face Hathaway. "Are we in agreement that there is no way that the moth was the actual experiment in whatever lab it escaped from?"

Hathaway nodded.

"Something got set off on accident. Shrink ray or something like that, firing willy-nilly. Has to be."

"I think so, too. Which is bad news for a couple reasons. This is where it gets into 'unknown knowns, known unknowns' type shit, Rick. Are you following me?"

Hathaway, in an effort to understand, bit down twice as hard on his lip. Ben could see that he didn't quite see Ben's point.

"I mean that we don't know what causes this effect. Could there be shrunken scientists underfoot, screaming at us to notice them before we squish them with our sneakers? Could a fifty-foot Deinonychus come hauling ass around the corner any second? We don't know."

Frustrated that he wasn't making himself clear, Ben tried wording things differently.

"We're racing into the midst of a shitstorm, and I guess what I'm trying to say is: don't be too sure you know the difference between a dirty diaper and a disinfectant wipe. The only thing we know for sure is that pretty much anything could be happening."

Hathaway nodded.

"It's an Agency thing," he said, and grunted.

They started to move.

There was no strategic way to climb the scaffolding without exposing themselves to view, so the two of them rushed as fast as they could to the stairway leading up to the roof. As they rounded the top corner, Ben's peeked out over the roof. The glade seemed empty, but Ben took little comfort from that. The scene on the rooftop was a mess.

The cage doors were all blown open – save for one, at the far end of the roof. Dry, papery bird carcasses and singed plumage drifted around like slips of paper wafting in the light wind. The desiccated skin of the birds crackled and crumpled in the breeze like cellophane, and Ben's stomach turned at the noxious crunching sounds. Hathaway began lightly calling out for the trapped scientist.

"Jeff?"

Hathaway's voice sounded pitiful and small in the crackling stillness.

"*Rick?*"

Jeff's voice resonated with incredulity, as though he didn't dare to believe that the signals coming from his ears could possibly be rooted in reality. Ben darted to the sealed cage. Hathaway joined him as quickly as he could, and they both gasped in astonishment when they saw Jeff.

His face was a study in the physiological effects of fear and adrenaline: all the color was gone from his features – making his dark brown goatee look jet black in comparison to his pallid flesh. His eyes were so wide they seemed to take up half of his face, his pupils reduced to tiny pinpricks. Yet that wasn't the primary cause of Ben and Hathaway's alarm.

Jeff had buried himself under a grotesque pile of dead birds in all states, from crows so lifelike that they looked merely frozen – like the work of master taxidermists – to crumpled husks of partially burnt feathers and bird skeletons too damaged for even an ornithologist to identify. Ben wrinkled his nose in disbelief and disgust to see that the bulk of the pile Jeff had pulled together to hide beneath consisted of bird legs and beaks. The birds they had belonged to had been burnt away completely, leaving only these hard, fleshless portions – along with dozens upon dozens of drifting feathers – behind.

"Jeff, good buddy!" Hathaway said.

From the evident relief in his voice, Ben remarked to himself, an outsider would never have suspected how much Hathaway hated Jeff.

"It's actually you. You're actually *here!*" Then his expression went blank with the onset of fear. "The bug-thing?"

he asked cringingly, sounding like a child looking to his parents for reassurance about the boogieman.

"It's gone," Ben said, showing Jeff the rifle slung over his back. "We should have a fighting chance against anything else."

Ben didn't know how much he believed his own words, but they seemed to have a calming effect on Jeff, who started brushing the bird carcasses and avian body parts off himself and rising to his feet.

"I'll try to come out, but the cats… did something to the cage. The door is… It's like, stuck." Jeff sounded tentative.

Hathaway tugged on the cage door, jiggling the handle with increasing violence, yet the door remained firmly closed.

"Hinge is melted. How the hell are we going to get you out of there?" Hathaway kicked the metal cage in frustration, and cursed under his breath at the pain.

Ben continued to look around the roof for something to use, some kind of advantage. Jeff and Hathaway kept trying to loosen the cage door.

"Of course that's not going to work, Rick," Jeff said, laughing manically as desperation took root. "We designed these cage doors to withstand a lot more pressure than the three of us are likely to put on it anytime soon, and you know it."

Hathaway cursed again.

"Well, that doesn't mean Ben can't at least *help!*" Rick hissed as he and Jeff tugged fervently at the door.

Ben shook his head.

"It would be a waste of effort. Besides, I've thought of a better solution."

Jeff and Hathaway stopped their tugging, and looked at Ben expectantly.

"You could go down the chute," Ben said, and waited patiently as the flood of objections washed over him.

"It's too small!" Hathaway said, agitation setting him hopping from one foot to another. "He'll get stuck."

Ben had wondered about this.

"Do you know it's too small? How small is it really? I haven't seen the inside of the chute myself."

Hathaway looked guiltily down at his feet. The message was clear: he didn't actually know. Jeff spoke, seeming to perk up.

"It's actually as big as a child's playground slide. Maybe not big enough to go down with *dignity*, but certainly not so small I'd get stuck. *Hathaway* here, maybe…"

"Shut the hell up, or you can stay in that cage," Rick said, red in the face. "Alright then, say he gets down into the building. We meet up out front. Great, we rescued Jeff. But are we any closer to wrangling the cats and getting this whole thing on a lockdown?"

"One step at a time, buddy," Ben said calmly. "Go ahead, Jeff. We'll meet you downstairs."

Jeff nodded, then a look of concern flashed across his face.

"Do we know if it's secure down there?"

Ben looked around, noting all the open cages. "I really doubt the cats would escape, only to flee back into the building they escaped from…" Ben trailed off, realizing what Jeff was driving at.

"The *rats*," said Ben and Hathaway in unison.

"*Bingo*," Jeff responded, tugging down on his shirt. "If those kitties were hungry, they may have worked their way down to the basement and had their fill. I know we keep dozens upon dozens of rats down there."

"Hundreds," Ben, who put in the orders himself, corrected.

"And we're probably not the only on-site project that keeps rats down there," Jeff said. "If we're the only research team at the Agency with a bio-component, then I'm a freaking goat herder."

Pettinger's voice crackled over the walkie-talkie.

"Wish we knew what the upper limit on their consumption was."

Ben groaned.

"I wish you knew *jack shit* about what you were doing when you set this project up, so I guess we're even."

Ben had been getting braver in offering his opinion to his superiors throughout the day, and Pettinger's vehement reaction caught him entirely by surprise.

"Drop the mad scientist crap, you smug bastard!"

Ben's mouth dropped into a wide 'O' as the berating continued.

"Nobody would know anything about goddamn anything *if we didn't try. Marie Curie, ever hear of her? Her fingers rotted right off her hands so that snotnosed kids like you could go get your arm x-rayed when you break it playing middle school basketball. Should she just 'not have messed with that stuff'* then, *since she didn't know what she was doing?"*

Ben flinched. What she was saying had struck home. She took a deep breath – crackling over the walkie-talkie.

"Your generation especially: *your smugness is inversely proportional to your accomplishments and expertise. The depth of*

your convictions is only as great as your reasons for having them are shallow and tenuous."

Hathaway looked uncomfortable as Pettinger continued chewing Ben out over the walkie-talkie.

"Let me connect a few dots about your generation for you, kid," she began

Hathaway reached up to take the walkie-talkie from Ben's hand.

"That's enough," he said, but the verbal onslaught continued.

Pettinger's voice had become a breathless rant, rushing out of her like the tidal wave of an unburdening confession. She was talking about Jay Leno and Conan, about Occupy Wall Street and Edward Snowden. Any coherent point she might have been trying to make was lost in the rush of her words and the complete insanity of her timing.

Ben grabbed Hathaway's wrist, locked his eyes on his. Hathaway read his signal well enough. *'Something's wrong.'*

Jeff started pointing agitatedly at the walkie-talkie, and then at his ear. The three of them listened. Pettinger's furious voice sat in the foreground of the transmission, but now that Jeff had pointed it out to them, the others heard it, too. A faint, intermittent crunching sound behind her words. Ben's face screwed up in concentration.

On the roof, the three of them had stopped listening to what Pettinger, who had clearly gone off the deep end, was saying, and instead focused all of their attention on discerning the confusing sounds in the background.

That's when Ben realized the mistake they were all making.

"Nayeli! Nayeli! Get out of there!"

Ben looked helplessly at the others. Their faces all wore the same expression: if Nayeli had been waiting for Ben's advice, it was too late. The three on the roof wasted no time. Jeff sent himself down the chute – his only possible means of escaping the welded-shut cage – as Ben and Rick thundered down the stairs to meet him by the North doors.

Twenty

It took Jeff no more than five seconds to come to regret his heroic impulse to hurl himself down the cat chute in his haste to come to the rescue of Nayeli and Pettinger. It took only two seconds for the fading light from the rooftop to dim utterly, and seconds later the already snug fit tightened. Jeff grunted, wrapping his arms over his chest like a mummy in an effort to reduce his form. As he worked his way downward, the passage became increasingly constricted.

He skidded to a complete stop. His sneakers had become jammed in the narrow aperture. Cold sweat beaded on his forehead. Jeff realized in a flash that he had probably been intensely claustrophobic his entire life, but never had an opportunity for self-diagnosis. Pushing outwards against the walls with all his weight and might, he attempted to drive himself down the chute as though he were climbing *up* it. He strained with exertion, and managed to propel himself a few more feet downwards.

His sweat-slicked hand slipped, and he lost his balance, banging his head on the pipe with a reverberating *clang*. His leg jerked in automatic response, and he slid a further few feet down the pipe, wedging his right leg painfully behind himself.

"God *dammit!*" he hissed.

His slippery hands pawed at the metal for purchase, but his palms slid uselessly. He couldn't get enough traction. Gritting his teeth, he eased the leg that had been bent painfully behind him back into place.

His goddamn *shoes*, they kept catching on the metal. His mental gears grinding uselessly, he began to kick his feat furiously out of fear and desperation. Once he had given into the fear rising inside him, it avalanched. His uselessly pawing hands thrashed in tandem with his feet until he heard a chain of curious *thunking* sounds, and felt a cold wind blowing against his face, and it occurred to him that he had loosed his shoes and cleared the bottleneck.

He felt calmness congealing inside him. He had done it! He had escaped his pitch black confines, wormed his way out of the building's infrastructure. The sense of triumph welling up inside him was short-lived.

He remembered what he was doing – *why* he had jumped into the dark pipe in the first place. Above all, he remembered the crunching, grinding sounds from the shed that they had all heard over the intercom – and as the darkness of the pipe began to sweeten with the first pale hints of the light to come, part of Jeff – with his shoeless feet and sweaty hands – wanted to try climbing back up.

* * *

The plan – for Pettinger and Nayeli – had been to remain at the shed. That plan quickly fell by the wayside. While Pettinger had been berating Ben over the walkie-talkie, Nayeli had grown instantly alarmed. Her shock at the surprising vehemence in Pettinger's voice almost distracted her fully from the faint sound at the limits of her perception. As she backed unthinkingly away from the raving Pettinger, she pressed herself against the wooden wall, and jumped in surprise when the entire wall shuddered with a heavy impact.

Pettinger, however, didn't seem to react at all. Nayeli, gripped by indecision, became paralyzed with fear. Once again, the shed wall shuddered. This time, a set of rakes and hoses fell off their hooks. Still, Pettinger stood ramrod straight, unresponsive to this new development, as she gripped the receiver and poured out a stream of insults into the walkie. Splinters flew out of the wall with the impacts.

Nayeli bent down on instinct, picked up a fallen rake, and held it like a staff, too frightened to think to draw the revolver she had taken. Soon, the far wall of the shed was being buffeted, as well. What the hell was going on?

Nayeli tried to pull Pettinger along, away from the shrapnel, but the senior scientist just kept growling into the transmitter. Pettinger was past saying anything sensible. A moment later, the senior scientist dropped the walkie talkie on the ground. Nayeli reached down and clipped it to her belt, but to her astonishment Pettinger continued yelling insults into her hand, as though nothing had changed.

A moment later, Nayeli screamed in panic as whole chunks of the wall flew inwards. She scurried up the shelving like a child climbing a tree and pressed herself flat against the top before peering over the edge. What looked like the muzzle of a large, ursine creature protruded through the gap in the wall momentarily before pulling back.

Nayeli couldn't believe it, though she knew that the Chippewa National Forest was home to several species of bear. The thick claws that continued rending the shed left no doubt, however: at least two large bears were breaking the shed walls down.

What could Nayeli possibly do? Pettinger was oblivious, beyond helping or being helped. Nayeli's hiding spot was worse than useless: if she had been able to get up there, a pair of bears would be able to get her down twice as easily. The voices of Jeff and Ben screamed in a tinny overlap through the small speaker of the walkie talkie: *'Get out of there!'*

The rake became insubstantial in her hands. It would only serve to provoke angry bears, not fend them off. The first bear had widened the jagged opening in the wall enough to stick its head through, and when it saw Pettinger, it bellowed. The sound reverberated inside the closed space of the shed, hurting Nayeli's ears. Pettinger was *still* focused in on the walkie-talkie she was no longer holding – the juxtaposition of her posture and her imminent danger looked absurd: like a sleepwalker in an old cartoon having a heated phone conversation with a banana held up to her head.

Naycli, desperate to help Pettinger in any way she could, began to prod her boss with the handle of the rake, to no response. The second bear, meanwhile, had made significant headway in demolishing the wall. The ceiling now hung down like a sagging ail as the north wall buckled and drooped. The collapsing roof pushed down on Elmyra's head, yet still her incoherent yammering continued unabated. Nayeli looked in all directions, desperate for something she could use. She saw a gap had opened up between the closest wall and the roof, where the building had begun to fall apart.

"Forgive me!" she said to Pettinger, not knowing what else to do, and pulled herself through the gap.

Her arms burned from the effort, but soon she was out and up onto the roof. The entire structure wobbled under her, and she knew she didn't have long before the thing collapsed. She looked above her, not daring to hope for what she found: a thick, low-hanging branch within her reach. She leapt for it, the bark biting into her hand with the tightness of her grip. Her already aching arms screamed with exertion, but soon she had made it to the trunk of the tree.

Only then did she dare to look down. What she saw made no sense. The bears had stopped attacking the shed. The pair were, in fact, sitting on their haunches like placated dogs, their tongues hanging out of their mouths. These were no black bears. Judging from the size, these could only be grizzlies. The two bears appeared to breathe calmly, and if she hadn't seen it with her own eyes, she would never have imagined that they had been ferociously demolishing the shed only moments before.

That's when Nayeli first saw them. Each bear wore a thick, red collar, with a metallic-grey box affixed to the side of their throats. A series of colored lights blinked in intricate sequences, lights chasing lights across the unit before repeating in a nearly identical order (but even from this distance, at this level of fear, Nayeli could see that no two sequences repeated themselves quite exactly). What the hell? It suddenly occurred to Nayeli that she was looking at one of the other top secret projects, from one of the other labs.

Just then, the walkie talkie on her hip burst into another round of screaming.

"*Pettinger? Nayeli? What the hell is going on out there!*"

"Goddamit!" she spat, reaching one arm down to twist off the volume on the unit. Her other arm sung a high note of agony with the exertion of holding her full weight. The walkie silenced, but the loud burst of noise hadn't gone unnoticed.

The larger of the two bears tilted back its head, and its dark, predator eyes slid up to meet Nayeli's gaze. She yelped in alarm, yet the bear didn't respond.

She furrowed her brow and pulled herself slightly higher up in the tree. The bear blinked slowly at her a few times before letting its gaze drop back down to the shed. What the *hell*?

Seconds later, Nayeli forgot herself completely.

"Elmyra!" she called down.

Pettinger had wandered out of the shed, and now stood limply in front of the two bears. She didn't respond to her name, or to the threat of the bears. Indeed, Nayeli watched in slack-jawed amazement as Pettinger took three staggering steps forward and placed a palm on top of each bear's head. The bear on the left twisted its neck and lifted its muzzle like a dog, allowing her to scratch under its chin.

"*Elmyra!* What are you *doing*?"

Pettinger's head cocked to the side. Slowly pivoting on her feet, she turned towards Nayeli and lifted her gaze. Her eyes seemed empty.

"What's going *on*?" Nayeli cried.

Pettinger's arm rose until her hooked index finger pointed vaguely up at Nayeli's perch.

"*Al baballa,*" croaked a scratchy voice only slightly resembling Pettinger's. "*Il bial byaballa.*"

Nayeli groaned. Something very bad was happening to her boss. One of the bears pushed itself up on its haunches and stretched. The other followed. The lights on their collars began to blink faster. The faint sound of an intermittent, high-pitched *beep* drifted up to Nayeli's ears as the bears lumbered up to the trunk of her tree.

Groggily, the first bear stood up on its hind legs and gripped the trunk of the tree with its paws. Deep gouges from the beast's curved claws scored the wood. The whole tree trembled with the thing's weight.

Nayeli, driven by sheer, terrified instinct, climbed higher. Despite not having scaled a tree in over thirty years, she scurried her way rapidly towards the top, not pausing to consider how this made her position all the more precarious. Soon, the second bear joined in on the fun, and Nayeli's tree began to wobble. How many pounds of weight could these two behemoths apply to the tree between them? How many *hundreds* of pounds of pressure were they able to exert?

The impression of apathy the two lethargic bears presented only made things worse. Nayeli was on the verge of being torn to shreds by two large carnivores which seemed almost torpid in their indifference. No desperate fire of hunger drove them on, no instinctive territorial urge compelled them to expel her from their area. Indeed, Nayeli discerned no feelings or reactions in the two creatures whatsoever. They seemed like drones, doing what they were doing only because they had received a signal which insisted that they must.

Pettinger, meanwhile, stood to the back, her arms limp at her sides. She fixed her gaze upon the ground. Nayeli could plainly see that, where her boss was concerned, no lights were on upstairs. Was her condition analogous to what had happened twice with Hathaway, or had the cats unleashed some other terror from a different laboratory?

By necessity, none of the scientists on the cat project had the slightest clue what was going on with the projects in the other labs, and vice versa. Just as a technician from whatever lab these remote-controlled grizzlies had come from would be baffled by the sudden appearance of a cat that could spin webs around people with its mind, Nayeli felt utterly at a loss as to the meaning and function of the blinking collars. And could *anything* under a technician's purview explain why her ordinarily level-headed boss now stood there slack-jawed, saying things like *"Il bial byaballa?"*

Nayeli didn't have much time to reflect on these thoughts. The bears continued shaking the tree, their effort intensifying. Though no sign of spirit or life was visible behind their glazed over eyes, when it came to physical effort, the two ursine hulks were going at it whole-heartedly. Dr. Reed could see it was only a matter of time before she fell from her perch. Minutes at the most. She needed to do something more drastic than simply cling.

She looked around desperately for anything she could use. Before her fear could mentally veto her plan, she grasped a thick limb from higher up in the tree that broke off and became entangled in the branches. Instead of wasting the weapon on the bears, who would have gripped it in their jaws and used it to pull Nayeli down, she hurled the heavy branch with all her might at the collapsing shed, hoping to create a diversion.

The tottering structure fell in on itself with a loud clatter. The bears didn't react at all. Nayeli cried out in frustration.

That was all she had, and it hadn't worked. Nayeli gripped the convulsing tree harder, and realized she was crying. She blinked her eyes to clear the tears, and that's when she noticed. The bears hadn't responded, but Pettinger *had*. Shaking her head, Pettinger put a hand to her temple and rubbed, coming to. After a dazed moment, she saw the situation immediately.

"Oh my God! What's going on?" she cried, finally aware of the bears.

"Elmyra!" Nayeli called down. "Watch out!"

*   *   *

One of the two bears became aware of Elmyra, as well. Now that Pettinger was out of her trance, she seemed to be fair game for attack once more. While its mate continued shaking the tree where Nayeli perched, this bear dropped back down on its front paws with dull *thud* and lumbered slowly towards Pettinger. It moved with no urgency, but Pettinger held no illusions. The beast was obviously capable of out-running her.

Pettinger's fear-stricken vision clarified. The veins of every leaf on every tree stood out in stark detail. A caterpillar crawled along a leaf. A long-abandoned bird's nest lay nestled in the crook of one high branch, shuddering in the light breeze. Pettinger saw how the grass trampled where the pursuing bear's heavy paw touched the ground sprung only partially back when the creature lifted its thick legs. Its black nose was as wet as the snout of a happy dog. Pettinger started to laugh.

The idea that her last thought would be a comparison of the thing that was about to kill her to an excited puppy – for whatever dark reason – amused her. She supposed that was a better way to go than drowning in fear. As the bear's face grew ever nearer, she found that her body's terror forced her to shut her eyes. With the thing was bearing down on her, she couldn't meet its gaze. She didn't have the heart.

Her eyes shut tightly, she took a deep breath and tried to make peace with the fact that she was about to die.

"*Al baballa!*" came an insistent voice, cutting through Elmyra's terror. "*Eel bib...* dammit! Oh! Right. *Il bial byaballa! Il bial byaballa! Al baballa!*"

It was Nayeli. Pettinger opened her eyes in surprise, and let out a yell of shock and horror. The bear's face was *inches* from her own. The hot, noxious carnivore's breath poured over her face like water. She wrinkled her nose in disgusted response. Pettinger's heart rate spiked upwards, and she trembled uncontrollably. The huge thing leaned forward, its open mouth leering towards Pettinger's head, and she knew that, whatever had caused the temporary lull in its attack, she was about to die.

Pettinger felt a rough, wet tongue slide up her face. She screamed, her eyes shooting open. The panting bear sat on its haunches before her, looking at her expectantly. She cut the scream off in her throat, not wanting to provoke the thing, but she couldn't shut off her terror as easily. As if trying to reassure her, the bear once more playfully licked her face.

"What did you *do*?" Pettinger asked out of the corner of her mouth.

Nayeli, relieved to find that the bear assaulting her tree had also entered this docile state, slid down the tree trunk and joined Pettinger. She approached the pliant beast gingerly, finally working up the courage to stroke the fur behind the bear's ears as though the creature were a massive puppy.

"I'm not entirely sure," Nayeli said wonderingly. "Whatever it was, it was what you did, only in reverse."

"What *I* did? How did we even get here? The last thing I remember is the tunnel."

Nayeli swore.

"You sort of… blanked out. Something like what happened to Hathaway happened to you. You were babbling some kind of crazy talk to the bears and they were leaving you alone."

Pettinger looked at the giant, collared beasts sitting lazily before her, and shuddered. Nayeli continued.

"Look, I know they told us to stay, but we need to get the hell out of here. I don't want to risk turning our walkie talkie back on around these things."

Pettinger agreed, and they turned and ran across the open field as fast as they possibly could, back towards the lab.

Twenty-One

To Ben and Hathaway's shock, Nayeli and Pettinger were running across the clearing, towards them, once they reached the base of the stairs. Hathaway clapped them both on the shoulders – oblivious to Nayeli's wince of pain.

"What the hell are you two doing here? We thought we had to save you! What the hell was that crunching sound?"

Pettinger cocked a thumb over her shoulder, at the bears in the distance, still sitting dumbly by the ruined shed on their back legs like dogs. Hathaway's eyes squinted in disbelief.

"It's okay," Nayeli said. "Their batteries are dead, or something."

Ben gave her a puzzled look, which she ignored.

"Where's Jeff?"

"Inside," Ben said, turning to look at the doors. "I'm not sure how safe it is in there."

"Where the hell are the security teams?" Hathaway said.

"Rest assured, when that alarm is sounded, the military will be all over this site in minutes. Just give them a little bit longer."

"If we last that long," said Hathaway, but he was laughing as he said it. Their moods were improving.

"Not to cross any professional lines," Ben said, "But what was with that rant about the younger generation?"

Pettinger looked wounded, and turned away. Nayeli spoke up.

"You heard her earlier, didn't you? She went all 'Hathaway' on us."

Now it was Hathaway's turn to look wounded. Ben quickly stepped in.

"I'm just glad you're alright now."

Nayeli spoke up.

"We've all gone through a lot, but now the important thing is that help is on the way."

Hathaway brightened.

"That's great, but what about Jeff?"

Their crests visibly fell. Ben shook his head.

"We have to get him out of this building. Saving Jeff was the reason we came out of the bunker in the first place. Dr. Reed, Dr. Pettinger: no sense risking all of our lives on this. I can't imagine how it would help. Try to get to a safe zone."

He turned to Hathaway.

"Want to do the action hero thing one more time?"

The older man grinned.

*　　*　　*

Ben and Hathaway raced to the front at their maximum pace – which was slower for Hathway than it was for Ben. When they caught sight of the door, they slowed to a tentative crawl. Jeff wasn't waiting for them there, as they had hoped, but even from a distance they could see that the doors had been propped open with someone's shoe. Cautiously, Ben approached and picked it up.

"I'd be lying if I told you I'd memorized all my co-workers' footwear," Ben said.

Hathaway squinted at the shoe.

"I don't think it's Jeff's. Too small."

"Whose could it be then? Who had left it here to prop open the door?

Hathaway tapped Ben's shoulder and pointed to a large display case just inside the nearby vestibule, mounted into the wall. A large, greasy arrow had been drawn in sweat on the glass, incongruously juxtaposed against the set of framed certifications and inspection approvals mounted on polished wood plaques hung inside.

"I don't know what the fuck happened, kid," Hathaway whispered, "but looks like whoever this shoe belongs to didn't stick around."

Rick eased the inner doors of the vestibule open and stuck his head through the widening gap. He inhaled sharply through his teeth, and pulled back, shaking his head. His expression chilled Ben – Rick looked like he was bargaining with himself, trying to mitigate what he had just seen. His mouth worked senselessly for a moment before he managed to stammer one word.

"*Charlotte.*"

Ben's eyes went wide, and he pushed his way through the door to see for himself. Instinctively, his hand rushed up to his mouth as his stomach dropped three feet inside him. Hanging from the now-flickering ceiling fluorescents swung *dozens* of twirling rats and birds, sagging down like rearview mirror dice and bound like miniature mummies in silky wrappings. Some squawked and struggled fitfully, many hung lifeless, while still others, dangling like wounded wraiths, writhed wretchedly in a languorous stupor, their eyes wreathed in foamy flecks of venom.

Ben's stomach settled, but fear still raged inside him. Adrenaline flowed through him, sharpening his senses, until he could feel the blood pounding hot inside the flesh of his ears.

Click.

Ben jumped at the unexpected sound, and felt like a fool when he realized it was the sound of him releasing the safety on his own gun. He chastised himself for nearly blasting a hole in the wall.

His senses seemed heightened but his reactions were dulled. Ben took another deep breath. He needed to get a hold of himself. He wasn't going to do any good blasting holes in things on accident.

"This is more than I signed up for, kid. Jeezus *gawd*. Looking at those things tied up like flies is making my head hurt."

Ben knew exactly what he meant. The impossible-to-internalize notion that a fellow mammal was responsible for the arachnid-like webbing filling the ground floor hallway struck such revulsion into them that the pair had been stripped down to their most basic, primitive instincts – the urge to *flee* beat at them, screaming from the base of their brain where things hadn't changed since the time of the reptiles.

Yet they had to find Jeff. It might not be what they wanted to do, but it was the right thing to do. Against all the overwhelming protestations of their own minds, they entered that nightmare hallway and pressed forward.

It took every ounce of control they could muster to keep their feet moving and their voices steady, to ignore the instinctive howling from the core of their being that told them to run from the lair of this insectile predator, but they soon managed to work their way to the ends of the hallway. Pushing open the swinging double doors, they froze in their tracks.

Sitting in the middle of the hall, calmly licking the back of her paw and drawing it across the top of her head, the cat called Charlotte sat peacefully grooming herself. Ben flattened himself against the wall, but that act alone was enough to draw the cat's attention. The green eyes locked on his and Ben felt, for the first time in his life, just how out of control everything in the universe truly was.

His mind flew aimlessly and desperately down the corridors of his life like a panicked bird trapped in a building. A distant memory of a time he had purchased an item online, only to grow furious as the weeks rolled by and it became apparent he had not actually been sent the item, began to wrap itself around his consciousness like a web. Ben felt the hot emotion welling up inside him like something fresh, felt the senseless outrage and entitlement washing over him. He actually started to laugh – standing there, pressed up against the wall as the cat calmly cleaned her fur – and remembered how upset he had been at the slight mistake.

Had he felt *owed* then? Had he thought it terribly unfair that something he paid fifteen dollars for took three whole weeks to arrive? The website, he remembered, didn't just indicate that you would be tolerant of their service, they *guaranteed* something they called *satisfaction*. Ben felt these irrational memories encircling his thoughts, binding his consciousness tighter and tighter within themselves. The thought of resisting never entered his increasingly constricted mind.

Had something as transient and insubstantial as a website, loaded onto a computer – a thing so delicate that it could be destroyed by anything from magnets to orange juice – really claimed to be able to *guarantee* something as significant as *satisfaction* for something as ephemeral as the idea of fifteen 'dollars' worth of green colored paper, which in fact only existed as a digital record on *another computer* at the bank?

'No one could guarantee that the atmosphere won't be ripped from the earth this second,' Ben thought, as insane laughter spilled from his lips.

He felt hands on his shoulders, but it felt like they only reached him through thick layers of gauze. His eyes remained locked on the cat, on Charlotte, who still groomed herself calmly. What lovely fur she had! No wonder she took such pleasure in keeping herself so clean and glossy.

The pressure on his shoulders had grown fainter still. He wondered (a little) what the strange, scrabbling feeling might be, but as time wore on, even that faint sensation seemed to recede far enough away from him to be safely ignored. As Ben's sense of feeling diminished, he focused more and more on the eyes of the cat.

The slitted irises of the cat weren't exactly spinning, he noted, but they were certainly doing *something*. Why was it so hard to tell what those eyes were up to, Ben wondered? They were swirling around, he finally decided, like the great, swiveling beacon of a lighthouse. They seemed to weave in and out of the space they occupied, two glowing lanterns enshrouded in a gently wafting fog.

Ben was transfixed by the pulsing gaze of the cat, the faraway sensation in his shoulders having long since faded completely from his mind. Gradually, the eyes of the cat likewise vanished into the underlying swirl of fog and vague numbness, and Ben surrendered to it: a cold, enveloping emptiness he was only too happy to embrace.

An ear-shredding howl ripped out of his cold mouth as what felt like a dagger of flame pierced his dulled flesh. The thin sound of his muffled scream widened, like a stream of light flooding in through an expanding tear. His vision, subsumed by the silent darkness that had enveloped him, erupted into a field of pure bright light. Heaving gasps escaped his lips as the flaming sting in his shoulder grew sharper.

Hands fumbled at his shoulders and arms, and he felt the tightness that ensconced him loosen. Blinking against the harsh brightness, he began to descry faint shapes. Ben coughed, and suddenly his limbs were free. He felt nails clutching at his chest, and realized that he was clawing at himself, tearing thick layers of sticky webbing away. He could now clearly make out the overhead lights wheeling above as he toppled backwards. He managed to steady himself just in time to prevent a tumble.

Hathaway clawed at the dense, clingy webs and swore through his teeth.

"Goddamn *sticky!*"

Ben's racing mind seized onto the tremendous pain that had ripped through his shoulder. It had been his lifeline back into the waking world of thought, but he couldn't understand what caused it. He steadied on his feet, and was shocked to see Hathaway puffing on an honest to God cigarette.

"I Keep 'em for emergencies, kid," his boss said huffily. "Don't tell the missus."

So *that's* what had caused the sharp pain – Rick had actually *burnt* the psychic webbing off of Ben. Ben had never been more grateful for addictive agriculture, and for him that was saying rather a lot.

"What about Charlotte?" Ben managed to ask between ragged breaths as the two of them ran down the corridor.

"That's the weird thing!" Hathaway said. "I don't think she had ever wrapped up something as big as you. It seemed to take quite a lot out of her. She was almost asleep when I caught up with you. She saw me coming, yawned, and moved off down the hall."

Ben swore.

"That was close!"

Hathaway nodded vigorously.

"God forbid we run across the mean one."

"Number six?" Ben asked.

Hathaway nodded again.

"Whatever the hell that bastard's name is. Call him what you want, but that cat wants to dine on *us*. You can keep the 'ick' out of his goddamn name."

As he spoke, Hathaway ripped a fire extinguisher canister off the wall.

"I'm not going to just start shooting at a housecat," he said. "Half of those things probably don't even want to hurt us. Better to have something to use as a diversion."

Ben agreed with the wisdom in this.

"How do you think Jeff's doing?" Hathaway asked as they neared the lab.

Ben shrugged. Jeff been left with no way out of the cage on the roof aside from going down the chute. If things had been a little more stabilized up there, Ben and Hathaway could likely have found some means of prying him out. At the time, when they thought they had to rush to save Pettinger and Nayeli from whatever was attacking the shed, using the chute seemed clever and resourceful.

Now, Ben and Hathaway were not so sure.

As they neared the lab doors, they could hear the muffled sounds of a skirmish inside. Ben looked over at his boss. Hathaway shrunk back, away from the door, before finding the resolve to continue.

Lifting the extinguisher high above his head, Rick prepared to kick the door down. The instant he pulled his leg back to kick, the door flew inwards like an airplane hatch blowing out at ten thousand feet. The air pressure pulled the pair off their feet. They clutched madly at the floor, Hathaway holding his extinguisher tightly in the crook of one arm while the whirling nozzle whipped around like a severed Hydra head. Howling air pressure sucked at the two of them, drawing them through the doors into the laboratory chamber beyond.

TWENTY-TWO

As Ben felt himself being drawn through the door, he noticed, as he clutched at it for purchase, the out-of-fashion pattern of the carpet. His fingernails screamed in pain, unable to hold himself back against the unnatural gusts sucking him inward. His chin struck the metal latch on the doorframe, and sparks shot across his field of vision.

Hathaway's extinguisher canister clattered to the ground, clanging loudly as it rolled through the tempestuous hallway. Ben's hands automatically clutched for whatever purchase they could find, his fingers slipping over wall tiles before he managed to take a hold of a small box mounted halfway up the wall. He looked down, and gave a small shriek to see that he was now about six feet from the ground.

The wind was so strong! He felt the grip of his sweat-slicked fingers slipping, and he watched helplessly as the box slipped away. Loose papers and folders flew past, buffeting Ben's face like a barn full of startled birds.

Ben's flailing hands grabbed unthinkingly for anything he could take hold of, and he finally managed to wrap his fingers around something that felt like a cord. Though he could sense his weight straining this makeshift lifeline, whatever it was, it seemed to hold. He clenched his eyes shut instinctively as post-it notes and plastic bags buffeted his face and cut his cheeks.

He felt the cord straining in his grip, as though it were nearing its breaking point. Ben groaned with effort, his arms burning and his legs fluttering straight out behind him. He looked like a tattered flag blowing in a high wind.

A high-pitched keening noise mingled with the sound of the howling gusts, followed by the tinkling shatter of exploding light bulbs. Hathaway's moaning voice cut through the howl of the wind. The lights in the hallway began to strobe as the bulbs, beset with flying shrapnel, burst in their fixtures. The shards of bulbs and fluorescent tubes joined with paperclips, packs of staples, and other dangerous detritus in flight. The debris in the air gathered in thickness, now able to inflict dozens of tiny cuts per second. Ben felt his grip on whatever it was he was holding begin to slip, and in that moment, a thought occurred to him: *why was he holding on so tight?*

Why was he so certain that floating in this shrapnel-filled hallway indefinitely would be an improvement over the alternative? Ordinarily, in a situation with that kind of airflow, hanging on would be the only correct solution. But this wasn't a blown airplane hatch, or some kind of industrial-strength ventilation system gone awry. He wasn't Toto, this wasn't Kansas, and the problem wasn't exactly a natural disaster.

Ben realized, as his aching fingers strained to keep their grip on their increasingly slippery lifeline, as he felt the stinging bite of paper cuts and debris battering his skin, he realized that letting go – though every instinct in his body and mind screamed against it – was just as likely to be the right choice in this unnatural situation.

Ben decided to release his grip on the cord in the wall just as his fingers were slipping, and as he flew down the hall, away from his lifeline, Hathaway's hefty steel-toed boot struck him in the temple, and he blacked out.

*   *   *

"Kid!"

It was Hathaway's voice, alright, but it sounded as though the man were speaking from underneath a pile of hundreds of soaking wet washcloths. Ben wrinkled his nose – the only movement he could make that didn't hurt – and coughed. When he did, his field of vision turned bright red, and the dull fire in his skull flared orange.

"Sweet *Nefertiti!*"

Hathaway loomed over Ben's slumped form like an anxious mother. Ben painfully forced open an eyelid.

"That's an old one," Ben wheezed.

"Goddamn you, kid."

Hathaway was grinning.

Ben inhaled sharply as he sat up. Everything hurt with a dull ache.

"Where are we now?"

The room was small and dark – lit only by the screen of Hathaway's phone – and smelled like damp concrete.

"Under the stairs, in the little utility room where the janitors keep their porn."

Ben rubbed his head.

"So we're already in the basement?"

Hathaway nodded.

"What happened up there?" Ben only remembered fitful glimpses.

"Vortex," Hathaway said. "In the next room." He shook his head. "You know why we aren't dead?"

Ben waited for the answer.

"Because when we flew into that room, that cat was *scared*. Two giant people, flying into a room with a little cat in it. And that's the one thing we can't forget here."

"What's that?" Ben asked.

"That these things are *cats*! We're talking about them like they are Talibani agents or something. Aside from the mean one, I don't think these cats *are* particularly violent. They certainly aren't trying to take over a government facility. We're acting like they are."

Ben rubbed his head, but said nothing. He was lost in thought.

"I mean," Hathaway continued, "you got to see it from the cat's perspective. She's sitting in the hallway, and the next thing you know – your unconscious ass is flying at her head at fifty miles an hour." Hathaway whistled. "I tell you, she was every bit as scared as you would be if a full-sized hippo flew in the window, coming straight at your face."

Hathaway took a drag on his e-cig, then continued.

"What set them off? My guess is the rats. Once these freaks got a full charge from pigging out on their first all-you-can-eat-buffet, they started… well, *freaking out*. Vortex wasn't trying to suck herself into oblivion – Charlotte wasn't trying to wrap you up in a web and *eat* you. These cats are just *full* – overflowing with energy, and I don't think they can help using it any more than a dry pile of leaves can help catching on fire when a match gets dropped on it."

"So what do we do?" Ben asked.

Hathaway struck his palm with his fist.

"We out *cat* them."

Ben scoffed. "You must have got knocked on your head there yourself, good buddy."

Hathaway dismissed this with a wave of his hand.

"Hear me out!" He started ticking points off on his fingers. "What usually motivates a cat? The only time you see a cat ever trying to do anything is when they are hungry or bored. The only functional difference between a cat with a full stomach and a doorstop is fur."

"These guys are young," Ben reminded Hathaway. "Cats are usually pretty wired for a couple years before they start slowing down."

Hathaway snapped his fingers, nodding vigorously.

"Exactly! I know these are young'uns, but do you remember when *you* were a growing little pipsqueak? You were probably exactly like these little bastards – a bottomless pit to stuff with food, but when you crashed, you crashed *hard*. People don't seem to remember how teenagers sleep like little coma victims until they have some of their own."

"So what? What good does that do us?"

Hathaway's eyes narrowed.

"You're a little piss-ant."

He coughed wetly for some time – a harsh, raspy sound – before Ben realized he was laughing.

"This is what we're going to do. We're going to get a ball of yarn and dangle it over their little heads. We're going to get a laser pointer and get them to chase it off a cliff. You see what I'm saying?"

A light went on in Ben's head.

"You mean like Judo? Work *with* the opposition?"

"*Bingo!*" Hathaway clapped him on the shoulder. "That's the ticket. Like freaking *Judo*. Use their momentum *against* them!"

Ben looked around the dim chamber.

"Did you have anything particular in mind?"

Hathaway's grin widened even further.

"Take a look at this," he said, wheeling around and pointing at squat, garbage can-like unit nestled against the wall under the stairs. "What's that look like to you?"

Ben frowned. To him, it looked as though an oil drum had had an affair with an ergonomic computer keyboard, producing an unlikely bastard-child.

"Like a Roomba on steroids?"

Hathaway snapped his fingers.

"You know, that's a good way of putting it. The thing is an auto-ordinance device."

The gears in Ben's mind clicked. The thing really *was* sort of like a Roomba on steroids. If an unusual or suspicious package or device was noticed on site, this thing would be fired up and dispatched to the scene, crawling along on its tank-like treads, to 'apprehend and envelop' the potential threat, and then, should it prove to be explosive, detonate it safely somewhere far from the site's buildings. This sort of device had become common at government facilities as worry about terrorism attacks had grown, and though Ben had heard of such things, he had never actually seen an auto-ordinance robot in person.

Ben gestured towards the device.

"Is this thing automatic pilot, or remote control?"

He wasn't surprised to learn that it possessed both modes of operation.

"So do we smear some mouse guts on its grill and run this puppy out there? *'Get her,'* kind of a plan?"

Hathaway nodded, pulling out his phone.

"Something like that. Got the thing loaded on here," he said, showing Ben the image on his phone's screen – it was a bright green night vision depiction of the room they were in.

Rick slid his fingers over the on-screen controls, and the egg-like contraption rolled forward a foot.

"Damn, like a remote controlled car!" said Ben, laughing.

"Let's not have too much fun," Hathaway said sternly. "Jeff's counting on us."

Ben looked down at the ovoid robot, its spindly, pole-like arms whirring softly around its 'head,' and felt his heart sinking again. If this comical-seeming device – which looked more like an exotic add-on to an ill-received Wii game than a serious life-saving tool – was their best chance, how good of a chance did they really have?

Twenty-Three

Jeff had never felt more grateful in his life than he did upon finding the place where they kept the key to the lab's shredding bin. The lab – like all government research facilities – was required to use a third-party confidential material disposal service for its sensitive document destruction. In government work, compliance was all. For this reason, there was a large, empty, fire-proof box for Jeff to hide in once he escaped the chute.

And a large, empty fire-proof box that he could lock himself inside was the only thing that could have saved him just then.

*   *   *

When, moments after his kicked-off shoes flew out the chute, Jeff himself came popping out, he found himself face to face with a cat. He didn't recognize which cat right off the bat, because he was distracted by the horrible, ear-splitting sound that filled the lab. Each alarm at the facility had a different tone, and even in his great state of fear Jeff recognized the shrill klaxon that meant *fire*.

He threw himself behind a desk to put some kind of barrier between himself and the cat. Jeff's mind started working. If there was a fire, he had to get out of there, but he would have to get past the cat. But weren't cats afraid of fire? Surely it could smell a fire if it was nearby. Didn't these things have super-sensitive senses of smell? Why hadn't it run away?

Jeff shuddered as he started to panic. What if this cat had *started* the fire with its mind? What if the cat started *him* on fire?

From his position under the desk, Jeff looked up and saw a small key rack mounted just underneath the surface of the desk: out of sight, but within reach of workers. A light bulb flashed on in his head. He ran to the waist-high to-be-shredded bin, unlocked it, and crawled inside. Pleased to find that it would snap shut without being locked from the outside, he had just enough time to seal himself inside the bin before the cat walked out from behind the desk.

He heaved a sigh of relief as he shut the door, but he tried to heave it quietly.

*   *   *

Because the sensitive documents all had to be destroyed off-site, there were no dangerous parts or metal blades inside the bin. It was simply a heavy box with a slot in it. Jeff *was* dismayed, however, to find that the warning of 'Paper and Staples/Paperclips *Only*' hadn't gone entirely heeded – he had sat down in something sticky and rotten smelling, and felt fairly certain it was a month-old donut soaked in week's old coffee.

Gathering his wits, he found that by sitting at the right angle, she could see a fair swath of the room out of the bin's slot. Grimacing at the soggy donut mush mooshing between his kneecaps, he looked around, his ears still grinding from the incessant braying of the alarm.

What he saw was not what he had expected. He thought it would be one of the scary cats – hell, maybe even the really mean one – but instead Jeff saw little Decibel trotting out. The tortoiseshell cat looked around, brushed an ear with a paw, and then something very strange happened. In one single, fluid moment, the fire alarm morphed into the sound of a cat sneezing, dropping rapidly in volume as it did.

Jeff blinked as the cat sneezed a second and third time. The fire alarm did not return. Jeff realized that he had sealed himself in this fire-proof box based on a faulty assumption. Before he could decide what rude thing to hiss at the cat through the slot, Decibel had trotted out of the room.

Jeff sat back, reassessing the situation. He felt a gross sensation on his pant legs and swore under his breath. He cursed his luck again, more vehemently, when he realized his foolish mistake. Though he had brought the key into the bin with him, he couldn't reach his wrist through the slot. His fingers only protruded up to his palm. He certainly couldn't reach around far enough to get the key in the lock and then turn it to open the hatch.

For whatever shortsighted reason, the third-party disposal service didn't bother putting an 'emergency release switch' on the inside of the paper shredding bin. Jeff's heart raced. There was no way to let himself out!

"I'm going to *die* in here!" he muttered, panic swelling in his chest.

At that moment, the lab doors flew open.

"*Dammit!*" It was Hathaway's voice. "He's not here!"

"Do you think he got stuck in the chute?"

Must have been Ben.

"That fucker is pretty lanky, but I guess he *is* bigger than a cat."

Jeff could hear the voices getting fainter.

"*Hey! Wait!*" He pounded the walls. "I'm here, I'm here!"

He could forgive being called a lanky fucker, and he would even be willing to buy Hathaway a drink and tell everybody on-site that the fat bastard was his best friend ever, if only they got him out of this foul-smelling prison. He didn't want to die in a shredding bin.

"Did you hear something?"

It was Hathaway. Dear god, were these shredding bins soundproof as well as fireproof? Why would they do that? He pounded harder.

"Help! *Help!*"

"Ben, wait!" Hathaway again. "What if that sound is Decibel and not Jeff?"

Oh *no!* They weren't going to save him because they thought he was a cat! That damn cat was the reason he had locked himself in this shed in the first place. For all Jeff knew, Decibel might still be walking around out there, and they'd see him and feel certain they hadn't actually heard him.

Jeff could just imagine Hathaway saying "Jeezus Gawd, I freaking knew it wasn't Jeff!" He bit his lip. This was terrible!

"It's freaking *me!*" he wailed. "It really is!"

Ben's voice came next.

"I don't think Decibel knows English. He can just repeat it. And besides, even if it *is* the cat, all he can do is make sounds. Worst case scenario is he deafens me with a fake rock concert, and that's small price to pay to try to save Jeff."

Jeff would buy them *both* drinks! That Ben kid was okay!

"It really *is* me. I'm not a cat!"

Their voices sounded louder now.

"Even I believe you now, Jeff. But where the hell *are* you? You sound like you're in a coffin."

Jeff could see their belts through the slot in the bin now. He stuck his fingers out.

"I'm in here!"

"Christ!" Hathaway for sure. "How did you get in… never mind. How do we get you out?"

Jeff pushed the key through the slot.

"Take it, take it! I can't reach through! I thought I was going to die in here!"

The key clicked in the lock, the bin's large grey door swung open, and Jeff tumbled out like a stowaway in a train's overhead baggage compartment.

"*Jeezus,* buddy! What in the blue fuck is that *smell?*"

*   *   *

Nayeli and Pettinger whooped and cheered as the security team rolled in: van after van of armored men and women with outfitted with firearms, flak shields, and other serious looking gear. Pettinger called out to them.

"Remember: only render them unconscious. *No* killing. Except for the grey and yellow one. If you see him… do whatever you have to do. Alive is best. But we prioritize human casualties over the subjects, obviously."

Their leader – a tall, fair-haired woman with a serious expression by the name of Marsha Strauss – nodded, pulling a sophisticated stun gun from a loop on her belt.

"What do we have to worry about with the grey and yellow cat? Any specific warnings?"

Nayeli shuddered.

"We're not sure *what* that one's limits are. I pray none of us find out."

Strauss shook her head, checked the charge on her stun gun, and called out to her contingent.

"Let's rush 'em, folks. Be on your guard, but remember: they're just cats."

As wave after wave of security team members passed them, Pettinger leaned over and whispered in Nayeli's ear.

"If only that were true."

*   *   *

As Ben, Hathaway, and Jeff walked at an even, measured pace down the corridors, the bomb-destroying robot rolling stolidly along behind them like an R2-D2 in dire need of Android Growth Hormone, Ben realized something.

"There's no way in *hell* that was Jeff's shoe."

"What do you mean?" Jeff asked, at first thinking Ben was referring to his taking off his shoes when he was stuck in the chute before realizing that Ben couldn't have known about that.

Hathaway explained.

"When we first came in here, there was a shoe propping the door open and an arrow drawn on the glass. Thanks to the auto-lockdown of the facility, if that shoe hadn't been there, we probably wouldn't have been able to get the doors open."

"So somebody is still in here somewhere?" Jeff asked, shuddering.

Ben hit the wall with his fist, shaking it out and regretting his impulsivity.

"We can't just leave them."

"Damn Ben, you should have been a Navy SEAL instead of an office assistant," Hathaway said admiringly.

Ben looked over at him.

"I'm not that brave. I wouldn't knowingly sign up for danger. But that's what we've got, and we've got to do something."

Jeff looked flustered.

"But they could be anywhere! Why would they go further from the doors? Why wouldn't they try to leave?"

"Either something was stopping them – that giant moth springs to mind – or they were trying to help somebody."

Hathaway snapped his fingers.

"Hey! We could try pinging them on the intercom. If they aren't locked in a paper shredding bin or something, they might be able to respond."

Ben perked up at the idea.

"That might also confuse any other cats that are still in the building. If they hear voices coming from *everywhere*, every room, it might disorient them a bit."

At that moment, an amplified voice echoed down the hallways.

"The security team is on-site. Please make your way to the closest exit. The security team is *on-site*."

Jeff leapt into the air, pumping his fist.

"We're off the hook! Whoever is in the building will be rescued, and we don't have to risk our lives!"

Even Ben, so brave and so willing to help, was grateful, grinning from ear to ear.

"Yeah, looks like it!" he said.

When it came down to it, even he would much rather leave all the dangerous work to the army.

187

They turned the corner, leaving the little robot behind, unheeded, the three of them wearing elated and relieved smiles on their faces, patting each other on the back and making promises to meet up for drinks later that night when they got finished debriefing the security teams, only to come face to face with Deinonychus, sitting in the middle of the corridor.

"*Row,*" said the cat.

And he meant it.

Twenty-Four

The grey and yellow cat could, through a haze of his seething anger, only make out two distinct forms standing in the hallway. An older human, with some kind of purplish glow about his lungs, whom he recognized as the one with the weak, malleable mind, and a second: a tall, lanky man. The cat hissed.

The two Namers oozed terror, and the thick emotion filled the hallway like a noxious stink. Then, to the cat's irritation, a strange, third being advanced. This seeming creature gave Deinonychus pause. Despite its bug-like movements, this new thing didn't radiate any signals of life. The creature, if that's what it was, looked to Deinonychus like a litter box with arms, and, as it rolled, it made a high-pitched *whirring* sound that offended the cat's ears.

The wafting odor of the two human's fear thickened in the hallway. The gathering clouds of it were visible to the cat's secret eye, forming a light lavender hue that drifted up to the ceiling. The sight and scent of their terror brought Deinonychus back to the business at hand. These two people (and their little dog, or whatever that thing rolling along on wheels was) had come along just when Deinonychus was starting to get bored. The cat had had his fill of birds and beasts, and he felt ready to try some larger prey.

The cat brimmed with energy, despite the massive amounts he had already expelled. The cat hadn't come back into this stupid, smelly building with the intention of eating these Namers. He had come to find his brother – the one the Namers called Leviticus. The humans obviously didn't know what Leviticus could do – that the little grey 'dud' was the most powerful of them all. Deinonychus, accordingly, despised him above all other things.

Deinonychus hated Leviticus all the more fiercely for being such a coward, despite his enormous powers – for being so damned *loving*. Deinonychus knew *Leviticus* would never stoop to using his power the way it was meant to be used. So what good was he? Deinonychus would kill him, eat his flesh, and take his powers for his own.

A simple plan, but the execution would not be so cut and dried. Leviticus knew what Deinonychus wanted. What's more, the grey runt had been making efforts to stop him. If it weren't for the smaller cat's mental meddling, Deinonychus would have already laid this entire place to waste by now. As mentally powerful as his physically puny brother was, however, Leviticus still wasn't strong enough to plug all the leaks of terror Deinonychus had bored in the fabric of reality at the agency plant.

Deinonychus still managed to briefly short circuit a number of human minds, unleashing most of the pent up havoc that had been bottled up here. Things were reaching a tipping point, and Deinonychus knew it. If he kept busy, Deinonychus would still be able to attain his goals.

And then these two stupid, terrified Namers walked in, looking like a perfect meal. Especially the bulky one. A feast that would give the angry yellow-and-grey cat an extra dose of energy, the opportunity to wreak further terror. One more pit stop on his way to world domination.

Deinonychus knew he was meant for nothing less.

* * *

And so the cat, sitting calmly on his haunches, began to marshal the dark power inside him. Deinonychus focused first on the tall one – he was probably faster than the fat one with diseased lungs. No fun letting the prey get away.

Like a germinating seed shooting out roots into fertile soil, tendrils of the feline's mental energy spread themselves – first inside, then outside – the cat's mind. The hall grew thick with the gathering power, like lightning about to strike. A painting rattled in its frame and fell off the wall. It wasn't enough. The cat concentrated, the two humans frozen in fear. Ceiling tile began to crack and crumble, the dust falling like volcanic ash.

Deinonychus gave a small *mewl* of pleasure as bloody streaks ran down the tall, lanky Namer's face – starting at his forehead, and slipping across his cheeks like massive claw marks.

The terrified idiot shrieked in despair and alarm, and the cat sank his mental claws deeper, relishing the man's naked fear. So weak, for something so large! Deinonychus renewed his attack, savoring the slowness with which he was able to work. These two fools seemed paralyzed by fear. They didn't even try to escape! As a cat, Deinonychus was not above playing with his food.

The cat focused on the blood dripping from his prey, blood which seemed to him to shimmer and dance with flashing patterns of light. It was *so good*, this Namer blood. Droplets of blood began to rush from the tall man's wound, flying through the air towards Deinonychus's open mouth. The spray of blood the cat had drawn out of the pumping veins of his human victim splattered his tongue lightly, revitalizing him. The Namer's gaze was wide with fear, his vision obscured by the blood running into his eyes – yet even as they were being attacked, the two tall fools did nothing.

A haziness came over his vision – as though a heat mirage stood between him and his victim. Deinonychus didn't like that. The cat saw the larger of the two fiddling with a small rectangular box in his hands. He switched his attention to the purple-lunged oaf. Satisfyingly, the tubby man immediately yelped like an injured kitten.

Weak. So weak.

Starting at the end of the hallway, light bulbs began to burst in their fixtures like bombs, each bulb growing nearer the Namers. The tinkling glass made a brittle *splashing* sound as it exploded. The cat liked the sound of breaking glass – it reminded him of shattering bones. As Deinonychus, enrapt in his bloodletting, kept at his work, the strange haze obscuring parts of his vision thickened. The effect had grown much worse, but the cat was focused on how much fun he was now having. What could mere haziness do to harm him?

In the meantime, the unnatural and ridiculous box had rolled closer to the cat. Not so close that he perceived it as a threat. Deinonychus barely permitted the approaching thing to register on his mental radar. He was too busy trying to rip off the tall one's ear. Droplets of blood flowed through the air like sideways raindrops. The cat lapped them up greedily. Waves of pleasure washed over his tongue. In the midst of these ecstasies, something happened that had never happened to Deinonychus before: something hit him.

Hard. The distorted, vaporous thing didn't just knock the wind out of him. It knocked it across the room.

One minute, the cat had been slowly carving his first victim, when the hazy cloud resolved into a vaguely human form. In an instant, that insubstantial, mirage-like shape launched a very substantial-feeling foot right at the cat's head. Pain streaked across his vision like fireworks, as Deinonychus saw the hallway spin end over end. A furious mix of surprise, anger, and agony escaped his lips in a caustic hiss before his painful landing in the shattered glass from the frame of the downed painting. A shard wedged itself in his front paw, and he screeched in anger.

He seethed, in a furious state beyond the edge of anger. The closest Deinonychus had ever felt to fear wrapped around his anger like a squeezing vine. Fear, and confusion. *What* had hurt him? What had happened?

In his short life, the few offenses against him had been swiftly dealt with. He had discouraged the playful fighting from his sisters and brothers, turning it into respectful distance with a few choice lashings. The insufferable gassing he had went through at the hands of his Namer captors had pushed him into bringing about their ruin.

In each of these instances, Deinonychus at least partially understood what had happened to him. More importantly, he had been able to see who he needed to punish for their transgressions. This time an unseen power had visited suffering upon him.

Suffering, Deinonychus could take. He was designed to both inflict and withstand it. For him, the true outrage was being *stopped*.

He had meant to do something, and some external force had halted him in mid-action. A force he could not see. An enemy he could not respond to. A reaction he couldn't take. He was beyond enraged.

Doors in the hallway flew open and caught aflame. The ceiling tiles, already crumbling in a wispy dusting, now tumbled down in smoldering sheets. Deinonychus leapt to his feet and howled like a tiny wolf, sending a furious bolt of energy at the tall Namer so powerful that it instantly burnt the pale thing's clever, clawless hand. The wretch screamed like a fabled siren, clutching at his now-useless left hand with the other.

Yet even that wasn't enough for Deinonychus, could never be enough. He was incensed. Nothing was supped to be able to hurt him. *Nothing*.

That doddering moron wasn't the one who had done this to him. That much was clear. The gangly, worthless, yelping Namer had done nothing in his life but simper and suffer. The fat one with the putrid lungs hadn't been the one to hurt him. He had merely stood there in shock, fiddling with a tiny box in his hands. The thought that the squat, robotic device might be responsible for the savage kick never even entered his mind, so ridiculous was the notion.

So where was the culprit?

Deinonychus's mind went for the first time to his powerful siblings – particularly Leviticus. Even that didn't seem right. This was something *physical*. And he, thinking cleverly despite his rage, felt certain it had to do with the Namers.

The fat one seemed to have lost interest in Deinonychus, focused instead on the funny little box in his hands. Deinonychus's first thought was to melt the box, but that wouldn't be good enough. The cat wanted to hurt the stupid Namer, not just ruin his things. After a few moments of deliberation, Deinonychus settled on the proper punishment. The pudgy fellow with rotting lungs began leaping about as though he were standing on an oven.

It took the frightened man a few moments to realize his footwear was burning.

"Jeezus goddamn *lord* in a box of *Chex-Mix!*" the moron shouted as he kicked off his smoldering, smoking shoes. "I just got these goddamn shoes!"

The cat didn't know what that meant, but he could sense the fear and outrage behind the utterance.

"Ben, kick him again! Kick him in the goddamned *head!*"

With that group of sounds, a strange image formed in the cat's mind. A younger, less grizzled, less stocky Namer's face floated into his thoughts. Who was *this?* The Namer seemed vaguely familiar to Deinonychus. But what should that matter? Obviously, the only two people here were the tall one and the big one who couldn't breathe right.

The emergency sprinklers began to rain down on the hallway, shocking the cat with an abrupt spray of cold water and infuriating him even more. Deinonychus, trying in vain to avoid the droplets, begrudgingly accepted that these credulous fools had a few tricks up their sleeves besides bleeding everywhere. The tall one with the burnt hand seemed grateful for the water, holding his damaged appendage up towards the rainfall. Deinonychus had to do something quick.

He might have all the power in the world, but he *hated* getting wet.

*   *   *

The haze began to fill his vision again. This time, the cat knew what to expect, even if he didn't know how or why it was happening. He tried to get a mental lock on whatever lay within the haze, and found he could not wrap his mind around it. As far as his mental powers were concerned, there was nothing there at all. Yet the cat knew better – or at least thought he did. If his mind couldn't get a grip on whatever was concealed in the haze, then maybe his incisors could.

Deinonychus flung himself forward as the miasma raced towards him. He bared his curved fangs and extended his dagger-like claws. Just when the cat felt his body strike something solid where his eyes told him there should be only nothingness, he furiously twisted his head and raked his claws. The immediate taste of blood was his reward.

His sense of victory was short-lived, however.

A rising scream of "*Ya!*" reverberated in his ears, and the cat felt himself being lifted off the ground by a full body blow once more. He snarled, sailed head over paws, and struck a heavy door. Tongues of flame licked at his fur. He scrambled away from the fire, which he himself had set in his rage, and rolled quickly and instinctively against the carpet in order to put out the tiny tongues of flame biting into his fur.

Panic gripped him. His coat was smoldering! He had to extinguish himself!

The instinctive drive to put out the fire overwhelmed his senses, causing him to react so quickly that he ignored the rather obvious fact that he was in no danger of burning to death while in the middle of a sprinkler downpour. After a bit of scrabbling and rustling against the carpet, he felt reasonably doused.

But he was also done playing games.

Before Deinonychus even bothered to register further environmental cues, he flung himself violently about, hissing wildly as he scratched out a furious net of anger in all directions. If something invisible was here, he had learned moments ago that it could be cut. That was all he needed to know.

The cat felt his claws tear into rough fabric, despite the evidence of his eyes suggesting that nothing was there. He squeezed his paw into a clenched fist. To his delight he felt the fabric tear in his grip. He opened his jaws wide, ready to bite at the unseen assailant, but his head exploded in a burst of stars as he tumbled through space yet again, carried by the inertia of an inexpert roundhouse kick.

What was happening?

The cat's fury was palpable. The hallway was thick with it. Pipes began to boil in the walls, their outlines revealed by the condensing sweat from their near-boiling heat on the tilled hallway corridors.

The cat could no longer see anything through the red curtain of his absolute anger. Glass display cases filled with awards began to crack. Emblazoned metal rectangles on plaques commemorating good safety practices for record amounts of years began to spark blue and green, to curl at the edges, and ultimately smoke and drip and ooze down the case walls like molten lava.

Deinonychus lashed out sightlessly, heedlessly, and this time his claws raked against something smooth. Something curved, that vibrated on the physical plane with the thrill and energy of what seemed like life. On a mental level, the cat could detect nothing whatsoever: none of the bits and blips and blops that crackled and cackled and snickered and bickered in the cat's thoughts, the mental representations of other minds, other beings, other species, other cats.

Deinonychus, when confronted by this new development – and particularly after having been repeatedly thwarted by the painful rebukes of the invisible Namer force – did the only thing he thought appropriate. The cat tried to bite the thing – mind or no mind – and the raging yellow-and-grey cat came to immediately regret his decision. His teeth clamped down on unyielding metal.

Not psychic metal, as had Chroma when she attempted to snap through the minds of the two collared bears, but real, desolate, permanent, unyielding metal in the most physical of senses. Deinonychus hissed in fury. Droplets of his spittle flew. Before he could back away and reorient himself, he felt twin arms of steel clamping down on him. He sputtered and clawed at the mechanical appendages, but to no end. They fed him into a cold, cramped maw, consuming him like a devouring a praying mantis feasting upon its prey.

As his sight returned, the cat howled in frustration. Darkness enveloped him. That irritating whirring had become louder now, and the angry and confused feline began to piece together what must have happened to him. The ugly, rolling litter box-like thing had engulfed him, ensconcing his body within itself. Only, unlike a proper litter box, this blasted thing had no way out. It was a trick.

Deinonychus's fury redoubled. The small ordinance robot trapping the furious cat inside rumbled along protectively as falling metal bars and chunks of the ceiling infrastructure, plummeting down as though they were as insubstantial as the acoustic tiling, buffeted the device's chassis relentlessly. The cat sent psychic claws of hate and mental lashes of fury rocketing around the hallway like pinballs. He blindly launched bolts of anger with no particular target.

The furious, insensible cat, however powerful he was, had no way of knowing in his blind rage that, aside from himself and the many fires – some of which now burned with rage and intensity to rival the cat's fury – he had set, the hallway was now empty.

Twenty-Five

The second wave of security forces rolled in, dismounting from the open-top, extreme-stretch Humvees in droves. Their leader looked to Pettinger and Nayeli for direction.

"Which are the B and C facilities?" the man, whose nametag read 'Cahill,' asked Pettinger.

He was referring to the other labs buildings, where research apart from the genetic feline project took place. Presumably, at least one of the experiments in either 'B' or 'C' had something to do with the school bus-sized moth that Ben took down earlier.

Pettinger directed the team, but did not envy their jobs.

* * *

The 'C' facility had a ring of frightened scientists standing at the front doors. Peter Cahill took this as a good sign.

"What's going on here?" asked a tall woman in front.

Cahill took that as an even better sign. If they didn't know what was going on, the facility was probably secure. A man in the back spoke up.

"Where did all these freaking *feathers* come from?" He appeared to marvel at the amount of squirrel corpses littering the field.

Cahill ignored him, turning his attention to the woman who spoke first.

"What's going on?" she repeated.

Cahill couldn't believe it: not that she would repeat herself, but that she could talk without moving her lips. Odd time to try out a ventriloquist act, Cahill thought. He was about to explain that there had been a breech at the other labs, when she repeated it a third time.

"What's going on?"

She had modulated her voice precisely the same way each time she spoke, sounding like a looped recording. Once again, she hadn't moved her lips, not even slightly. As Cahill struggled to understand this, the woman scientist's face creased in confusion.

Cahill was soon distracted by an incongruous comment in the background from another scientist.

"What's a good little kitty like you doing at a government facility? You must be miles away from your little bitty home!"

The gears clicked in Cahill's mind, and he spun around. A small cat, its black and white fur practically begging to be stroked, stared at them intently.

"What's going on?"

"Fascinating!" said more than a few of the scientists, in near unison.

Cahill moved slowly, trying not to startle the small thing. So far, it hadn't seemed particularly dangerous, and he wanted to keep it that way. Reaching into his equipment belt, he began to pull out a tranquilizer gun.

"What a good little kitty!" came a scientist's voice.

"But you still haven't answered my question!" said the tall woman, apparently over her shock at being mimicked by a cat.

"*Shhh!*" Cahill responded quietly, hoping they would all take the hint.

The scientist who first called out 'good kitty' made a step to move forward, seemingly to pet the two-tone creature.

"*Stop!*" Cahill said, louder than he would have liked to.

The cat flinched, but otherwise did not move. Cahill let out a breath.

"Please, everybody – there has been a breech in 'A' lab, at least. Likely 'B,' as well. Even if there hasn't been one here in 'C,' this is a serious situation. I need you all to remain perfectly calm and still."

"Perfect calm, still. 'B,' 'A,' calm," repeated his voice in a clipped stutter.

This time, the cat was unmistakably the source of the sounds.

"Remarkable!" exclaimed three of the scientists.

Cahill, weary of the scientists' clustered hyperbolic remarks, drew the barrel of his tranquilizer gun clear of his belt and brought in line with the cat.

"Doesn't that seem a little excessive?" said an older man with a grey-flecked moustache.

A colleague jumped into the discussion with a useless interjection in defense of the cat.

"See, here now!"

Cahill felt lucky this cat didn't seem particularly violent, as these scientists clearly didn't grasp the severity of the situation. In fact, he thought rather more colorful thoughts of approbation than that, but kept them to himself.

"Stupid pocket protector wearing geeks are going to get us all killed!" intoned Decibel, in a voice disturbingly like

Cahill's. "Po-tweet, weet!" added the cat, in imitation of the closest bird.

Cahill quickly loosed the dart into the creature's shoulder. Decibel dropped at once to the ground, his paws momentarily flickering in the air like a dog dreaming about rabbits before his prone form stilled.

He turned sheepishly to the other scientists.

"I wonder where he heard that one?"

Most didn't seem to buy it, but the revelation that a house cat could not only reproduce their voices but evidently tap in to their thoughts distracted them from any resentment they might have felt towards his remark. Cahill shrugged.

"If you haven't had any problems in there, I'm going to get to the 'B' facility. Head to the evac units, and please report anything you might see immediately. This is a life and death situation."

*   *   *

By the time Cahill and his team had arrived at the entrance to the 'B' facility, Strauss's team was already inside. He got her on his walkie.

"Cahill party on backup, entering facility now. Anything we should be aware of?"

He paused, waited.

"Strauss, this is Cahill, over?"

No response. He looked back at his team.

"Shit."

Just as he prepared to enter, the walkie talkie in his hand crackled.

"*I'm here,*" came Marsha's gruff, no-nonsense voice. She spoke very quietly. "*Radio silence for now, for the love of god. We're on the far west wall of the first floor. Get here as fast as you can. Over and out.*" The radio crackled again.

Silence.

"Shit," Cahill repeated, before leading his team further into the building. This wasn't going to be good.

* * *

Pettinger and Nayeli had joined the other scientists and workers, led by a rear echelon of the security team. The group eventually made their way to two large bus transports which had just rolled up. Each of the two enormous, armored vehicles was fitted with massive, angular grille guards mounted on the front – similar to the type used on safaris to protect jeeps against damage from big game.

Only much larger.

A bloody sheen of organs and slimed coated the wedge-like protuberance of the front bus's grille guard, and Nayeli shuddered as she stared at it. She didn't want to imagine what the grille had forced its way through on the way here.

She and the other escapees boarded. A short, jittery man spoke from the front of the first bus over an intercom system piped into both vehicles. The evacuees learned that a tightening, circular throng of animals ranging in size from mice to cattle had surrounded the forest headquarters of NUCPA. From miles away, animals streamed towards the facility in thickening groups. When viewed from the air, the sight was as physically disturbing as it was intellectually ungraspable.

The power of Deinonychus's mind had grown along with his lust for power. As energy had flown into his body, his ability to lure ever more distal, ever larger prey sharpened. So great had his powers grown that the problem was no longer

203

confined to the physical NUCPA facilities. This situation had slipped out of control and threatened to engulf the entire region.

"Cow," explained the rattled looking driver, in response to Pettinger's quizzical look at the gore-coated grill.

No, thought Nayeli – she definitely didn't want to know more about the animal gore coating the grilles. Her stomach felt like it had been caught in a bear trap.

Soon, all the increasingly terrified scientists had boarded, and the buses wheeled around in the clearing to exit. Nayeli and Pettinger were in the front bus, which bore primary responsibility for cutting through the ring of mindless, lemmingized animals. The hope was that the second bus, traveling in the slipstream of the first bus, would suffer less from the impacts.

"How bad has it gotten?" Nayeli asked the driver.

"It's getting worse, but it was already pretty bad."

"How many, erm… *cows* did you see?"

"Five. I have a feeling there are a *lot* of cows in ditches around here with broken legs right now."

Pettinger whistled. This *was* bad. How long before this situation got out of the bottle? How long until the public demanded an explanation? How far outward had the cat's radius of influence stretched? They had to hope that the security teams could defuse the situation in time. The alternative was too dark to contemplate.

The busses finished pulling around, and the driver at the head of the small convoy revved up the engines as he prepared to leave.

"Hold on, people," he said into the intercom. "I have a feeling this is going to be a bumpy ride."

*   *   *

Ben and Rick hadn't fled the scene once they had trapped Deinonychus – they ran deeper into the building. In the mad scramble of the hallway's fiery destruction, the team unintentionally split up. Jeff went the back, instinctively fleeing the building, while Ben and Rick, driven by a sense that they had to find whoever it was who had left the shoe and the hastily scrawled arrow at the entrance, had gone on ahead.

By now, Hathaway no longer needed Ben's constant disapprovals to motivate himself. His blood might have been pumping and his heart racing, but Rick felt better – and better about himself – than he had for years. At the end of another branching hallway, the duo slid to an almost comical synchronized stop as they spied another arrow on another glass case, this one pointing towards the stairwell. The timing of their sighting was miraculous – the sprinkler system activated by the fires was literally washing the greasy arrow away as they watched. Another few seconds and it would be gone completely.

The pair didn't wait long enough to watch that happen, and barreled up the stairs. Hathaway cursed when the door closed behind them with a loud *snick*.

"Are these one-way doors?" Ben asked, a sinking feeling in his stomach.

Hathaway nodded.

"Auto-locks, kid!" he hissed. "Hope nobody needs us on the first floor again. Those doors are designed to survive a terror attack."

Ben struggled to orient himself. He only dimly remembered floor plans seen just prior to a fire drill. These half-recalled maps swirled around inside his head like a spinning video game display. Things weren't adding up for him – he had only worked here a few weeks, and this wasn't the kind of place where they encouraged the new hires to wander the hallways.

Ben couldn't tell where he was, exactly, but one thing became apparent rather quickly: on every floor, the stairwell door had been sealed with the same auto-lock mechanism as the first.

With each flight of stairs they climbed, their hope of escape diminished. The second, then third, and then fourth floor doors wouldn't budge. Beginning to despair, they were left with no options but to head to the roof, where, to their relief, they found yet another shoe propping open the door to the outside.

They slapped themselves on their foreheads, realizing their foolishness. There was an outside stairwell leading from the roof down to the ground. Whoever they had been trying to 'rescue' hadn't been trapped – they had simply walked down the scaffolding to the ground below. The shoes had been left in the doors, along with the arrows on the glass, to help *others*, in case the security breech escalated and the doors were sealed shut from the inside.

Ben and Hathaway had risked their lives for nothing, but in the end it was the foresight of the person they were trying to save that helped them to escape alive. Give a penny, take a penny.

The smell of smoke grew thicker in the air.

"That bitchkitty downstairs is going to be a cooked goose in a minute, bud," Hathaway said, shaking his head. "But I can't claim to feel too bad about it."

Ben nodded.

"I'd say our part in this little action-adventure sequence has reached its conclusion. You're a good person, Mr. Hathaway," Ben said, his voice suddenly going strange. "Just try to forget all the douchey things I said to you today, at some point. Preferably before my first performance evaluation."

Hathaway just grinned.

"*You're* a good person. On my own, I would have just ran like a baby and let everybody die." A confused expression crossed his face. "A baby that can... run. *Jeezus*, you know what I mean."

Ben smiled back, and they pushed the door to the roof open. They darted across the rooftop to the scaffolding, noting the military-style off-road vehicles filling the clearing – long, jeep like vehicles with open backs containing seats for at least a dozen crewmen a piece. Feathers and moth down billowed around them.

The pair on the rooftop could just barely make out Jeff running below. He had already made it about halfway to the busses. He stopped to look over his shoulder, and began waving frantically when he saw the two of them. They waved back ecstatically.

They had all made it, after all.

Hathaway pointed to the two busses in the distance, whistling at their train-like angular grilles.

"That's some serious *shit*, son!" he said, sounding proud.

The pair were so wrapped up in admiring the 'cavalry,' that they almost didn't hear the tiny mewling sound coming from one of the cages as they passed. With all the doors to the cells hanging wide open or lying flat on the ground – not to mention all the havoc that had been wreaked on the site – they had just assumed the cages were empty.

It was Hathaway who paused.

"What?" Ben said, eager to get off the roof and into one of those evac busses.

Hathaway put his hand on Ben's shoulder, silencing him, and cocked his head.

"There it is again!" Hathaway said, snapping his fingers.

He started looking through the cages, until he found what he was looking for.

"It's little Leviticus!" he cried out. "The good kitty!"

That strange change had come over his voice again – Ben's boss reverting to something like baby talk. Ben didn't think this was mind control, like whatever Deinonychus had done to Hathaway and Pettinger. Ben just thought that the cute grey cat brought out what little innocence survived in his jaded middle-aged boss. It made him smile, even if they were in a hurry.

Hathaway went over and began to pet the small cat on its head. Quickly, Rick's cooing voice turned to a sharp one, full of concern.

"He's sick!" said Hathaway.

"I'm not surprised. He probably got attacked by one of his more fearsome siblings. As cute as he is, he didn't seem all that powerful."

Ben was surprised by the dirty look Hathaway shot him over his shoulder.

"You're as bad as that Pettinger. I don't care how '*powerful*' he is, he's a good cat. I'm not going to let him die up here. If he's 'just a cat,' then I claim him as a pet *right now*." Hathaway scooped the little fellow up. "You didn't see this, you got me kid?"

"I don't know if that's such a good idea, I mean–" Ben began to stutter.

"I said '*You got me, kid?*'"

Hathaway left no room for argument. He wrapped the cat up in his coat.

"How are you going to sneak that thing into the evac bus? What if Pettinger finds out?"

Hathaway just shook his head, waving the problems away.

"We'll figure it out. He's little, after all. He's just a little, *liddle* guy."

Hathaway poked at the cat, wrapped inside the coat.

Ben didn't like this. He kept up his arguments.

"What if this is another trap? What if this cat is just more cunning than the rest? Uses trickery instead of brute force?"

The two of them – along with the swaddled cat – moved to the scaffolding. Ben was running out of time to make his case. Hathaway responded, and Ben saw it would take more than time to change his boss's mind about bringing the contraband cat.

"If he's eviler than he looks, it could be as serious as coming home from the grocery store to find he's eaten all the speaker wire in my house." Hathaway jabbed an emphatic finger. "Ben, if he can't do anything weird with his mind, what evil plan could he possibly have? He's just using his 'cunning' to get off the roof of a burning building – and by 'cunning,' I suppose I mean the fact that he is so sick he can barely move and I feel sorry for him."

"You're the one who is all about following regs to the letter," Ben said, trailing off.

Hathaway continued cuddling the faintly wriggling cat cradled in his coat. Ben could see it was no use. Hathaway looked up at him for a moment. They both started for the steps. Ben saw there would be no further argument.

From the way Hathaway held the balled up coat in his arms as though it were a baby, however, Ben hardly thought that this would be the end of the matter. If his boss really did want to sneak the contraband cat out of here on a government transport, he was going to have to think of something better than wadding up his coat.

Whatever Hathaway decided to try, Ben wanted no part of it.

Twenty-Six

Cahill and his team had only made it three doorways into the 'B' facility, and already the air had grown thick and pregnant with negative energy, like the hum filling the air before a lightning storm. Once the team had made it past the initial foyer, just into the hallways, it became very apparent that the experiments here were under heavy lockdown. Or had been, at least, until very recently.

Whether unsealed by fleeing scientists or things that Cahill didn't want to think about unless he had to, it seemed that almost every containment hatch and security entryway in the building had been blown wide open. Steam issued from some in curling wisps. Loud clattering noises poured from others. Some hatches exuded a pale and ghostly light, in hues of red, green, purple. Ultraviolet lights for disinfecting bacteria, infrared-spectrum lights for cultures of deep sea vent algae. Every type of radiant energy suffused the facility.

The mingling steam, swirling lights, and unsettling sounds merged together to form a sickening miasma of otherworldly uncertainty. Cahill could hear the blood pumping in his ears as he led the team further into the building. The sense that any number of code W's – unknown unknowns – could jump out at him at any time gripped him.

On top of that, Cahill felt a deep rumble, like the spinning of massive turbines in a hydroelectric plant. Though the thrumming that ran through the frame of the building may have been near the edge of perception at first, its increasing intensity was unmistakable. Cahill wondered what the equipment producing that rumble did. The thought that the powers-that-be deemed it safer to leave the works running during this emergency rather than shut it down didn't fill him with confidence. All these factors conspired to put Cahill at the very edge of his limits. So, despite Cahill's deep training, he cried out in alarm and nearly dropped his weapon when he rounded the next corner and confronted two massive, unexpected grizzly bears.

The hulking creatures reared up on their hind legs, their tall heads scraping the ceiling fire sprinklers. They bared their fangs and howled with ear-splitting alacrity.

*   *   *

For roughly five minutes, the first evac bus rumbled along through the woods at full tilt. It had encountered dozens of waves of smaller woodland creatures, but so far only crashed through a small farm's worth of out-of-place animals. The driver had informed them over the intercom that this was actually smooth sailing compared to the journey to the labs.

A moment later, he had less pleasant news. Aerial reconnaissance had sighted a final, massive wave of animals – by far the largest yet. And this ring was closing in fast. With the speed the bus had amassed, it wouldn't be long before the moment of impact.

The reconnaissance copter would do its best to assist them by attempting to taking out – via tranquillizer darts – the largest of the approaching animals.

Nayeli, bracing herself near the back of the bus, heard the approach of the copters and the frenzied herd of beasts at the same time – insistent rotors and the loud braying of horses mingled together. She and Pettinger pressed up against the windows to get a better view. Unlike most of the coats on the bus, they had been on the team studying the cause of this phenomenon. The pair also knew this was their last chance to study the cats in real-time. After this, they would be back to working on mere genes. The living cats were simply too dangerous – far more powerful than anybody on the project had ever dared to imagine.

Nayeli, feeling partly responsible for the madness surrounding her, had to wonder if the raw genes themselves might end up being an even worse evil. How would a human being – filled with conflicting impulses and ideological motivations – react to an infusion of this kind of sheer power? A sound interrupted her thoughts: a squawk erupting and then cutting off, followed immediately by a thud. Moments later, a faint crunch came from beneath the back wheels.

Another chicken.

Behind them, in the distance, a deep rumbling, percussive blast like a thunderclap rolled over the forest like a tsunami wave. Heads on the bus wheeled around as a wall of smoke rose above the tree line.

"Is that the lab?" asked dozens of concerned voices simultaneously.

So there it was, then. The defense team had been forced to pull a Code A. 'A,' for 'Annihilate.' That blast and rolling cloud of smoke could only mean that the NUCPA facility had been destroyed in an immense conflagration.

Nayeli didn't know whether to be sad or happy. Tongues of flame now were visible above the tops of the trees.

Her work materials had been destroyed, the last several years of her professional efforts wasted, but Nayeli was, she quickly decided, glad.

In the seat next to her, Pettinger thought about the mug her niece made for her in pre-school, three years before – long a main-staple of her office, a daily relic of her professional life,

213

and now surely blown to smithereens – and decided that, though she would miss the mug, she felt as Nayeli did: more like smiling than crying.

Dr. Elmyra Pettinger didn't think she wanted her niece growing up in a world where it was as easy for humans to destroy as it was for them to hate.

TWENTY-SEVEN

Deinonychus felt the ever-increasing heat radiating through the metal of canister which entrapped him. Whether it came from the fire outside or had flamed forth from his own wrath, however, he couldn't tell. Nor did he care. His blind rage became a howling wind, a thousand spreading cracks of hate and destruction speeding outwards. Like the growth of mold in a time lapse photo, tendrils of his rage expanded outwards exponentially, with him at the center: a white-hot nucleus of anger.

The entire structure trapping him began to rattle. Seams of light ripped through the darkness in claw mark patterns. Deinonychus's face locked in a snarl of fury as the structure around him ripped to pieces.

Things had not gone anything like they were supposed to. He faced the very real danger of death or serious injury for the first time in his life. The prospect did not agree with him. Everything was backwards. *He* was supposed to be the dangerous one. The cat had been reduced to a trapped, twitching ball of sparking, wrothful indignation.

The chassis of the robot began to split apart. Seeing the light of the world outside only made the cat angrier. He couldn't believe that he had been *trapped*. He needed to get out.

The seeming earthquake in the hallway stilled. The streaks of flame running down the hall's walls and carpet slowed their sprinting spread down to a mere crawl. Instead of working to continue the general destruction, Deinonychus focused his mental efforts on widening the claw marks he had scored into the steel canister imprisoning him. The ordinance robot shuddered and tore apart like sheets of plastic wrap. Soon, the metal walls had been utterly shredded, and the metal can fell open like a metal flower as it split down the sides.

In the center of that flower's gleaming, metallic petals, Deinonychus tilted his head back and bellowed an unearthly cry of frustration. The smallness of the young housecat belied the continent-sized mass of loathing unmasked in his voice. Now that he had freed himself from the robot, the remnants of the ceiling sprinkler system resumed buffeting his fur with water.

He snarled again. Was everything in this disgusting world out to get him? He narrowed his eyes and stretched his front paws out before him, then began trotting down the hallway.

*   *   *

As he sauntered along the flaming wreckage of the corridor, the cat's entire demeanor rapidly changed. He trotted down the hallway with seeming calm, his fur shining. Smoldering woodwork dropped all around him as the myriad fires spread, but it didn't faze Deinonychus. The cat ignored the sights and violent noises around him as he sniffed out a way to the outside, taking his lead from the path the clean air travelled as it escaped the building.

Here at floor level, he was beneath the accumulating clouds of smoke and soot gathering near the ceiling. He stepped lightly over the debris in his path, his tail held high. He looked almost serene. Even the constant fur-soaking drizzle seemed to no longer irritate him. Outwardly, Deinonychus gave every appearance of indifference.

In fact, he was marshaling his strength: focusing his mental tendrils before shooting them into the outside world.

His mental eye swept over the landscape like an invisible searchlight, seeking out the humans who had wronged him. Those who had trapped him in that little can would soon be his victims. His thoughts made one pass over the lands and found nothing. He made a second search, widening his scope. This time, he found something.

Deinonychus was confused. He *had* managed to find the tall Namer on the grounds outside: running away of course, an act which seemed typical of these spineless Namers. But where were the other two? There could be no doubt in Deinonychus's mind now that there were two others, not just the purple-lunged older man the cat could see. Whatever kicked Deinonychus twice and locked him in that rolling metal box hadn't been nothing.

He meowed in triumph when, at last, he caught a mental scent of the fat, crusty-lunged Namer. Progress. The man was up on the roof. Deinonychus sank further into his own mind, focusing all of his mental will on the purple-lunged fool, and finally found what he was looking for. The cat saw only fractured images – like trying to look closely at the contents of a room solely via the diffuse reflections from the myriad scattered shards of a shattered mirror – but he *could* see, and what he could see was the thing he was looking for.

A stranger peered out from behind the squat man's unsuspecting gaze. Two green, sparkling eyes saw out through the wheezing man's own. And the cat could finally make out, through the conduit of the Namer, what he himself couldn't detect.

The smoky, fog-obscured figure remained hazy, but nevertheless Deinonychus could now see the shape of the male Namer. See, and thusly target. Deinonychus, however, wished examine this mysterious person first.

He wanted to know what it was that had kicked him before he killed it. Who was this Namer, and how could he escape being seen? Deinonychus had never encountered such a thing before. And it wasn't as though he looked particularly special, now that the cat could see him.

Not as tall as the person running across the field, and not as short as the large, coughing one with the faint purple aura of disease. Nor as *old*… but that couldn't be why Deinonychus wasn't able to see him. That didn't make sense.

Deinonychus could hear the bird embryos growing in a nest almost a mile away, without even listening for them. Age had nothing to do with his ability to perceive. And this wasn't just a mental blockage. Even with his waking eyes, this Namer was invisible. What could possibly explain that?

The cat thought furiously as he neared the closed door of the building. He approached, and blew it off its hinges. It lay shattered in the grass before him, haloed by a wide spray of thick safety glass.

Clearing his head of all such thoughts, Deinonychus stepped clear of the building's vestibule. Who really cared why this infuriating human hardly registered to the cat's mind, or why he didn't seem to be visible? Worrying about *why* things happened or didn't happen was what *they* – the pitiable humans – did.

Deinonychus did not need to know why or how the man had attacked him. Blurry or not, hazy or no – the not-tall-not-short Namer would be dead in a minute. Deinonychus would make sure of it.

That was all that mattered.

TWENTY-EIGHT

"Don't move!"

Strauss's voice crackled over the walkie. Cahill and his team, frozen in formation about twenty feet in front of the bears, listened in mute, dull horror to the loud hiss of her voice over the speaker. Cahill's eyes had locked on the two bears – if that's what they even were. They sure looked like bears, but the strange machinery on their collars – not to mention the vacant, absolutely absent look in their eyes – made him suspect that, by now at least, they were something else.

Something that just used the bears.

"They seem to react instantly to movement," Strauss continued, via transmission. "They also respond to local sound. The walkies seem okay, though. They don't react to them at all."

Cahill wanted to respond that, now that his team had gotten themselves into a life-or-death situation trying to save her, Strauss didn't exactly sound like she needed help. He managed, however, to stop himself before he opened his stupid mouth and pissed off the bears. Cahill's leg began to tremble with fear, and he focused on willing his body to stop responding to the terror. The wrath of those bear-things was just one gasp or jerky shudder away from killing the entire group.

"Now listen to me," Strauss said. "We're trapped down in the basement. That whirring sound? Some kind of major system down here is shutting down. Every readout down here is saying the system is about to reach critical mass. We got sealed in, and the controls to deactivate the failsafe locks are on the outside of this chamber. The air is going to be pumped out of here in four minutes to 'minimize thermal dispersion.'"

The walkies crackled loudly for a moment before Strauss continued.

"There's nothing we can do to stop it and there's no way we can get out without your help."

Jesus! Sweat poured down Cahill's forehead. He wanted to wipe it away, stop it from stinging his eyes, but he didn't dare move. He couldn't do anything but stand there as the near motionless bears filled the hallway before him.

Strauss went on.

"There's a row of security camera screens on the other side of the barrier from us, and we can see you on one of the monitors."

Cahill wanted to ask her why, if Strauss could see them, she hadn't warned them they were about to walk into to a gang of cyber-grizzlies.

Cahill dragged his eyes away from the bears, and noticed the camera up in the corner behind the two beasts, up where the wall met the ceiling. Cahill sighed inwardly. He didn't see how her seeing them could possibly help him now.

Strauss's voice crackled through the speakers again.

"Three and a half minutes," Strauss said, the clear helplessness in her voice echoing throughout the hallway.

Cahill, dripping with sweat and forced into motionlessness, gaze fixed on the muzzles of the enormous bears, didn't see what he could do about it.

*   *   *

Ben and Hathaway ran as quickly as they could down the scaffolding and out into the clearing, meeting up with Jeff near the third and final evac bus. The newly reformed trio clapped each other on the shoulders, feeling victorious in their mutual escape. The moment passed, and they headed to the bus.

Ben kept his eyes on Jeff. A few times, the taller man glanced at Hathaway. Ben waited for Jeff to comment on Hathaway's bundled-up towel. He never did.

Ben realized Jeff was too frightened and excited to care about a wadded up coat, and for the first time it struck him: his boss might actually be able to get away with taking the cat. The idea didn't comfort him. Ben's glance drifted to the towel, and he thought he saw it squirm slightly. He bit his lip – Hathaway's obsession with that damn cat was making him nervous.

Ben didn't know what his boss saw in the puny grey thing that was worth risking his career – and possibly his life – over.

* * *

Tendrils of consciousness snaked out from Leviticus's mind and out into the world around him. The small, grey cat shifted his body slightly. He could barely move.

He felt all sort of wadded up; his body constricted, but in a surprisingly pleasant way. Leviticus's was wrapped in something soft and warm, something that felt safe. What's more, he could feel the unmistakable good will of the person cradling him. The man's pure intentions radiated outwards, spreading a kind of mental warmth. It was – like the soft, fuzzy fabric enwrapping him – strangely comforting.

After everything he had been through, Leviticus felt somehow safe, in a way he had never felt before. Someone held him, and loved him, and wanted to be his friend in a simple, unassuming, undemanding way. A purr started to rev away in his throat as his happiness spread through him, and the wrappings of the towel were squeezed pleasantly tighter in response.

Though he didn't know where he was going, Leviticus could feel – with absolute certainty – that he could trust the Namer carrying him. The cat tried to let the worry ebb out of his body and mind. It should have been hard to stop worrying, with his murderous brother yet to be stopped, but Leviticus found himself sinking into restful apathy. The threat of Deinonychus didn't get to dictate the way Leviticus felt every hour of every day.

The waves reflecting back from his brother's depraved, spiteful mind told the story of a somehow chastened and humbled cat. Things didn't always go Deinonychus's way, after all. Leviticus didn't think that the newfound Namer friends around him needed his protection against his older brother just now. Leviticus let his mind's eye rove over the surrounding land in a vast mental radar sweep, looking for signs of trouble or anything else of interest. Not in the hopes or fears of finding anything, but out of sheer force of habit.

His thoughts were stopped by a wall of fear, as though his mind clanged against the metal of a fence gate. In a nearby building, at least a dozen Namers stood stricken with terror. Some were frozen – unmoving for fear of their lives – while others moved agitatedly about below the earth, struggling to find some way out. Leviticus couldn't understand the mechanics of their situation, but he saw plainly enough – with the eye in his mind – what held them back from their goal of survival.

Two huge animal-things menaced the motionless group. Great beasts reduced to mere vehicles for the will of something other. Leviticus couldn't clearly sense what that other thing was… but it seemed to live inside a box stuck to the beasts necks, a tiny, cold contraption filled with lights, stuck deeply into their flesh and with wires running throughout their ursine bodies. Metal entwined with nerve endings, forming an arachnid tangle of machine and monster.

Leviticus felt suddenly weak. He was already exhausted, famished. The grey cat wanted nothing more than to relax in the loving arms of this Namer and let this group of people take him far away from here. Leviticus could see, however, that his work was not yet over.

He had to help the trapped Namers – it was against his nature to ignore their suffering and let them die. They would not die. Not if Leviticus could help.

His purring died away as he focused his mind on the wires inside the huge beasts' skulls. His eyes narrowed to slits, an otherworldly light glowing inside them that illuminated dark interior of the coat enwrapping him. His feline mind gathered itself into a net of psychic thunderbolts, turning his concentration into countless daggers of energy: intense, bristling, electric power which he stabbed with sudden violence deeply into the bleeping boxes on the distant grizzly bear-bots' necks.

His fading mind shot out from him like lightning, jolting the wires of the monstrous bear-things unnatural inner-cables, shocking them at the points where they enmeshed with the animals' nerve endings. With each jolt, pain flared up inside his own body. Leviticus's eyes fluttered closed, consciousness pouring out of him. He fought to remain awake – to see into the building, to ensure safety of the trapped Namers. The grey cat kept right on shocking the beasts, oblivious to his own suffering, until the moment when his energy ran out completely.

His last waking sight was a mental vision of the endangered Namers cheering, running through the building, safe and free. The ones in the hallway, Leviticus sensed, could now save their trapped friends in the basement. All would be well.

Leviticus felt pleased with himself. His responsibility had been fulfilled. Despite the sharp pain in his head, he had no trouble passing into an exhausted but contented sleep, his protective powers temporarily extinguished.

Leviticus slipped into unconsciousness, another small rivulet of blood snaking out of his mouth, at precisely the moment when his snarling brother Deinonychus erupted from the 'A' lab, a stampede of dying birds and mammals bursting around him like fireworks.

Bolts of crackling energy burst around his head as the hateful cat galloped at full speed towards the trio of Namers. The sleeping Leviticus, aware of nothing, could offer no help. They were on their own.

Twenty-Nine

Cahill and Strauss's teams barreled towards the outside doors at full speed. Despite the providential malfunction of the bears' cybernetic apparatus, the two security team's time was short. The 'thermal dispersion' systems couldn't be deactivated, not even after Cahill had arrived on the scene.

He and his crew had been able to free Strauss and her people from the inner chamber before the air pumped out out – barely making it out of the basement in time themselves – but no amount of hammering on the controls could deactivate the overall destruct routine. The entire 'B' building was going to go sky high in a matter of sixty seconds or less.

Still, the mood in their new, larger amalgamated group was rather upbeat. Both teams had narrowly escaped certain death, exchanging it for a slight chance at survival. Certainly an improvement.

Yet, despite this good fortune, Cahill's mind was vaguely troubled. As the group of security professionals raced along the flaming hallways, desperate to escape in time to avoid burning to death, Cahill *still* couldn't understand what had happened with the robo-bears.

* * *

Just minutes before, Cahill and his team had stood frozen in the hallway – the bears, mere yards away, locked in a similar attitude. A motionless standoff, both sides eyeing each other but making no moves. Then, with a sudden, lurching change in the room's atmosphere, the two hulking creatures tilted back their heads and bellowed as one entity, revealing teeth so long they made Cahill's mind swim with horror. Several of Cahill's team members, dashing quickly to action now that the bears moved first, had taken aim, but the bears rushed from the room before any among the security detail could fire.

With no signals of their intention, the two hulking behemoths bolted from Cahill and his astonished crew, taking off down the hallway. An instant before, Cahill and his crew had been staring death in the fangs, and now they were alone in the room. Cahill shook his head clear.

The clock was ticking. Strauss and her team were still in danger. Cahill didn't have the time to process what may have happened. He doubted he would understand it, anyway. He wondered if the coats running these experiments would even have understood.

Cahill led the team deeper into the complex, towards Strauss. Bears or no bears, they were running out of time. Assuming that he could figure out how to free her and her team once they got there, they had only minutes to spare.

*   *   *

Now, with that scant time nearly depleted, it seemed all wasn't lost, after all. Cahill managed to free Strauss's group with the failsafe override controls almost effortlessly. The combined group sprang up the stairs at breakneck speed. The basement door swung itself shut a moment after the last of the team burst through it. A loud *woosh* behind them made it clear that they had only just escaped an agonizing death via depressurization and suffocation. Still moving at top speed, the team made it all the way back to the main corridor where, at the end of a final hallway, sat the front doors. Only seconds remained before the self-destruct sequence detonated, but the exit was close at hand.

There was actually a slight chance they would all survive the impending blast.

With only seconds to go, the rumbling in the floors became a thick, heavy rattling. The walls shuddered and cracked. Bits of plaster fell from the ceiling in drabs. Strauss somehow doubled her speed, and Cahill fought to match her. A sparking 'EXIT' sign fell off the wall, nearly striking one of Strauss's troops.

The front doors – in truth only about twenty yards distant – looked more than a mile off to Cahill. The reluctant feet at the end of his scissoring legs felt like blocks of unyielding stone. The very air itself seemed to slow him down as he pushed himself forward. The temperature in the hallway rose as the self-destruct spun up through the ignition phase. A wall of heat radiating from the impending blast pushed him from behind.

Their escape was going to cut it close if it was going to cut it at all.

Thirty

Deinonychus charged like a fireball, like a comet streaking across the ground. Ben tracked the movement, struck incredulous by what he was seeing, unable to react. Ben was looking at something utterly divorced from nature, from reason, from the sane, rational world of the possible.

Ben saw an ephemeral form flowing through the air, a great, vaporous umbra riding out behind the charging cat like a billowing standard. The shape grew and solidified as the cat barreled along. The beast's true form: his inner power and hunger for infinity revealed, cast outward like a monstrous shadow by the mentally blinding rays of the cat's psychic energy.

For all his appearances, Deinonychus was not a housecat. Not really. Something bigger, something worse saw out from his eyes. The heart of a nightmare beast beat in his chest.

Ben heard not the clamor of padding paws thudding lightly against the grass, but the thundering footsteps of a galloping beast larger than a lion. The claws in those fingers, no matter what they might have looked like, were really the size of rapiers. In truth, the rows of teeth set in those terrible jaws were curved, cruel daggers.

Ben didn't see a housecat running towards him, but his doom. Deinonychus: terrible claw. The worst thing in the world.

A hulking predator, its green eyes glowing, raced at Ben across the mists of prehistoric time; a kind of carnivore that hadn't hunted humans for ice ages bared its fangs at man for the first time in hundreds of thousands of years.

Ben's eyes, locked on the approaching cat, felt too heavy to ever move again. His pupils began to pulse in his eye sockets, to somehow swirl in his iris. He felt the soles of his feet grow down into the grass like hungry tree roots.

As Ben stood petrified, flesh seemed to coalesce around Deinonychus like a growing thundercloud, wrapping itself onto the cat's expanding frame and adding to his weight. Ben's eyes flashed and pulsed as the impossible seemed to happen in front of him: as the vicious animal stampeded across the field, the small cat grew to become the reflection of his own terrible self-image. A wreath of fire crackled around the growing cat's head like a mane of flames.

Somehow, all of the cat's rage, hate, and energy were coalescing into a physical form: a fire-crackling monster of hate and hunger and instinct crisscrossed with lave-cracked fissures from which sick, orange light poured and curling, putrid smoke wafted.

And Ben, his feet grown heavy and his eyes blank and pulsing, was powerless to even move, let alone retaliate.

*   *   *

Cahill and Strauss, like the leaders they were, insisted on being the last of their teams to exit the building. As their turn came at last and they darted through the door together, they felt the expanding heat from the hallway pushing them out like inexorable, invisible arms. Their teams, now halfway across the clearing, never stopped running, and the two leaders didn't either. The heat licked at their heels as they raced through the field. Their arms flew up automatically, protecting their eyes and head from the onrushing blast overtaking them from behind.

The sound of the explosion was enormous. It stabbed thick battering rams of air deeply into their ear drums. Flames rocketed skywards, a great *woosh* which seemed to come from all directions at once. The expanding wall of fire engulfed everything visible for a moment before it began to dissipate. Squinting, Cahill tried to make out the scene in front of him.

It wasn't working out for him. Cahill blinked a few times in disbelief. It seemed that a great streak of fire was rushing through the field in front of him. How could that be? If fire from the explosion behind him was so strong that far up ahead, then how had he and his team have survived?

He rubbed his eyes as he ran, and looked again, and he still saw it: a massive fireball shooting across the field. He struggled to understand. The fire's angle was all wrong. He traced the flame's trajectory. It led back to the 'A' building.

Cahill, starting to piece together what was happening, swung his head back and saw that the fireball's path took it straight towards a group of three NUCPA workers, all standing with their jaws agape near the second evac bus.

"What the hell *is* that?" Cahill wondered aloud as the fireball sped onwards.

*   *   *

Hathaway tried to pull Ben along by his wrist, but it felt to Rick as though the younger man were rooted to the ground. Hathaway waved his hand frantically in front of Ben's face, hoping for some sign of life, and saw to his horror that Ben wasn't just unresponsive – he looked *incapable* of response.

His eyes pulsed in an otherworldly rhythm, his pupils expanding and contracting, his face expressionless. Hathaway glanced back up, and saw that the cat was somehow growing in size as it approached. Bigger now than the biggest lion, the creature continued its frenzied gallop, closing in across the yards that separated them. Even from this distance, the hatred in the cat's eyes was unmistakable.

Hathaway's ordinarily colorful interjections failed him.

Jeff had already started to run, his atavistic fear of death outweighing any sense of responsibility for protecting his friends. Hathaway, however, couldn't consign Ben to die like that – even if the best he could do was to die alongside him. Hathaway held the small bundle containing the temporarily-forgotten Leviticus tight against his chest with his left arm, and continued pulling at Ben with his right. It was a futile, purely symbolic gesture by this point.

The speed with which Deinonychus, in all his otherworldly fury, now bore down upon them gave them no hope of escape, even if Ben suddenly regained awareness. Hathaway gulped deeply, bracing himself against the coming impact.

Pressure grew in his ears. Hathaway dropped the coat to the ground, pressed his palms against his temples, and moaned in agony. His head felt like it was splitting open. His entire body shook. The entire clearing seemed to thump and tremble at subsonic frequencies, like something gigantic was stomping nearby.

Even the cat felt it. The surging form of Deinonychus's massive new body stopped dead in its tracks, mere yards away. Something else had come to the clearing, something heavier than anything that had ever set foot there.

Lumbering through the forty foot blazing wall – all that remained of the smoldering 'B' building – two colossal forms emerged from the fire, running at a full tilt. Flames streamed off them like water. Their ursine bodies had been transformed by the dying gasps of whatever size-modifying experiment had created the monstrous moth. The effect was devastating.

Before their run in with the mass-altering device, the pair of creatures had been among the largest natural land predators currently extant on the planet. Now, they had grown into demon monstrosities larger than the greatest predatory dinosaurs ever to walk the earth. The rumbling of their growls echoed throughout the woods, louder than jet engines, as they stampeded from the flaming wreckage.

In that moment, as Hathaway covered his ears and Deinonychus's attention turned to these new interlopers, Strauss and Cahill ordered their teams to open fire at the twin bears' towering frames. Ben shook his head clear, recovering from the strange hold Deinonychus had held him in.

The cat wheeled around to face these new intruders, his grudge against Ben and the Namers temporarily forgotten. At once, snaking threads of blue flame began to entwine themselves around the thundering legs of the onrushing bear titans. Smoke sizzled off their fur. The cat's mental attack, however, didn't seem to be slowing them down.

Ben, now fully snapped out of his stupor, began pulling at Hathaway to go. Hathaway smacked him away and rooted around on the ground for something before finally joining Ben in racing to the bus.

"He's sick!" Hathaway grunted as they ran.

"What are you talking about?" said Ben.

He could barely hear the older man's words over the din of the clash behind them. Ben, in his fear, had forgotten about little Leviticus.

"He's bleeding from his mouth," Hathaway said, as though the health of the cat was a more striking development than the skyscraper sized bear-robots.

Before he could elaborate on his concerns, a tree to their immediate left burst into flame. The scurrying pair of government workers, feline stowaway in tow, darted onto the bus. They found Jeff waiting near the door with an urgent look on his face. Shortly after that, Cahill and Strauss flew through up the steops, the very last of the on-site team to board.

"Get us out of here," Strauss told the driver, who didn't need to hear it twice. "This whole place is going to be firebombed in five minutes, tops."

The scene shrank behind them as the yowls of the bears grew in shrillness. However big they might be, from the retreating bus it seemed as though Deinonychus, in all his power, might now be getting the best of them.

In all the excitement, nobody noticed the small bundle Hathaway held in his lap.

Thirty-One

Deinonychus had been so close – he had almost been able to taste the flesh of his foolish Namer quarry. However blurry the young man might have looked, once the hate-fueled Deinonychus had locked onto his scent it became a simple enough matter to run him down. And right when the denouement was at hand, and victory was assured, it had happened. Those two monsters arrived and challenged Deinonychus's supremacy.

Despite being interrupted from taking his revenge, Deinonychus found he wasn't in the slightest bit offended. The two mammoth monstrosities that emerged defiantly from the burning wreckage of the 'B' laboratory seemed like splendid adversaries, and Deinonychus was able to pivot the focus of his rage on a dime. He almost gratefully wheeled around to face the two bear creatures. Here, at long last, were opponents worthy of his power.

They towered above him. Their heads, far above the trees, cleared even the top of the multi-story 'A' lab. The cat, in his gluttony and outrage, had grown to the size of an SUV, yet the behemoths he now faced held the size advantage to an obscene degree.

Deinonychus's confidence didn't flag for a second – because he knew that no living thing on the surface of the earth could harbor a rage that burnt brighter than the hatred flaming in his heart. Mental whiplashes of loathing and destruction shot out from him and twisted up the tree trunk legs of the bear-creatures. Their howling cries reverberated through the woods.

The bear on the left made a sound like a giant sneeze, and the odd box on her neck, sizzling with blue bolts, began to flash red. The creature twisted her body in a way that was painful to look at. She thrashed, her elephantine legs crashing down again and again like the mad kicks of a bucking bronco. Sprays of dirt and earth flew as her claws dug into the earth. A sizzling, crackling cacophony broke out as the box on her neck pulsed faster with crimson flashes.

The bear on the right didn't pause to look after its companion, but just kept rushing onwards. As the towering thing approached, Deinonychus's bitter heart brimmed with instinct for battle. He lashed out with more mental claw swipes, and as the beast reached him he sank his real claws – now swollen to the size of heavy police flashlights – through the fur of the multi-story creature and deeply into her leg flesh.

The towering monster gave a cry of alarm and pain. Trying to pry Deinonychus's jaws from her arm, she twisted her great neck and snapped her jaws at the cat. By the time the immense bear began to swing her paw – shaking it as though trying to shoo a fly – to rid himself of Deinonychus, the furious cat had already made its way to the bear's back, climbing up the back of his intended prey by digging in with his claws.

The other bear, her neck-box sparking and crackling, continued to moan in feral agony as she thrashed senselessly around the clearing. Deinonychus had damaged her cybernetic components so badly that the system malfunction was finishing what the cat had started. The fish-out-of-water flops of the bear nearly crushed Deinonychus, now clinging to the other's back. Deinonychus slashed at the thrashing bear's nearby face with his dagger claws.

Blood shot out from the gaping slash wounds, and flew at once against gravity and into Deinonychus's mouth. The cat's anticipation was palpable. Deinonychus expected the best possible nourishment yet for his dark power from that blood – it was the blood of a sinister hunter such as the world had never seen! What greeted his lips, however, was surprisingly thin, and held none of the life energy of the ravenous monster inside it.

Tasting the weak gruel that passed for the beast's blood was a bitter disappointment. Deinonychus had been counting on a meal greater than anything he had yet to taste from these two massive quarries. His rage – however deep – was not self-sustaining. He had required the life force of nearly every small animal in the woods for miles around to affect his escape from the ordinance device, and in his anger at the Namer who had kicked him, and his subsequent quest for revenge, he had expended almost all of what was left.

Deinonychus *needed* more energy, and in these two massive monsters, he had thought that he had found it.

Yet in terms of Deinonychus's psychic power, the energy he got from eating these monsters' living flesh was no stronger than the powers he got from munching a bowl of dusty kibble. Already, his otherworldly size began to dwindle. He couldn't sustain an attack against two creatures of this size for long, not without energy to fuel him. His rage had begun to boil off inside his heart, replaced by a new feeling: fear.

He might not be able to extract vital energy from these two beasts, but he *had* to kill them – or he would be done for. Deinonychus howled in rage as his newfound flesh steamed away in his exertion, but even with the major setback of finding that he couldn't count on any new energy from these monsters, he remained determined and confident. Even in the fog of his anger, he had enough predatory cunning to hatch a new plan.

He ceased racing along the back of the bear, and cried out to the other, injured monster. He dug his claws into his ride's hide and held on as it shook its great bulk like a wet dog in an effort to loose the cat. Deinonychus hissed as he struggled to keep his balance.

The other bear stopped galloping about in pain and turned on Deinonychus, sparks flying in ever greater bursts from the box attached to its neck. The look of anguish in its eyes was boundless – Deinonychus reasoned that it must be in great torment from whatever was happening to it. The raving thing roared at Deinonychus, and charged at him as he sat on his perch.

Deinonychus tensed his haunches, preparing himself to act with split-second timing, as the crazy-eyed monstrosity launched itself at him, incisors splayed open. With a mighty *swish* of his tail for balance, Deinonychus overleapt the charging thing's head and landed between its ears, just as the bear took a deep bite from its oversized compatriot – a bite meant for the cat.

The cat sent a whirlwind of burning energy out from inside himself, his unnaturally oversized body shrinking appreciably as the energy left him. But he had managed to flay great, spiraling welts of singed skin off both his opponents in the process. The claws of the bear Deinonychus had tricked flexed in her pain, raking even more skin off her double.

Deinonychus ran down the side of his new mount, dozens of pounds lighter than he had weighed when he ran up the other's leg. His body had contracted, and he now looked gaunt – in need of a meal. He could see that the two bears were thrashing in mutual confusion and pain for a moment, and so he dared to cast his mind about for some small sustenance.

A bird, perhaps. He found what he was looking for in the skies above – living energy. He thrust his mind deeper, probing for the essence he needed, when the truth of the matter struck him like a thrust fist. This was no *bird* flying through the air above.

It was a pair of Namers.

They were flying faster than any bird ever had. How could that be possible? Their speed was too great for Deinonychus's mind to maintain his lock on them, covering immense distances in a very short span of time. Their path, however, seemed clear enough to the cat. The pair of flying Namers headed straight for the glade at top speed.

Deinonychus felt a sudden twinge of fear. Whatever these soaring humans intended, it was nothing good – and it didn't bode well for the cat. He was every bit as afraid of the unnaturally flighted humans' potential power as the Namers had been at encountering mere cats that could affect the world with their minds alone.

Deinonychus was brought back to the present moment as gargantuan foot crashed down inches from his head. He hissed, sending a bolt flying up at the eyes of the approaching bear, and ran off to the edge of the forest. Behind him, a giant cloud of dust and sparks rose up, temporarily blinding and disorienting the bears. As he ran, Deinonychus's frame shrank, his remaining supernatural flesh steaming off his bones like smoke as it floated away to join the maelstrom of dust churning behind him.

By the time he reached the forest's edge, he could be certain he had managed to lose the bears. He had also receded back down to his normal size. The experience taught Deinonychus a valuable lesson – if he wanted to obtain and sustain such enormous levels of power, such intense expansions of his normal abilities, he would need a lot more than a swimming pool full of squirrels and blue jays.

He would need the power that slept in his brother's heart. He needed what was inside Leviticus. Once he had feasted on his brother's life and energy, he knew he would be able to take his enlarged, enraged, *true* form once and for all – to take it and *keep* it.

Deinonychus cast his mind out like a net. He felt the slight *ping* of his brother's enormous potential up ahead – growing fainter all the time. Evidently Leviticus was already escaping, putting distance between himself and his murderous brother with every second.

No matter. Deinonychus would be able to feel his brother at any remove, so great was Leviticus's power. Feeling for Leviticus's mind was like determining which direction the sun lay with one's eyes closed. Deinonychus took comfort in knowing that no matter how fast the grey runt ran, his brother could not escape him.

He heard a sound he did not recognize: the sound of helicopter rotors. The flying Namers were close. His head filled with clicks and pops, and he had a vague sense that if he did nothing to interfere with the work of these Namers, he wouldn't have to worry about being pursued by the bears. The Namers didn't like them any more than he did. The cat bolted through the woods, trying to put as much distance between himself and the laboratories as he could in what he instinctively felt were the final moments of consequence.

Seconds later, his instinctive suspicions were proven valid as a mushroom cloud of flame rose in the air behind him. The bears, he could feel, had been utterly obliterated. The Namers hung in the air over the now-destroyed facility, looking for any survivors in the outlying woodlands through some sort of far-seeing eye mechanism.

Now, thought the cat in his feline way, it was safe to kill them. A moment later, blood fell on the cat like rain, traveling through the air from afar like a flock of birds in flight, as the helicopter spun into the raging fires below. Two dusty, skeletal husks in flight suits, still strapped into their seats, were all that remained of the two people within as the copter's fuel tanks caught fire. The machine burst into a thousand tiny pieces of wreckage.

It was a small meal, but to the famished Deinonychus, it was a start.

Thirty-Two

The urgent excitement that helped to keep Hathaway's feline stowaway undetected when he boarded the bus began to fade as the evacuees bumped their way through the woods. As the general sense of fear waned, Hathaway's nervousness grew. Thanks to Deinonychus's attack, he hadn't had the opportunity he had expected to hide Leviticus in something better than his jacket. Hathaway felt the little guy squirm inside the bundle as he awoke.

Rick's eyes caught Ben's, and the look of disapproval – no, *disappointment* – on the younger man's face made Hathaway wince. Ben sighed, and his face softened.

"I understand *why* you did it. I just can't believe you actually did," he said quietly.

"Come on and *help* me, Ben!" Rick replied.

A bit too loudly, judging from the heads that turned to look. Lowering his voice, Hathaway continued.

"I mean, what do I do here?"

Ben shook his head with the air of a person being asked for advice on how to get out of a situation that they themselves would never willingly enter into. 'This is your mess: *you* clean it up,' his gesture seemed to say. Realizing how difficult he was being – to his boss, no less – Ben tried to take a more consoling approach.

"The best you can do is just lay low, get off the bus in the middle of the crowd, and hope that the little guy doesn't wake up and start meowing his ass off."

Hathaway nodded vigorously, taking hold of this idea like a drowning man grabbing a life raft. It was at that precise moment that Leviticus woke up and started wailing in the loud, plaintive tones of a hungry infant.

*   *   *

"Don't do *that!*" Hathaway pleaded.

When he got on the bus, he had realized that if his little bundle was discovered, it might have serious repercussions for his career. He hadn't considered, however, what would happen to Leviticus.

"I'm sorry, but – like you – I have my orders," the driver – a senior NUCPA military liaison named Sgt. Raul Alvarez – said, checking his gun's safety. "Some of us actually have to follow them."

Hathaway winced in shame, but his posture was still defiant and defensive. Alvarez continued.

"You know better than almost anybody how serious this all is. I can't *believe* that *you* broke Agency regulations… for a cat!"

The highly military-seeming driver was clearly not happy about being forced to shoot a small housecat in the head in the middle of the woods. Neither was Hathaway.

"But this one is just a normal cat! He doesn't deserve this!" Hathaway pleaded.

Ben, in the back of the bus, frowned. Seeing his boss like this made him feel sick inside. Ben had to admit – however grudgingly – that he felt bad for the cat. He didn't want to feel bad – he *wanted* to think that this was all Hathaway's fault. He wanted to truly believe that Hathaway should have just left the little guy passed out in his cage, and let him be put out of his misery in the firebombing.

Now, as the small grey creature in Hathaway's arms reached up to put a paw on his boss's nose while Hathaway tearfully pled with the merciless driver, Ben wasn't sure what he felt. He inwardly cursed his boss for putting him in a position to feel what he was feeling.

This whole thing was a mess.

"I'm sorry. I can't risk our lives like this and defy orders – not after this has become such a major national security breech."

Alvarez put a reassuring hand on Rick's shoulder, a strangely frightening gesture considering the automatic pistol in his other hand.

"Look, I think this whole thing is crazy, too."

Hathaway's expression changed, seeming to pass on to the final stage of grief: acceptance. His gleaming eyes blinked, he sniffed a little, but was nodding.

"I was a damn fool, thinking I should save this little guy. It's just, he's just such a *little* guy." He shook his head, standing up straighter. "Here you go."

He handed Leviticus, who was still stretching his front paws towards Hathaway's face, to the driver.

"Just do it where I can't see it."

"Of course, Rick."

The driver folded his free arm around the cat and made his way out the door.

Hathaway shook his head as he worked his way past the mix of reproachful and sympathetic gazes to his spot at the back of the bus. Plopping his weight in the seat next to Ben, he sighed mournfully.

"Damn fool. I've been a sentimental old idiot."

Ben put his hand on his boss's shoulder.

"Don't beat yourself up. You were just doing what you thought was right."

Hathaway looked at him, starting to nod. The loud report of a gunshot echoed through the woods. Hathaway's lip quivered as he momentarily fought his tears, then he buried his head in his hands and began to cry.

*   *   *

Sgt. Alvarez had, in his long career, been forced to shoot countless ordinary targets, and several unusual ones. Nothing in his prior experience, however, had prepared him for this act – throwing a juvenile housecat onto the forest floor, and firing a bullet directly into his skull. It was the most cold-blooded thing he had ever had ever been forced to do, and as much as he could, on some level, understand Hathaway's motivation in trying to smuggle the cat out, Sgt. Alvarez deeply resented being put in this position.

The cat squirmed against his body, and Alvarez found himself in the unpleasant position of trying to soothe the thing, to calm it down to the point where it would hold still long enough for him to kill it. The disappointment Alvarez felt in himself was literally making him feel sick to his stomach. He coughed, suppressing the surge of bile that rocketed up his esophagus. He turned his head to look back as he walked, and saw the bus only faintly through the obscuring trees.

Not much farther to go now.

The grey cat in his arms meowed again, its voice high and plaintive. Alvarez looked down at it, an act he had been attempting to avoid. The golden tag dangling from its collar gleamed brightly in the sun. 'Leviticus,' read the tag. Alvarez looked away from the expressive green eyes staring into his own.

"Come on, cat," he said, like a frightened kid whistling in the dark to divert his fear. "You couldn't possibly understand."

In response, the small grey thing, evidently called 'Leviticus,' meowed again. Alvarez tried to change the subject.

"So, with a name like 'Leviticus,' you must be a pious kitty?"

He instantly regretted referring to the thing as a 'kitty.' It made what he had to do seem all the more like what it really was.

"Alright, enough of this crap."

He set the cat down on the ground. Alvarez had hoped it would start running immediately, giving him the urgency and cause to reflexively shoot it. Instead, the cat just stared up at him with baleful eyes.

"Oh, jeez."

Alvarez lifted the gun's muzzle and aimed at the kitty – *no,* the cat. Not even that. He aimed at the target. He *couldn't* bring himself to shoot it if he thought of it as a 'kitty.' He had to let it just be a target.

Images flooded into his mind out of nowhere, images he didn't understand. He stood there for a moment, shocked by the vividness of the vaporous scenes taking shape inside his mind. He worried that it might be the onset of a stroke or a seizure or something.

At first, none of what he 'saw' was coherent, but as the images grew brighter and more vivid, they took on lucidity. Bars against the sky, treetops waving in the breeze. Concrete floors. Alvarez shook his head and blinked his eyes, and still saw a hodgepodge of images swirling kaleidoscopically before his eyes, with that small grey cat in the center of them, the only constant.

The cat!

Could it be that Hathaway's little stowaway – supposedly one of the 'duds' that had no especial power – was doing this to him? That Hathaway had been wrong about the creature's supposed lack of abilities? As Alvarez thought these things, the forest resolved once more around him, resuming normality. He looked over his shoulder, and could just make out a few sparkles of sunlight on the metal of the bus through the trees. Everything was as it should be.

"Not letting *that* happen again, you creepy bastard."

Alvarez squeezed the trigger, his guilt largely assuaged after the bizarre supernatural episode the cat had visited on him. Satisfied that he had killed the cat with his expert shot, he quickly turned on his heels and left the carnage behind him, returning to the bus.

The small, grey body of Leviticus lay split open and motionless on the ground, his skull cloven in two by the bull's-eye shot to the head.

THIRTY-THREE

The cat, moving cautiously, made his way through the woods. His prey still seemed unaware of his presence, and he wanted to keep it that way. The compact creature he pursued was happily drinking water from a clear, trickling stream. The red-furred thing's impossibly fluffy tail darted around in the air like a moving exclamation point, reflecting the simple happiness of its owner.

The cat felt sorry for his intended meal. He wasn't the sort to toy with his food, and he didn't relish the idea of taking another life without purpose, as did so many other cats. The reason for this was quite simple – he identified too much with the prey. Their thoughts were all too vivid in his mind as he went in for the kill: their sudden fear, the rush of adrenaline, the terrifying last moment when all hope was abandoned. It was too much – it took all the instinctual joy out of the act of feeding.

The cat had been quite content with the dry, crunchy food given to him back at the laboratory facilities. While perhaps not the juiciest of imaginable foodstuffs, it had nevertheless sustained him and assuaged his hunger without any of the guilt or horrendous imagery that accompanied his more *au naturel* repasts. And it didn't taste nearly as bad as his demented brother seemed to think it did.

Leviticus coiled his haunches beneath him, preparing to pounce on the squirrel.

He refused, rather proudly, to use his mental talents to render the act of hunting any easier than it would have been for an ordinary cat. He considered that cheating. His high-minded chivalrousness had seen him going hungry more than a few nights.

Now that the squirrel was within his grasp, Leviticus just wanted to get things over with quickly. He had more reason to hurry than just guilt and revulsion at the 'overheard' sensations that accompanied each act of murder. His terrible brother was only a day or two behind him at most. It was of his brother Deinonychus, the only other surviving littermate, that Leviticus thought as he sprang through the air.

Somehow, imagining that it was his brother's shrill thoughts of alarm, terror, and pain filling his mind instead of this guiltless squirrel made the act of twisting its neck and swiftly ending its life slightly more bearable.

*   *   *

What had happened days before, when he was last with the Namers and they had escaped the lab together, still confused Leviticus. He awoke inside a strange type of long, metal animal. The creature seemed to gallop at an incredible pace without lifting its feet.

Leviticus found himself wrapped in rags that smelled awfully of Namer sweat. There were at least thirty Namers in the long, thin beast along with him – including two that he recognized from back at the lab. The larger of these two held him through the jacket. The other was the younger one, the one who took those strange orange pills.

Leviticus couldn't understand why the Namers seemed so much less nervous than he imagined they should be. They were all trapped in the stomach of a great, whale-like beast that was sprinting through the trees with unbelievable speed. A loud, deep rumble suffused the interior of the creature – assuredly from the beast's breathing and heartbeat. The sound terrified the small, frightened cat, reinforcing the tremendous size of the animal that had somehow consumed him, along with all these Namers, while had had been asleep.

As the cat shrugged off the remnants of unconsciousness, he considered his options for survival. As of right now – though he had apparently been eaten by this huge creature – he was whole, intact, and not yet bathed in the digestive juices and enzymes of the massive beast. If he played his cards right – by, say, causing the creature to vomit him up – he had a chance to survive.

He had to try *something*. He couldn't understand how the Namers could just sit there, so accepting of their fate that they weren't even struggling.

Leviticus didn't stop to consider that he could feel no real mind from the bus. Even if he had noticed this fact, it might not have meant anything to him. After all, there was only the most rudimentary flicker of a mind in those bear-things, and they had been dangerous enough. For Leviticus – awakening to an unknown world of strange smells and horrible, metallic monsters – the time for reason had passed.

It was time for action.

The only action he could take, at first anyway, was to get free from the bundle of rags he had been ensconced in. Yet that act, which he had assumed would be so simple, proved more difficult than he imagined. As soon as he began to writhe and wriggle, the arms of the Namer holding him wrapped tighter around him, holding him in place. Couldn't the man holding him see the danger they were all in? They were all lucky the giant Auto-Beast hadn't already digested them, or cut them to the death with its fangs when it had swallowed them.

Unwilling to sit there and wait for death, as all these Namers seemed content to do, Leviticus began to cry out. That's when his circumstances changed, and when they did, they changed very rapidly.

*   *   *

Seconds after Leviticus started meowing at the top of his feline lungs, the rumblings of the giant creature ceased. With a final growl, the beast silenced itself. The sudden stillness of the air felt oppressive, like a wet, heavy blanket. The bundle enwrapping him started to shift and heave.

A Namer whom Leviticus did not recognize was attempting to wrest the bundle away from the man holding him: the nice man who seemed to like Leviticus more than the other Namers did. The two were having some kind of argument which Leviticus couldn't quite understand, as it involved neither claws nor hissing. The cat still had no difficulty recognizing it for a fight – he had never heard Namers use voices like that in ordinary speech.

The tone of the man holding him went from angry to pleading, his register climbing several steps as he begged the second man for something. Or to *not* do something – it was all very unclear in Leviticus's mind. The cat wished they would stop their petty arguing and set to work at getting out of this giant Auto-Beast. They really ought to be working together, at least while they had a common enemy. The pleading, however, continued, and Leviticus felt himself wrested away from the grip of the familiar, friendly Namer.

This other one held him more tightly, with a vehemence that surprised the cat. Layers of wrappings were peeled back, and, now exposed, the cat blinked in the harshly bright light assaulting his eyes. Once his eyes had adjusted, and he could finally see again, he noted that the Namer holding him was sighing as he carried the cat up to the front of the bus. Leviticus's heart beat faster.

This man was going to help him escape!

Leviticus meowed with glee. The man touched something on the inside of the vast, worm-like creature's face and the entire side of the creature's head peeled back. Leviticus marveled at a creature that kept its mouth on the side of its head.

Gratitude surged through his heart and mind. He and the others would escape the mighty predator after all. Soon he was free.

As the man who carried him off the bus walked past the head of the creature, Leviticus looked deeply into the long thing's great, silvery eyes. It seemed to be asleep. The cat shuddered – he wouldn't want to see those eyes when the thing was awake.

The man took a dozen or so steps into the forest before Leviticus became aware that none of the other Namers were following. Why didn't they run away, too? The thing's head was still split open, the fissure clearly wide enough to escape through. Yet all of the others just sat – some staring out windows as he was carried away, others talking to each other.

No sense of desperation. No instinct to escape. None of it made any sense.

It was then – as his sense of immediate threat dissipated and he cast his mind out to the Namer to try to understand what was going on – that he first became aware that the Namer holding him had no intention whatsoever of 'saving' Leviticus.

No, the Namer holding him was convinced, for reasons the cat didn't understand, that Leviticus was grave danger to them all. The man walked like a man carrying a venomous snake – worried that, at any moment and without provocation, Leviticus would strike. The cat couldn't comprehend this fear, but now he worried he finally grasped what was happening.

It all began to click into place. Now that the fear of being eaten alive had left him, he realized that *none* of the people on the bus were afraid of the thing, despite being clustered inside it. The animal must not have eaten them, after all – the Namers just had some curious symbiotic relationship with the much larger, long, alien-seeming monster with two silvery, blank eyes.

What they *were* worried about, he felt, was *him*. Was he dangerous? Was he going to do something to hurt the Namer that was carrying him? And some were worried about… worried about… It was hard to read.

'Would he suffer?' Suffer? Leviticus didn't understand, not at first. He looked into the mind of the man who had held him in his coat, and saw the vivid image of himself *exploding*, his head vaporizing into a mist of blood and grey fur that flew in all directions. What awful idea was *this*?

He looked into the mind of the man holding him now, and saw something similar. The conflict inside this Namer was terrible. The man was filled with resolve, regret, despair, terror. A mix of negative emotions and fear that stung the cat to try to contemplate.

It would be impossible for Leviticus to pick through those emotions and make sense of their combination. He felt helpless, in the arms of a monster. His brother's territorial need for dominance and lust for prey, Leviticus could understand. Perhaps it was not comforting, but it was natural.

This Namer, on the other hand, was a fireball of unnatural 'obligations' and 'duties' and 'principles.' The man who now held him scared Leviticus more than any animal could have – because the cat could see that this man was such a bundle of contradictions that he would do something he hated, that he thought was wrong, thinking it was somehow 'good' – and though he would hate himself for doing it, he would also feel proud for 'getting a hard job done,' and expect praise from his peers for his selflessness in performing an odious and repugnant deed.

This constellation of opposing feelings was an abomination to the feline's instinct-based sensibilities, more monstrous by far than a hungry carnivore who merely refused to starve.

Leviticus fought against the fear rising inside him, and tried to think of a plan. Fear was the last burst of futility felt by someone meant for a meal. Shrewd, bold moves calculated with innate instinct and executed with finely sharpened claws were what turned bad situations into opportunities.

The man set him down on the forested earth and took a few steps back. Leviticus looked around, rapidly developing a sense of his surroundings. He made a mental snapshot of the glade before fixing his large green eyes on the man, who looked more miserable than ever. Leviticus knew he had to do this quickly, but he was so frightened that the act of focusing his mind took every ounce of effort and skill he could muster. Images started forming before his eyes. That was all well and good, but Leviticus needed the Namer to see them, not him.

The gun came up, and the cat instinctively recognized it as the intended instrument of his destruction. Fighting the urge to flee – an option which would surely fail – he tried to clear his mind, to concentrate on the goal at hand. At last, as the barrel swung in line with the cat's head, Leviticus felt something give in the man's mind. That first hard push had been made. The cat could sense the shifting images taking shape in front of the man's eyes, wafting around the his consciousness like billows of smoke.

The Namer blinked in confusion. Leviticus, given an opportunity to hope, dared for the first time to think his plan might work. Passing his hands before his face, as if to clear his field of vision, the Namer pivoted to the side, aiming the gun down at a point on the forest floor at nearly a right angle to Leviticus's true location.

It was time. If Leviticus waited around to see what happened, he might not be able to sustain the illusion. He already felt too weak to run, so he settled for slowly slinking through the pine needles, away from the man and away from the bus.

Away from everything he had ever known, which wasn't saying much.

He jumped, startled, when the shot went off behind him, his sensitive feline ears burning with the loud report of the pistol. Leviticus, releasing the psychic hold from Sgt. Alvarez's mind, had no doubt that the thing that made that sound would have been his end. In the distance, he heard the Auto-Beast roar back to life and pull away. He was now, for the first time in his short life, utterly alone.

Thirty-Four

For the first few days Deinonychus fended for himself in the forest, he believed the only reason for speed was the head start Leviticus had on him. Even if the larger cat traveled at maximum speed, his younger brother, thanks to his stint on the bus, was already days away. The going was easy enough – he found plenty to eat, though he instinctively restrained himself from becoming a gluttonous fireball of destruction. Why he did so, he couldn't exactly say – until the fourth day of his journey.

His instinctive restraint when it came to 'charging' his mental energies proved to be well-founded. Though the cat didn't understand exactly what happened, NUCPA realized that their firebombing technique might have failed to eliminate all the subjects. The helicopter crash was sort of a hint.

Though far from definitive proof that one of the subjects was alive, that accident had nevertheless precipitated a full-scale search of the surrounding area. Every available team was on the job. On the fourth day, the search finally caught up with Deinonychus.

*   *   *

The sound of copter rotors was the first sign of human activity the cat had encountered since the fateful last day at the lab, and his ears perked up when he heard it. It was night time, the moon high overhead, and the cat had wandered through the tangle of trees with wide, seeing eyes. His nocturnal vision might have been the best natural sight in the woods that night, but now that the Namers were sending in their toys, natural was no longer the only game in town.

High above, the high-pitched sound of rotors drifted down to him, reminding him of the massive flying thing he had felled back at the lab. Deinonychus cast his mind up, surprised to find no Namers up there this time. The sound grew louder as the rotors approached, and still the could feel no biological intelligence behind the noise.

Cautious for the first time he could remember, the cat shrank behind a rock and watched as a peculiar thing descended from the tree tops. To Deinonychus, it looked like some kind of dangerous insect – eight dangling legs, and eight whirling rotors up top. It made an insectile hum and lowered itself to the ground. It was an alien sound. A sound that, when taken with its arachnid appearance, made Deinonychus instantly distrustful of the thing.

The cat had no way of knowing, but the device was an octocopter, a modern type of reconnaissance device. It had been equipped with infrared-and-heat-sensing-cameras, hyper-sensitive microphone arrays, and more. This particular model had eight rotors – hence the term 'octo-copter' – and was the size of a small dog.

Smaller versions, the more common 'quad-copters' –each little more than the size of a rat – were also on his trail. The batteries of these smaller models were prohibitively short-lived, and the purpose of this larger unit was to get a rough estimate of where the quarry was, before the NUCPA team sent a ground transport to disperse a cloud of the smaller versions from close at hand. The octo-copter, then, was just an outlier of a more complex system that would be dispatched when the government finally got a positive *ping* from the 'bloodhound unit.' These copters were an example of one of the many things researched and created at NUCPA decades before being 'invented' in university campuses and revealed to the world years later as a private creation, like so many of their discoveries.

*   *   *

Deinonychus only knew that the whirring, humming, spider-like monstrosity that descended from the sky to hover above him in the glade instinctively revolted him. He saw plainly enough that his hiding spot behind the rock wasn't protecting him from being the sight of the buzzing creature: the whirring thing hovered a moment, then slid through the air towards him like a hummingbird. Though it *wasn't* a hummingbird – there would be no meal here – Deinonychus swat at it as though it were.

Several rotors and two cameras snapped off the spindly looking thing in a burst of blue bolts and yellow sparks with his first mental swipe. Deinonychus didn't know whether to be amused or alarmed. The cat hadn't counted on the strange thing being so easy to break, and certainly hadn't expected the small electrical explosion.

This was kind of fun.

Deinonychus watched with some interest as the small servomechanisms powering the positionable cameras swiveled madly in their sockets for a brief time before slowing and eventually stopping. He trotted up to the fallen thing and swatted playfully at it a few times. His third paw-swat set one of the onboard cameras waggling in one last burst of electrical output, causing the cat to jump backwards with surprise.

Deinonychus had no doubt that the Namers had sent this – the same crafty humans who had sent the fire-dropping sky bird after him only to fail spectacularly had resorted to attempting to track him down using this humming, buzzing little creature. The bug-like fellow did manage to find him, but it had cost the thing its life.

Deinonychus pondered – if the Namers could be in league with a thing like this, they had the power to do almost anything. Deinonychus could take no chances – there was every possibility that this bug-thing had managed to transmit some kind of message to others. The longer the cat stayed in the neighborhood, the more danger he was in.

He knew now what he had to do. His plan became clear. First, Deinonychus would get ahold of his talented but pacifistic little brother and steal his energy. *Then*, and only then, would he start trying to take on the world of man.

*   *   *

"Was that him?" Jeff asked, scarcely able to believe that they had picked up Deinonychus's trail after so many days, still less using a device as ridiculous-looking as the octo-copter.

"Nope," replied Pettinger, staring at the screen in near-disbelief. "It's a cat in the middle of a National Forest that looks just like him who can destroy equipment with his mind."

"Har, har."

Jeff sulked for a moment, but the luck of their find and the urgency of their next steps quickly overtook his bruised ego.

"So is the Horde close enough to deploy?"

Pettinger shook her head.

"Getting there, though," she said. "It'll be in his area within an hour or two. Then we're in business."

'The Horde' was their term for what the equipment specialists kept trying, unsuccessfully, to get the NUCPA 'A' facility science team to refer to as 'The Flock' – a semi-autonomous group of the smaller quad-copters that travelled in tandem with a tank-like base, where they could return to charge. Nayeli got the creeps from the system – when a cloud of those quad-copters were in the air, they reminded her of a cave full of electronic bats. The idea was to reduce the negative impact from the limited battery life of the quad-copters by getting a general lock on the target with the larger, more rugged octo-copter, and then sending in the Horde, complete with its un-manned base-unit (which resembled a large truck on all-terrain treads) and letting the little buggers loose.

The sheer number of quad-copters that made up the Horde – or 'Flock,' depending on which department of NUCPA you worked in – were supposed to make it impossible to escape them once they had locked onto you. Avoiding the locked-on Horde, either through subterfuge or sheer luck with drained batteries, was theoretically impossible. Nayeli wasn't sure that she liked the idea that this mission – perhaps one of the most important in NUCPA history – was the first field test of this technology.

She shook her head and sighed. It seemed tragic that NUCPA's most important task to date would be this mission: stopping the fallout from their own botched experiment.

"Let's just hope those little hummingbirds are up to the task," she said.

Dr. Ron Elliot, the person who had designed the Flock system, tisked disapprovingly at the science teams lack of faith.

"You'll see. What happened with the octo-copter was just a fluke."

"*Fluke?*" said Pettinger incredulously. "I think you'll find that, as far as that cat is concerned, destruction is no fluke."

Elliot waved his hands.

"You misunderstand me. In many ways, what happened to the octo-copter was exactly the type of thing that has kept this technology from being useful the field. It was expected." He rubbed his palms together, like a greedy child about to dip into his Halloween spoils. "What makes the *Flock* so much better is that, through sheer number, through sheer *perseverance*, we can overcome all those traditional obstacles. Believe me, if this Dino Mucus or whatever his name is can destroy the whole *Flock*, he must be the worst thing to ever happen to the world."

Jeff bit his lip and, using every ounce of energy he could muster, managed to stop himself from muttering: 'That's what we're trying to *say*.'

*   *   *

Hours later, the moon long since sunk behind the trees, Deinonychus had left the metal skeleton of the odd bug-thing in the dust, far behind. As he walked on, about a mile east of the road to avoid any undesired chance encounters with rolling humans, a vivid mental image came to the cat.

A vision of him drinking water from a stream while countless tiny gnats buzzed around his head. Vexing him. Taking the pleasure out of the simple act of drinking. He hissed at this thought and the feelings it conjured. Why should he have such a vision now?

He drank his fill of water not long before, and was nowhere near a stream. He couldn't understand it. The next second, he heard the buzzing sound faintly filling the night air around him, growing louder each second. The bugs were coming.

He strained his eyes against the darkness, unable to make anything out. The sound was real, though. This was no mental mirage; the cat was sure of it. There was something else, too. A tone hidden within that high-pitched buzzing. A sound of such high-pitch that human ears couldn't have made it out.

The squeal reminded Deinonychus of a group of peculiar flying creatures he encountered a few nights before –strange flapping things with the ability to send out high-pitched clicks, and then hear the echo in the form of a picture. Deinonychus marveled at the way they painted mental pictures of the space in which they flew with sound, along with the things in it. It was not, Deinonychus thought to himself while munching on the head of a bat he managed to snag, all that different from what he did with his mind. Deinonychus used mental clicks instead of sonic ones, but the principle was basically the same.

Having thusly encountered natural sonar, Deinonychus did have a rudimentary sense of what it was he was hearing when the sonic grid laid down by the Flock's sensing apparatus – however faintly – reached his feline ears across the intervening distance. He instantly grasped the implications, and it put him on his guard. What were these things making this buzzing, clicking racket? They weren't bats. That was immediately obvious.

The cat felt sure the sound came from many small things rather than from a single source. Yet, Deinonychus felt no mind behind them. The sensation of finding living things with no mind inside them was becoming more and more common for him lately.

Then he saw the first of the tiny, buzzing devices emerge through the trees. It looked like a smaller version of the octocopter he had killed earlier. Then he saw the next, and the another, and then another. Deinonychus mewled in alarm as a veritable *swarm* of the things crowded around him, hovering up and down like angry wasps.

He struck out at them, sending energy out from within himself to batter the closest of the bug-like nuisances, but even as they fell to the ground, twitching and useless, three more came to take their place. Deinonychus meowed, annoyed, as the cloud of gnat-like drones thickened, doubling in number, then tripling.

The cat, working himself into a panicked frenzy, slashed with his claws *and* his mind now. He knocked more and more of the humming oddities to the ground, but became tired and winded in the process. Expending so much mental energy in destroying lifeless things that couldn't replenish his reserves taxed him, and he began to realize the very real danger he was in. He didn't want to think what these creatures would do to him if they managed to knock him into unconsciousness. The mental image of the things swarming all over his prone and lifeless body goaded him into further action.

Mere brute force, he realized, would never work against these things. There were too many of them. Deinonychus needed a more subtle plan than '*kill!*' Biting back the instinctive rage that threatened to overtake his reasoning faculties, he strove to notice some detail or nuance about the swarming vermin he had as yet overlooked. Hissing fitfully, he despaired of seeing something that he could use to his advantage amidst so many identical, whirring drones.

One flew close to his ear and sliced a notch in its pointed tip with its rotors, and he flung a blue bolt of electricity at it. The thing fell in a spiral dive, satisfying but exhausting to destroy. Deinonychus needed to escape these things soon, or his uncontrollable rage would overtake his fatigue, and he would be done for.

That's when he noticed a peculiar sight: two steady streams of the drones, flying in single file. One line of humming things joining the group, the other leaving it. Both lines led the same direction. Deinonychus had a flash of insight, and, seizing onto this idea, ignored all else to follow that trail.

The buffeting, baffling cloud of insectoid quad-copters did its best to vex the cat, but now that he had an inkling of a plan, he wouldn't allow himself to be lured into anger. He couldn't afford to let their insistent buzzing distract him. As the cat built up speed, the cloud of drones attempted to enclose him like a net composed of a thousand flying bugs working in unison.

The cat, sensing his impending triumph, would have none of it. Deinonychus's feet flashed as he galloped his way to the strange source – to the place from which the drones came and to which they went. He had the sense that, once he got there, he could find a way to paint the forest with the insects' regret and splash whatever passed for their vital fluids onto the earth.

Thirty-Five

The mobile base unit that powered 'the Flock' was fully automated, but as this mission was a matter of vital importance to national security – in addition to being the first real field test for the technology – Sgt. Alvarez and Dr. Elliot had trailed the device in a two-seat All-Terrain Vehicle. Alvarez was filled with mixed emotions – he felt, to his surprise, an almost childlike excitement about seeing the quad-copter swarm in use for the first time, tempered by an uneasy sense of foreboding at the prospect of going back into the woods to face another one of those peculiar cats.

Alvarez still felt 'off' after the peculiar way everything had shifted and changed when he terminated that contraband cat, and he the coats on this project had given him to understand that the cat they were tracking down now was much more formidable. Alvarez didn't like this creepy shit. Yet, upon seeing the actual functioning of the automated drone mini-copters, much of that uneasiness dissipated.

"It's like being at Kitty Hawk, in a way," he marveled appreciatively to Elliot, who visibly swelled with pride at the compliment.

"Well, we weren't the first to invent multi-rotor micro-copters, but our team was the first to create this self-sustaining system."

Elliot pointed at the skyline, at the stream of quad-copters beginning to return from the target's location.

"There's the first round of returners. Coming back for a re-charge."

Alvarez watched in wonder as the conga line of copters alighted on the charging deck of the base unit – which looked like the deck of a miniaturized aircraft carrier. Dozens of tiny circles covered it. These, Elliot explained, were the induction charging pads. They worked in much the same way as the most cutting-edge cell phone charging mats. The quad-copters would land on a circle and instantly start charging, without the need for plugs or connections. This inductive charging technology was practically a requirement for the self-sustaining system.

Even as a stream of copters returned with their batteries nearly depleted, a second stream of the tiny drones rose from the interior of the base and flew on a parallel course back to the site of the target. An endless, automated loop. The sight was impressive, and more than a little eerie, Alvarez had to admit to himself.

"You know," Elliot said, "I was head of the team that designed this system, but it still sends shivers down my spine to see it working. There's something sort of…"

"Alien?" Alvarez offered.

"Yes," Elliot agreed emphatically. "That's the word. Something *alien* about all this."

Alvarez quickly changed the subject.

"So how many of these things are there in the base unit?"

"Two-hundred and eighty-eight. Two gross." Seeing the look of astonishment on the other's face, he quickly explained. "Of course, most of those will likely never get used. They are backup, part of the full autonomy of the system. The Flock is designed for worst-case scenarios."

"Christ! How do you make so many of those things? They're so intricate."

"The latest three-dimensional printing technology," Elliot said. "It's getting pretty damn advanced. I try to keep up on all the latest developments in that arena, and I'm *still* surprised at the stuff they can do these days."

An insistent beeping sound demanded the attention of the two men.

"Damn," Alvarez said. "I had managed to forget that this isn't *just* a science experiment. They quads have locked onto the bugger. Now we have to get him."

The proximity detector reported back that the Flock had indeed found the small, domestic creature who supposedly represented one of the greatest threats to the security of the homeland the American government had ever faced.

Elliot whistled in disbelief as the photo – a composite image compiled from the infrared cameras of the many circulating drones – resolved on his monitor.

"Umm," he began. "I'm just a lowly nanotechnology engineer, but that looks exactly like a housecat to me."

"Trust me," Alvarez said, "I know how you feel, but I ran into one of these things – one that supposedly couldn't even do anything, and it started playing tricks with my mind. It just looked at me, and everything went wobbly. I felt a lot less guilty about shooting it once it started pulling that shit." Alvarez whistled through his teeth. "And from what they tell me, this cat here is responsible for destroying the entire Colburn Agency facilities. All *three* buildings."

Elliot couldn't believe that. To his mind, it was far more likely that somebody had made a mistake and simply found a way to blame it on an external factor. *System Offloaded User Error* was his team's terminology for such mistakes.

Still, it was his job to act as though he believed the official line – that a *cat* had somehow destroyed an entire government facility. He was happy to play along if it meant he could kick start the field testing of his pet project. This mission had bumped up the Flock's first deployment by several months.

Elliot couldn't understand, now that he was looking at the supposed 'threat' on his monitor, what the big deal was. He certainly didn't get how Alvarez, the military liaison, felt even the slightest bit worried. Elliot supposed that Alvarez – coming from a military background – had been trained to go along with what he had been told better than Elliot had. But all this talk of a cat 'playing tricks with his mind' rankled Elliot's sense of logic. That was clearly just a placebo effect from all the loose talk of 'dangerous cats.'

Elliot could believe in all manner of scientific advances, and he knew that some of the things being studied at the NUCPA labs were very 'out-there.' But those had all involved *real* science – interfacing with the nervous systems of living things, creating forms of electromagnetic radiation that had effects on the atomic states of matter to allow the mass of objects to be expanded or contracted, and things of that nature. What Pettinger's team was claiming was pure bunkum: that they somehow discovered a *gene* for psychic energy.

That claim was preposterous. End of discussion, as far as Elliot was concerned. And while they may have duped the suggestible Alvarez – not to mention NUCPA's funds appropriation board – with their tall-talk, all Elliot saw outlined in vibrant colors on his thermal camera monitor was a housecat slinking through the woods.

A housecat that was clearly afraid of the thick cloud of quad-copters surrounding him, no less. Elliot suppressed a laugh at the sight of the cowering cat shrinking against the ground as one of the copters swung by his head.

"Some monster," he remarked to himself.

The image juddered roughly, showing tumbling images of treetops. The frames tore at random, as though copter after copter had been knocked asunder, out of the appointed pattern. The composite image no longer cohered. Every inch of the monitor showed a different sight, from a different viewpoint, and all of them were spinning end over end. Elliot flinched, but held his breath as the integrated output of a large percent of the passing drones resolved once more. Large chunks of the screen had returned to normality.

"What the hell was that?" Elliot cried.

The cat hadn't done anything to any of the copters, hadn't touched a thing. The cat had just kept slinking forward, making its way through the cloud of autonomous copters. Yet at least ten of the small, mechanical things had plummeted from the sky. Elliot could see them in the video feed, lying on the ground useless, receding into the background as the cat slunk onwards.

"I *told* you," Alvarez began, but then the monitor buzzed with light as what looked like blue lightning bolts fizzled and flickered over the image.

Elliot gasped in astonishment.

"What's happening? Some kind of interference?"

Alvarez shook his head.

"You *really* didn't think this was going to be a big deal," he said in amazement. He laughed. "Well, time to learn the hard way. We have to go get that critter. Now, before he does any more damage."

But Alvarez was wrong. They didn't have to go anywhere. At that moment, both scientist and military man flinched as they heard a familiar sound. A sound that had never seemed so frightening to them before: the loud 'meow' of an angry cat, coming from just over the hill.

*   *   *

Striving against the onrushing clot of cloying quadcopters was one of the most irritating ordeals of Deinonychus's short life. He was a cat accustomed to having his way, to being in charge, and during this effortful journey he had been forced to live as others do – bombarded by annoyance that at times bordered on danger, and filled with a sense of impotent worthlessness in the face of an expansive, mysterious world. These bug-like aggravations were the last straw. As he crested the hill and laid his eyes on the strange hive of these gnat-like creatures, he felt his spirits perk up, along with his tail.

Not only had he found the nest of the annoying bugs, but there were two Namers here – at last, food for his powers. Deinonychus would need all of the energy he could get to dispatch the infernal cloud of lifeless drones buzzing around his head. One of the Namers pointed in his direction: they had already spotted him. The cat wondered if perhaps they were in league with the insects. Deinonychus quickly cleared his head of such thoughts as he realized that the Namer wasn't just pointing at him, the man was pointing *something* at him.

Deinonychus didn't waste time wondering what it could be, and sent the last of his energy flying towards the unsuspecting man, who instantly doubled over in pain. There was a loud, thunderous *crack*, and the other Namer hopped and squealed in agony. Deinonychus didn't understand what had happened, but the feelings of misery flowing out from the mind and body of this second Namer – whom he had not touched – were unmistakable. The second man's injuries put him in an even better mood.

Deinonychus was as yet too weak to draw their blood and energy towards him. He would need to take the first few bites in person, as it were. Still wary, but with ever-growing confidence, the cat trotted forward, increasingly self-assured in ignoring the pestering menace flitting around him and able to focus, for now, solely on the flesh he soon would taste. Another drone whizzed past his hurt ear, nearly clipping it again, and he snarled in anger and increased his speed.

The keeled-over human seemed to have recovered, and was fumbling for the gun he had dropped. The other, still screaming and howling, had inadvertently kicked it away with the foot that had *not* been blasted apart by the unintended rifle shot. Elliot cursed and swore at Alvarez for shooting him, but did nothing to help. He was in too much pain.

Elliot's injured foot looked like a rack of spare ribs after a stint in a blender, like a bag full of pulled pork that had somehow come to life and was now trying to escape the man's shoe through a massive blasted out hole. The smell of hot blood wafted to Deinonychus over the shortening distance, quickening his instincts and exciting his hunger. Still, he had to be wary about these two Namers – at least at first, until he had his fill and got his mental claws back.

* * *

"Dammit all, Elliot!" Alvarez cried, crawling towards the gun like a crab.

That cat was almost on them. The gun seemed to have, after Elliot's involuntary thrashing, skittered an impossibly long distance away.

"Damn *you*, you bastard! You shot me! You shot *me*!"

Elliot was fuming and whining, and seemed to have forgotten completely about the danger posed by the approaching cat. This rational, understandable, and severe physical injury distracted him from dealing with the unwanted reality of a psychic cat at a very opportune moment, as far as his shattering worldview was concerned.

"Didn't the military train you not to shoot people in the goddamn foot?"

The buzzing of the drone copters grew louder, and Alvarez looked up with dismay to see the cat only yards from the gun. His stomach still agonized him – what had that damned cat *done* to him? In his state, he seriously doubted his ability to get to the weapon before the animal intercepted him.

Alvarez felt a surge of relief, therefore, to see Deinonychus bolt right past him and towards Elliot. As he made the last few feet and picked the weapon up, Alvarez realized what a fool he had been for worrying – psycho-terror kitty or no, the furry beast didn't know what a gun was. Why would he?

A second later, as he was wheeling around to blast the four-legged freak, he heard a loud wailing.

"Get off me!" a revolted Elliot cried as the cat slurped at his decimated foot.

Elliot gave a small, bunting kick with his intact foot. The cat retreated a few steps, more cautious than injured.

"Now I've got you, you little bugger," Alvarez said, taking aim at the small animal.

The cat hissed, and Alvarez's wrist drooped as the metal of the gun handle seared into his flesh. Instinctively, he tried to drop the gun to end the pain, but it was as though his hand was glued to the pistol grip. He screeched in terror, his throat filling with screams.

Alvarez could smell the sickening, charred odor of burning meat, and knew it was his hand he smelled. He was too frightened and in too much agony, despite all his military training, to take aim at the cat. He didn't have the presence of mind to realize that he could, in all likelihood, end his suffering by ending the life of the cat and severing its psychic hold on him.

Elliot, meanwhile, was locked in another losing battle. Now that Deinonychus was upon him, all the quad-copters that were programmed to lock onto Deinonychus were buzzing around *him* now, and in his adrenaline-fueled state, he was irrationally waving his arms like mad to shoo them away. The only effect his futile efforts had was to allow their many rotors to inflict myriad small, papercut-like gashes on his arms, from which blood began to ooze at once.

The cat, meanwhile, was in a state of exultant pleasure, lapping up the falling droplets and growing ever stronger. Elliot keeled over, a sudden and intense pain ripping through his insides. It felt as though he had swallowed a ball of fire, a fire that was rapidly spreading throughout his body.

He collapsed to the ground like he had been shoved roughly by a giant, invisible finger. As the unseen force ground his face into the pavement, he felt a gentle but raspy tongue lapping at the cuts on his arms. He squealed in outrage and agony, but remained unable to do anything but wiggle helplessly, like a fish tossed into an empty bathtub.

Behind them, quad-copters began to explode one after another. Tongues of flame erupted on each of the induction charging pads in turn, successively catching fire like the consecutive procession of falling dominoes. Alvarez's high-pitched screams of agony grew to a fever pitch, catching Deinonychus's attention and irritating the gluttonous cat. He didn't want his triumphant feast ruined by the ridiculous shrieks of his prey. With a sickening crunch, Alvarez's flailing limbs flew wide before bending back unnaturally with a further harsh *crack*, and he stirred no more.

Elliot's own screams had turned to paste in his mouth. As terrified as he was, he found himself powerless to move or resist, and now he was unable even to cry out. His formerly heaving chest had stilled, and he was quite incapable of taking even a hitching breath. As he felt the first sharp pain of cat fangs tearing into the already sliced flesh of his arm, his vision and consciousness began to go mercifully blank. The last thing Elliot saw were the wide, terror-gripped eyes of Alvarez, staring lifelessly back in a frozen grimace of horror out of his motionless face, while drones fell uselessly from the sky like exploding hail around the two men.

Deinonychus filled his stomach, his sleek fur shining, as Elliot's field of vision went blank, and the pain ended.

Thirty-Six

Leviticus had, over the course of two months, wandered through all of Chippewa National Forest and much of Minnesota, heading south for over two-hundred miles, to wind up in a cornfield on the outskirts of Minneapolis/Saint Paul. The trip had taken him some time, but it was pleasant enough. He had never felt in any real danger, and in the interim he had found a great compromise when it came to food.

Leviticus had learned to become a scavenger, feasting on recently deceased birds and squirrels along the way. Once he had found a dead deer, and hadn't moved on for two days – until the stench of rot and the cloud of flies buzzing around the carcass had grown too thick to tolerate. Leviticus realized he had been tempting fate, when it came to his brother, by lingering so long.

His new habit of foraging for already dead meat saved him from having to deal with the disturbing flood of fearful thoughts and painful feelings that accompanied killing a prey animal. Carrion wasn't very tasty though, and gave off hardly any psychic energy to speak of. Once, meat Leviticus scavenged made him sick for two days.

Leviticus would ordinarily have never made such a large journey. He felt pressured to ignore his instinctive feline urge to mark up a home territory and stay there and defend it, pushed by the eventual but inevitable intrusion of his brother's mind. Every few days, like clockwork, the fringes of Deinonychus's radius of influence would touch upon the edge of what Leviticus could sense, and he knew that he had to move on.

Leviticus had dared to hope that, with the destruction of the strange Namer facility where he and his littermates had been imprisoned, his troubles might have come to an end, forever imprisoned in his past along with the memories of his dead brothers and sisters. Leviticus sensed that the danger of he and his siblings being used for some deeper, darker purpose had passed. But, the first time he felt his brother's mind seeking for him from afar, he realized things would not be so simple.

The end of the danger from the Namers didn't change the fact that Deinonychus possessed a glut of power and an almost limitless reserve of bad intentions. Leviticus knew that if his brother caught up with him, and managed to best him, that the apocalyptic outcome would be much the same. The world would most assuredly be better off if Leviticus just kept going.

That's why, when Leviticus was nabbed by a young Namer while he slept in a fallow cornfield on the edge of Minneapolis / Saint Paul after his months-long journey, Leviticus didn't have high hopes that things were going to turn out for the best.

When he awoke and found himself inside a cloth prison, Leviticus could hardly believe it. After a moment's thought, he wondered how he could have been so stupid as to not expect it. He had been placed in a downy jacket by one of four, rather scraggily looking Namers and taken into a smaller version of the Auto-Beast than the one that had barreled through the trees back at the facility. Leviticus just hoped this bunch had better intentions than he suspected they might. The signals coming from their minds seemed okay, but Leviticus had learned never to trust Namer intentions.

Even assuming his Namer captors had his best intentions in mind, he still would be unable to move onwards, to continue fleeing from the confrontation that his brother wanted to force on him. The four people took him back to a dingy, ill-kept house on the edge of Saint Paul, holding him – much as Rick Hathaway, now on unpaid administrative leave, had done – wrapped in a coat. Upon first entering the house, Leviticus was at once assaulted by a strange mix of smells.

Even the grotesquely rotted deer carcass hadn't smelled quite so strangely. It wasn't that the house smelled *bad*, per se – Leviticus's olfactory sense just didn't know what to make of the mix of smells. A slight odor of stale cheese; the harsh chemical smell of three different kinds of shampoo; the electric smell of a home theater audio receiver left powered on for a week; not to mention the scent symphony coming from the poorly-stocked refrigerator: a sharp and sour mix of hot sauce and ketchup combining with chocolate milk and grape jelly in his nostrils.

Leviticus hardly knew what to make of it.

And that was just the smells. The whirring of what seemed to be a hundred tiny fans from four different desktop computers situated throughout the house; the steady '*tick, tick, tick*-ing' of battery-powered wall clocks; the humming of refrigerators; the sudden billiard ball breaking sound of the ice maker dumping a new load of frozen goods into the hopper – all these various, foreign elements combined to create a complex, dense aural backdrop. The profusion of unknown, unnatural noises hardly made the frightened housecat feel at ease.

He sensed no ill-will on the part of his captors, however alien the environment seemed. On the contrary, they Namers acted incredibly excited to have found him. The feeling would have put him at ease if it weren't for the constant background concern of his brother's approach. As Leviticus adjusted to their house, he realized he would be able to settle down and feel happy in that setting, if only he weren't consumed by the knowledge that he was leading Deinonychus straight to these people.

*   *   *

"I thought it was *your* turn to feed him, Tone-control!"

Tony grit his teeth. He had never liked Mike's nickname for him.

"Well, it wasn't. But it shouldn't be a question of whose turn it is, anyway. I just looked at his bowl and saw it was empty. That's all the more it takes."

"Well, he's got his food and water now. *That's* the important thing, right?"

Mike had an absurdly goofy, hopeful look in his eyes. Tony found it hard to stay stern in the face of it.

"Yeah, I guess, man."

Tony reproached himself inwardly. Why couldn't he try to impart even the slightest sense of responsibility on any of his roommates? Because he was a pushover, he realized. A softie. His 'gentle reminder' form of encouragement, didn't seem to have any effect on his trio of roommates, all college seniors, like himself.

Tony had worried – when he first found that grey cat in the cornfield across from the University of Minnesota's rurally situated agricultural extension campus – that things would go pretty much as they had: that he would be the only one of his roommates to actually take care of the little guy. Yet, he had to admit, it really wasn't all that much work. Scoop some food into a bowl, pour some water into another bowl, and once a day scrape the cat's waste out of a box. Took about three minutes a day.

And in return, the spirits of the entire house had brightened. Mike, who had been mopey for three weeks since a particularly nasty break-up with his last girlfriend, went from being insufferably depressed to seeming almost ridiculously cheerful, all on account of that furry little fellow they had picked up near school. Nobody had wanted to confront Mike about his depression – particularly since they all sympathized with him – but he had really started to take the rest of the guys down with him. The cat arrived in their lives just in time.

As he scooped the grainy, brown and red cat food pellets into the paw-emblazoned bowl, Tony considered just how odd their little Leviticus was. First was that name, carved on an enigmatic round, golden tag. A name, but no phone number. That was odd, almost as odd as the name itself.

What really struck Tony about the cat, however, was the peculiarly piercing way it would look at him and the others. Almost immediately, upon arriving at their home, it seemed to trust them. Tony, the only member of the household who had owned pets before, looked on in surprise at the speed with which Leviticus adjusted to his new life with them.

Particularly, the cat seemed attracted to Mike. Mike, who had most needed cheering up. If Mike were sitting watching TV on the sofa, Leviticus would jump up into his lap and put his little paws around the despairing young man's neck. Though he was friendly with them all, the cat seemed to sleep primarily on Mike's feet, and meow the loudest when Mike came home from classes for the day. Tony noted how Leviticus would leap up onto the back of the couch and stare out the front window, about ten minutes before Mike came home. Then, when Mike pulled up and got out of his car, Leviticus would make excited little mewls.

What Tony *didn't* notice – not at the front of his mind – was how Leviticus would jump up ten minutes before Mike's arrival no matter how early or late Mike came home. It was as though the cat knew precisely when Mike grew near.

Just a few days after bringing the cat home, Mike's entire disposition underwent a one-eighty turnaround, leaving his depression in the dust. The coldness that had descended upon the romantically wronged student thawed by degrees as Leviticus flung himself at the young man. The almost pathetic eagerness, on the part of the cat, to show Mike love had melted whatever had hardened in the young man, and the other three members of the household were happy to be back in a state of near-equilibrium once more.

Yet, Tony noted, that didn't mean that Mike cared about the cat in an *operational* sense. When it came to things like petting, hugging, or picking up the cat, Mike had things covered. When it came to more mundane aspects of living with a feline, like feeding him or cleaning his litter box, then the gig fell to Tony.

Which, Tony grudgingly admitted to himself, he supposed he could deal with. The cat may have favored Mike with its affections, but it was pleasant to all of them, and didn't do many of the annoying things that Tony's previous cats had done – like puke on their blankets, scratch their furniture, or try to jump up on the razor-thin HDTV and claw at the screen for purchase when they realized it was too narrow for a perch.

No, it seemed that in all matters, Leviticus was a very well-behaved cat indeed.

*   *   *

Deinonychus, at long last, came to the edge of a great city of Namers. He felt the glow of his quarry from somewhere close at hand, only a handful of miles away. Deinonychus wondered what changed.

For the longest time, it had been a game of cat and mouse with his brother. Deinonychus would draw near, his brother would sense him and move on. Then Deinonychus would run to catch up, catch a whiff of his brother in the distance, and – even as he approached – feel his brother slip away yet again.

For days now, however, that had not been the case. For days now, Deinonychus drew ever nearer, and his prey remained stationary – completely stationary. Leviticus didn't seem even to roam about. He seemed *confined.* All to the good. Now Deinonychus had arrived, and things would soon be resolved. The puny runt would be his.

Then Deinonychus could *really* get started.

THIRTY-SEVEN

Leviticus couldn't believe just how much he enjoyed life with the college students. Thoughts of his murderous brother hadn't exactly slipped his mind, they just became easier to ignore after a while. The positive feelings of the people around him were so much *stronger* than the faint signals his distant brother gave off. When he first befriended the household, he had singled out the sad Namer. He couldn't quite understand what had depressed the Namer so – Leviticus had been 'fixed' shortly after birth, and had no sense of sexual politics.

What the cat *could* understand, however, was feeling sad and left out. Leviticus, on his long lonely march through the woods, had felt much the same way, if for different reasons. Leviticus had responded warmly to the change in mood his affections brought about in his new Namer friend, and the two formed an instant bond.

Leviticus could tell that these people had only the best of intentions for him. Indeed, it became evident to Leviticus that the arrangement that now existed between them – where he, the cat, would dwell with them while they fed and took care of him, in exchange for his affection – was considered quite normal to the humans.

This initially struck Leviticus as a marvel. One thing he had never felt back at the lab was the sense that things were *normal*, that the way he and his siblings were living was what they were meant to do. Upon developing that feeling in the house with the students, he grew to cherish it and the stability it allowed him to feel.

Always, in the back of his mind, sat the fear of his approaching brother like a coiled snake waiting to strike. For over a week, he was able to push it out and focus on the thoughts of his new family and the altogether new feelings of belonging.

Soon, however, Leviticus felt it in his mind. A growing heat like a rising sun. He could ignore it no longer.

Deinonychus was coming.

*　　*　　*

When it happened, the four students were all away at class or work. Leviticus had to go *now*, before Deinonychus got any closer, or he would be risking the lives of his new Namer family. It tore at Leviticus's heart – he didn't want to imagine their mood upon coming home and finding him escaped, not one bit. Yet, for the moment, the cat had more pressing problems.

Actually managing to escape the house being chief among them.

It had been weeks since Leviticus had eaten anything from outside, anything *alive*. The first time that his new owners had plopped the contents of a can of what they called 'wet food' into his bowl, Leviticus got his hopes up that the dead flesh would confer *something* of the power of living things into him, something that he could store for the battle ahead. Yet, as delicious as the meal proved to be, whatever power resided in the animals that had gone into the can was long since diluted.

Leviticus's power to peer into the minds of other and touch their thoughts didn't require living energy to feed on. But he would be utterly unable to move the heavy physical objects that barred his way without some kind of blood meal. For a small housecat with no powers in a sealed house, escape can be nigh on impossible. He felt Deinonychus approaching, and knew that his murderous brother could sense him, as well. It was just a matter of time.

Leviticus tried everything he could think of. He clawed through the window screens, only to be stopped by the glass of the window. He tried stretching up on his hind legs and fiddling with the strange metal knob that his human family members always worked to open the door, but its secrets wouldn't give themselves up to his slippery claws. He pawed at the bottom of the doors, hoping to find some way through the crack, but quickly realized that such efforts were futile.

He sat disconsolately by the front window, meowing plaintively in despair, when he saw an older man in a blue shirt walking up the front drive. The man held a heavy bag filled with slips of paper, and Leviticus recognized him at once. That man came to the house almost every day, ever since the cat had arrived. He usually came right up to the front door and pushed some papers through a small slot in the door. Leviticus, realizing this man was his only chance, waited until the man had come right up to the house, and then swung into action.

Flinging his mind out from himself, he wrapped it around the letter carrier's consciousness and pulled it tight like a net. Taking control of the mailman's arm, he reached up and punched the window as hard as he could, sending spider web cracks throughout it. It hurt the man greatly, but Leviticus tried to bargain with himself: it wouldn't hurt the man as badly as Deinonychus would, should he catch them here. He swung the other man's arm again and again, as hard as he could force him, to until the cracks widened and shards of glass began to rain down.

Looking out from his picture window perch, Leviticus saw the blank, vacant stare on the mailman's face as the cat willed him to do these things. Hopefully the Namer would have no memory of this experience. The window now sufficiently shattered, Leviticus had man pull out the remaining shards by hand and drop the jagged chunks of glass onto the grass outside. Leviticus could feel himself growing weaker with the frantic effort of this latest trick. As soon as the gap in the window was wide enough, Leviticus sent the man along down the street, slowly relinquishing the grip on the other's mind once he had moved a safe distance away.

Leviticus sprung through the newly shattered window, landing adroitly on all fours. Ravenous for sustenance, he began to look around for food. It didn't take him long to find a chattering and immature squirrel – a squirrel who perhaps didn't fear the cat as much as he should have, out of naïve inexperience. After that quick meal, Leviticus used his growing powers to eat another squirrel and a pair of birds. He felt terrible about killing them, but he needed to replenish himself. He pushed himself to gulp down the energy of their still beating hearts, fighting the guilt and revulsion. The situation was bleak – Leviticus didn't have time to pity his food. Not now.

If he couldn't stop his brother Deinonychus – today in this very city – the whole world would know what it meant to be prey.

* * *

Deinonychus felt the light of his brother's mind flare with brightness. The cat puzzled at this. He hadn't gotten *that* much closer to Leviticus, had he? Deinonychus increased his pace. This nasty place was a hard environment for a cat unaccustomed to the city to navigate. Surely the placid and meek Leviticus couldn't be having any easier of a time.

Reeking Auto-Beasts spewed fumes, growling down countless paths that seemed to crisscross every inch of the land that that wasn't covered in giant Namer boxes. Namers coming, Namers going. Namers walking itty bitty dogs.

Deinonychus had been trying to keep a low profile, but, as he felt his brother's mind grow stronger and brighter, and begin moving away, his rage snapped. The next dog-walker who came by, calling him 'cute little kitty,' cried out in horror seconds after passing as their tiny little Yorkie's ears shriveled as though burnt. Its incessantly wagging tail withered from tip to base like a lit fuse.

The woman shrieked, dialed a number on her cell phone, and began demanding an ambulance for her dog. The cat, a block down the street, had already forgotten about the incident. His mind was elsewhere.

Deinonychus couldn't understand why Leviticus had been so stationary for so long, and only now began to move away. The only possibility the angry cat could see was that Leviticus realized his murderous brother was coming, and had been frightened. Deinonychus couldn't blame him there: he *should* be frightened.

But why couldn't he have just sat there and waited for death? Deinonychus, sick of waiting, snarled. But he didn't lose all hope. It wouldn't be long now, even if he was trying to run away. Deinonychus increased his speed.

*   *   *

Leviticus ran as fast as he could, through backyards and alleys. He intended to stand and fight his brother soon, but he wanted to put as much distance between him and his housemates as possible before that happened. Leviticus couldn't help but think that there would be a lot of collateral damage when the final conflict finally happened, and he strove to find some place that seemed devoid of Namers or activity.

He wasn't finding it.

This strange place of the Namers – this sprawling city ringed by suburbs – was dense with Namer structures. Vast fields of Auto-Beasts slept in rows. Namers ran past in jogging outfits. Namers in sweaty groups toiled to build new structures. Namers stood chatting by the side of the road.

There was no place Leviticus could see that looked fit for a showdown. He remembered the vast empty field where he had been found by the students, and yearned to go back there. The cat paused. He had just seen a group of Namers building a new structure, but now he saw all the Namers leaving. Clapping each other on the back, slamming car doors. Going away.

An expansive, mostly open building, crisscrossed with interlocking girders and encircled with cranes and bulldozers, left vacant by the people who, moments before, had been working busily. Leviticus didn't know how long they would be away, but he knew how long he had. His brother would catch up with him in a matter of minutes.

Situated between several other buildings, the construction site was nonetheless surrounded by a massive lot. There was more space separating this structure from the others than the grey cat could find anywhere else. With the time he had left, this was the best option. Leviticus darted inside, where smells more caustic than any he had experienced in the student's rental home instantly hammered his sensitive nose.

The cat sped up the stairs, sliding to a stop just in time to prevent himself from running out the open end of the second story. This unfinished environment was disorienting. Though that might help in the standoff against his brother, it was just as likely to be a problem for him as it would be for Deinonychus. Leviticus strove to retreat to some vantage point before the inevitable happened, to give himself the best opportunity possible before the arrival of his brother.

A long, echoing meow bounced off the exposed metal of the building's girders, ricocheting up to him from the entrance, and Leviticus knew his time was up.

Deinonychus was here.

Thirty-Eight

THE FINAL CATDOWN

Deinonychus could smell his beastly little brother now – smell him with his *nose*, and not just his mind. The cretinous runt had wandered into an unfinished building that was, in many places, little more than a metal skeleton. Deinonychus couldn't imagine that his brother would be able to find many hiding places.

Deinonychus coveted the power inside his brother, desired it for himself, but while it was *in* his brother, he didn't respect it. He knew that his puny little brother was too afraid of his own might to be a danger. Too enamored of peace to bring war. Too hurt by other's pain to visit it upon them. It made Deinonychus feel like coughing up a hairball to imagine the immense waste of talents that his brother Leviticus represented.

Well, soon all that would be put to rights. Very soon now the world would know the likes of a power that did not slumber, of a might that did not fear the taste of pain. Deinonychus's claws clicked on the cement floor of the building. His tail swished in the air behind him as he crossed the threshold. The dying sun cast a long, twitching shadow out in front of him.

It was coming: the moment he had been waiting for. His mouth watered in anticipation of the meal he soon would take. More nourishing to his soul than to his stomach, but satisfying enough for both.

He called upon the reserves of energy he had stored up for this moment, and the faintly glowing outline of Leviticus's footprints – delineating the path his younger brother took when 'hiding – started to materialize in the dusky light of the building. The glimmering prints led the stairs, and Deinonychus followed them. His brother's footprints evaporated as soon as the cat passed them, while still others up ahead then flickered on. Leviticus thought he could hide, but Deinonychus knew better.

There would be no escape.

The iridescent shape of a cat appeared before him, and Deinonychus hissed in surprise. This couldn't be right. It wasn't a cat. Only the *edges* of a cat were visible, shining with a greenish-blue light. Inside, the shape was pitch black.

Not to be daunted, Deinonychus strode up to the strange ghost cat, which sat on its hind legs placidly, and hissed again. The shimmering cat-shadow merely tilted its head and extended its neck to Deinonychus in a friendly gesture. Deinonychus took a step closer, and the cat lunged forward. Braced for an attack, Deinonychus registered disbelief to find that the ghostly cat simply bumped its head against his own.

Something in that gesture seemed vaguely familiar to Deinonychus. He sniffed the other, but there was no scent. No surprise there. The shadowy, shimmer-outlined figure seemed completely insubstantial. Deinonychus hadn't expected the spectral cat to be able to touch him, but it had. The cat repeated its playful head-butting gesture, and this time, Deinonychus knew where he remembered it from. It was his littermate – the one who died. It had been months now since Deinonychus – or indeed anybody – had seen this cat. Yet here he was, in glittering, spectral form.

The cat, the spirit of his dead brother, made a further friendly feline gesture, but Deinonychus decided he'd had enough. He was not in a playful or friendly mood. Particularly not to his siblings, and especially not his *dead* siblings.

He intended to add Leviticus to that list, and this ghostly joker was just getting the way. Rebuffing the ghost cat's advance with a swiftly batted paw, Deinonychus leapt on the flickering form of his dead brother in a feral rage. He landed with an unexpected *smack* on the solid floor, the spectral form of his dead brother having vanished like a puff of smoke blown away on the wind.

Deinonychus, fully expecting a fight, whirled around madly. He looked hurriedly for his foe for several moments before allowing himself to believe that the ghostly thing had truly vanished. Deinonychus growled – a low, long, gurgling sound. That had been his first experience with spirits, and he hoped it would be his last.

He snorted through his nose deeply a few times, regaining his composure. After a moment, his purpose returned to him, and his eyes once more adjusted to see Leviticus's footprints. Deinonychus didn't have much further to go – there, at the end of the hall, stood, quite calmly, his brother.

*   *   *

Leviticus wore a peculiar, speculative look. He, too, had seen the form of the unnamed brother in the darkness, and wondered what it could mean. He felt a strange sense of hopefulness upon seeing the form of his affectionate but deceased brother appearing there, extending gestures of familial acceptance to his brother Deinonychus. That sense was dashed when he saw his murderous brother leap on their brother's otherworldly form, scattering it like a dust cloud.

At that, Leviticus's sense of hopefulness and wonder curdled inside him and turned to rage. Never before in his short life had Leviticus *wanted* to lash out, to inflict pain. Now that he had reached that point, he wasted no time. Deinonychus looked up, and saw him. Leviticus's eyes flamed with a green, feline brightness.

Deinonychus snarled and hissed, but approached cautiously. Leviticus rose up off the floor, a shimmering mist of interlocking green and red eddies swirling around him. Deinonychus's pace slowed even more. He hadn't expected any resistance. Deinonychus hadn't expected anything, really, except to find his skulking brother and then take his fill of his blood.

Leviticus, however, had been put in a foul mood. His brother had given him so many reasons to feel rage. Seeing his brother's ghost offering love and companionship, only to be rejected with violence, made him realize what was entirely missing from his life. Leviticus had forgotten how comforting the feel of another cat nuzzling up against him could feel – not just another cat, but *family*.

Leviticus felt no sense of family whatsoever for the spite-filled thing skulking before him now. Leviticus had no idea how the spirit of their dead brother managed to appear before them just now, or if he would ever be able to do it again. Seeing that Deinonychus's reaction was to *destroy* that amazing gift of love and fraternity which had been offered to him across the gulf of death itself made Leviticus see red. His eyes flared, in his anger, to an almost obscene brightness.

Because all that – no matter how badly it offended Leviticus's sensibilities – wasn't the real problem. No, all of that *might* be able to slide – to be chalked up to the one bad sibling out of the litter, the one bad seed in the lot – if it weren't for Deinonychus's relentless, destructive *ambition*. The cat thought he could rule the world, and if something couldn't be ruled, it ought to be destroyed.

Leviticus didn't understand how Deinonychus couldn't see that his conception of 'power' consisted of nothing *but* the ability to destroy. Destroying everything until there was nothing left: *that* was the extent of Deinonychus's 'ambition.'

The pointlessness of it was enough to fill Leviticus with a burning rage – a rage that knew almost no bounds. Leviticus had seen the types of kindness the world could harbor. He had seen happy families of all types – deer, birds, people. He had seen the beauty in the color of the flowers and heard the cheerfulness in the songs of the birds. He had felt the love in the Namer's hearts, and understood the fear that pain caused.

Leviticus knew that the point of the world wasn't to *rule* and destroy it, but to grow *in* it, along with it, to be a part of it. His foolish, power-obsessed brother saw none of this. He understood *nothing*. And here he was, at the tail end of a chase of hundreds of miles, come to claim Leviticus's life. The audacity, the *outrage* of his brother's tenacious chase was enough to send Leviticus into a comet-like flight of fury.

Leviticus looked down on his brother from a height of ten feet, floating in a glowing ball of energy and anger, and even as he hated his ruinous brother – as much for what he was forcing Leviticus to do as for what he was himself – part of Leviticus pitied him. Pitied all the things Deinonychus would never understand, all the obvious things his oblivious brother couldn't see. Then Leviticus caught the glint of hatred in his brother's eyes, pure hatred. A hate so full it was overflowing, a hatred tinted with envy and arrogance and impatience at not having what he wanted *now*.

Upon seeing that look in his brother's eyes, all the pity in Leviticus's heart evaporated. Now the fight was upon them, and Leviticus could do without pity. Because the one thing he didn't see in his brother's eyes was fear.

*   *   *

Deinonychus had to admit that he was a little surprised to see that his brother was actually willing to fight. As Leviticus rose into the air, wreathed in iridescent mists, part of Deinonychus was actually pleased. This would be no simple battle: *this* conflict actually stood a chance of being worthy of him and his immense skills and talents.

As the shine around Leviticus intensified, Deinonychus's eyes glowed a bright orange of his own. A mane of fire burst into flame around his neck. Visions passed before Deinonychus's smoldering eyes – visions of a world in flames, filled with the pained screams of an unlucky few kept alive only to amuse Deinonychus with their suffering. Greed flashed like the light of an electrical storm in his eyes. Blue sparks crackled around him like fireworks.

The cat felt his claws growing, his skin stretching, his muscles thickening, his brutal fangs sharpening. He had saved almost the full energy of every kill for weeks for precisely this moment, and he was nearly bursting at the seams with power. He focused his rage like a laser at his brother, and, having coiled for the strike, sprung with body and mind at his levitating foe. His deadly claws were extended, his razor teeth ready to strike, and every sparking volt of his horrific force aimed squarely forward at Leviticus.

Thirty-Nine

Deinonychus readied himself as his body – aflame with hatred – flew through the air, his eyes shut tightly against the coming impact. To his alarm, he felt nothing, and after some seconds opened his eyes to an unexpected and disturbing sight. He could see *nothing*, save for a brilliant bluish-white glow. He hissed and found himself unable to move. Plunged into a sudden, unexpected panic, he strove to make out any details in the harsh, featureless light that surrounded him.

Two green eyes flared like coals in the bright void. These massive, luminous orbs were the only things visible to Deinonychus. He hissed in outrage. Leviticus was doing this to him!

He strove to move his limbs, to no avail. Deinonychus's anger turned swiftly to fear as those eyes grew in intensity and size. No longer the eyes of his smallest brother, they were now the eyes of an ancient beast. The eyes remained all that could be seen, the skull-splitting brightness that ensconced Deinonychus enshrouding the rest.

That unbearable glare grew yet more intense, and Deinonychus howled in pain and fear. Just as suddenly as it had overtaken him, the light dropped away like a curtain. Deinonychus couldn't tell where he was, but he certainly wasn't at the construction site anymore. He looked around him, and realized with a sinking stomach and breaking heart that he was at the top of a distressingly tall building. The earth stretched out into the distance in all directions, nearly five-hundred feet below, while Deinonychus himself stood on a flat surface of gravel no bigger than city block.

Nearby, other tall structures reared to the sky like outrageous trees. Deinonychus whirled and whirled around, looking for his brother. He could see him nowhere. Deinonychus didn't know it, but he was now over five miles from where he had been before, on the roof of one of the tallest buildings in downtown Saint Paul.

And he was alone.

*   *   *

Leviticus's skull felt as though it had been split open. His eyelids fluttered open as he gave a faint 'meow' of pain, and he was less than half surprised to find himself back in the same cornfield where he had met his Namer family. He only dimly understood how he had gotten there. The sun felt brighter on his back than it had when he had entered the construction site, and the cat wondered at it.

Sunset had been approaching when he fought his brother. Now it was bright again? Had he slept through the night?

It had been, in fact, three months since his encounter with Deinonychus. Nobody had been there in the cornfield to witness the sudden appearance of one small, grey housecat out of nothingness, or they would have undoubtedly scheduled a meeting with the University counselor. School, as it happened, was now out for the summer. Leviticus didn't know it, but his Namer family of students had all gone back to their respective homes for the next few months. Leviticus had a sense that some time had passed since he was last awake, but he had no clue how much.

Leviticus had attempted to cast his brother into the Void, and, though he did not know it, he had not entirely succeeded.

His plan had been sound. There was no other way, Leviticus reasoned, to deal with Deinonychus once and for all, to ensure that his murderous brother never had a chance to realize his sick ambitions. Leviticus looked around, smelling the air and enjoying the breeze.

Not knowing that his family had split up and left the area, Leviticus, his head still aching, decided to stretch out at the edge of the field, and take a nap. Maybe they would be here for him soon.

*   *   *

Deinonychus had to find his brother, find him at once. Leviticus had played some kind of dirty trick on him, and there was no way Deinonychus was going to let him get away with it. The yellow and grey cat probed his own mind, and was surprised and delighted to find that he still had almost all of his mental reserves.

That was all well and good. But what had happened? He cast his mind out, scouring over the face of the planet. Nothing. Frustrated, he realized he could feel Leviticus nowhere. Deinonychus had no sense of the passage of time. He did not know that two months had passed since his confrontation with his brother.

It was not yet summer, school was still in session, but it was two months later than it had been when he had fought with Leviticus. These facts were unknown to the cat. He thought that, at the most, hours had gone by.

He certainly didn't realize that Leviticus wouldn't be emerging from the interstitial plain from which he had flung Deinonychus to this far place and time for a further month. Deinonychus could search around all he wanted, but for the time being, Leviticus was effectively nowhere. And he was going to stay that way for a while.

Quickly taking stock of his surroundings, Deinonychus saw one of those ugly rectangular panels that the Namers often walked through with the help of a trick involving their hands and a curved protuberance on the slab. Deinonychus wasn't in a very tricky mood, and, advancing on the door, he blew it open with his mind and passed through.

It took him to a stairwell. He quickly descended, where he came up against another door. It, too, flew off its hinges, breaking the plaster of the opposite wall. Leviticus entered, and found himself in a long hallway. It was empty. Leviticus certainly wasn't there.

Deinonychus, filled with anger, confusion, and a desire to *do* something, realized he would have to find his brother all over again before he could finish him. He thought deeply, sending his mind out with greater effort than he had ever attempted. Nothing, save for exhaustion, was the result.

Nothing *anywhere*. He cast his net wider, wider, maddeningly *wider* – still nothing.

Hatred grew inside him, eating away at his thin grip on sanity like a corrosive substance. Where was he? *Where was he?*

Deinonychus had followed Leviticus, and found him, and fought him – for *what*? Where was his prize? Where was his due? And now, he had to do it all again! He had to do something even harder, this time, for now he could sense his brother nowhere.

But why should Deinonychus even *have* to? *He* was supreme! Not his runty little brother. *Him.*

Deinonychus's anger grew inside him, his sense of entitlement overmastering any sense of cunning or instinctive deviousness that remained inside him. *Why?* Why had what he worked so hard for been taken away from him? Deinonychus fumed and stewed like hatred incarnate, and, as he ruminated on the appalling outrage that was his failed quest, that hatred fanned out from him like a mushroom cloud. It enveloped first the hallway, then the building, then the entire block, and then the blocks adjacent to him.

While Deinonychus stewed with fury, people began to drop in their offices like dominoes. Telephones fell to the ground in mid-conversation. Foreheads smashed into computer monitors and keyboards, typing an endless stream of 't's and 'g's and whatever other letters the unlucky victims' heads happened to strike.

Envelopes were dropped. Elevators were not stepped out of. Soon, cars suddenly bereft of guidance began to crash into each other, clogging the street around the building where Deinonychus was trapped.

Hydrants were collided with, spraying jets of water which began to hiss and boil almost immediately. Benches where fresh corpses sat waiting for busses that would never come became uprooted by crashing cars. Pedestrians collapsed to the crosswalks and cement in mid-stride. Panes of glass shattered outwards, raining shards down for hundreds of feet to slice through the bodies of the fallen like a hail of daggers. Flags fluttered to the ground from the tops of buildings, their edges smoldering.

Inside the building, the oblivious cat approached the next door, bashing his nose against it with full inertial force. He hissed in anger and shock, confused that it hadn't opened. Deinonychus snarled at the impudence of the door that thought it could defy *him*. Deinonychus could be stopped by *nothing*. Sitting back on his haunches, he aimed his mental force at the door, and let loose. In his mind, he felt his volley strike the door like a small, gently lobbed pebble bouncing off a sheet of metal.

What? *What?*

He tried again, and this time he felt nothing. *Nothing at all.* In his mind, he raged and screamed, demanding the door open. Open *now!* Soon he was clawing at the door, trying to bite his way through it. He had spent all of his mental energy on his petulant fit, and was just now beginning to realize it. Soon he was meowing plaintively, stretched up on his hind legs, pawing at the knob.

He looked, though he didn't know it, exactly like an ordinary cat. He didn't realize it, but now – at least until he ate something alive and full of energy, he *was* an ordinary cat.

The thought would not have sat well with Deinonychus at the moment.

Forty

After a day of waiting in the cornfield, Leviticus decided to attempt finding his new family's house on his own. He wondered, now that the pressure of worrying about Deinonychus was off his mind, what had gone through *their* minds when they discovered that he had left. It must have come as a great shock. Leviticus meowed guiltily as he remembered the broken window and the hurt mailman.

He eventually made his way back to the right neighborhood, but finding his old home proved difficult. For one, he could feel none of his Namer family's minds, and had to operate on smell and sight and sense of direction alone. Soon, however, he found himself trotting up the sidewalk that led to the front door. There was a new pane of glass in the window, and a sign inside, writ large with those funny lines and squiggles that Namers seemed to love to put all over their things.

Leviticus sniffed at the door, finding, to his surprise, only the faintest traces of the odors of his four human friends. It smelled as though they hadn't been here for some time. Thoughtfully, Leviticus looked up at the sky, glancing at the leaves on the trees. With the answer beginning to take shape in his mind, he sniffed at the air. The smell of pollen and plants had changed, along with the angle of the sunlight. The leaves were bigger, thicker, older.

In a flash, the truth of what must have happened revealed itself to him. He had, in his efforts to send his brother away, brushed up against the Void itself. He was now a bit downstream on the river of time from where he had begun.

And his human family? Where were they? In that moment, it entered his head that he might conceivably never know. The realization weighed heavily on him, and with a small '*row*' of discontent, he curled himself up, tried to ignore the dull ache in his head, and lay down disconsolately on the sidewalk in front of the door of the house that was no longer his.

*   *   *

Ronald Morgenstern was pretty tolerant, as landlords go. He hadn't even gotten angry at his four young tenants when they broke the window and made up the unbelievable cover story that someone must have broken in and then decided not to steal anything. He had just taken the money out of their security deposit and laughed a little to himself about the indiscretions of college students.

His wife tried to tell him that renting a perfectly fine house to a group of students like that would result in more wear and tear than he should bother to put up with, but heck: the guys had to live somewhere, and they were more than willing to pay. For his next tenants, however, he thought he might try to get folks that might stay on the lease longer than nine months. Finding new tenants every year didn't sound like his idea of fun.

As he finished up his work on the hot water heater in the basement, Morgenstern climbed the stairs and gathered up the rest of his tools. Making sure that everything was in good order, and that his 'FOR RENT' sign was still securely stuck in the window, he opened the front door and gave a small gasp when he saw a grey cat curled up there.

"Hey there, little kitty," he said in an unconsciously sing-song voice, the kind one might use to speak to an infant. The cat raised its head and looked at him with baleful eyes. A narrative thread began to emerge in Morgenstern's mind.

This cat was just sleeping in front of the door? Immediately, he suspected the college students of having fed this cat – caring for it like a pet until it had gotten used to them – and then just abandoning it when they moved away. College students were like that. His wife had tried to warn him. Well, breaking windows was one thing – but Morgenstern couldn't stand the idea that they had abandoned a perfectly innocent cat.

"That settles it," he said, bending down to the pet Leviticus's upturned head. "Moira was right: No more renting to students."

FORTY-ONE

Terror in the Twin Cities

A Shocking New Technology Devastates Downtown Saint Paul

(AP) DOWNTOWN SAINT PAUL WAS HIT BY AN UNPARALLELED TERRORIST ATTACK ON MONDAY, WHICH UTILIZED PREVIOUSLY UNSEEN TECHNOLOGY AND CLAIMED MORE THAN EIGHT-HUNDRED AND FORTY LIVES. THE DAMAGE IS ESTIMATED TO COST MORE THAN HUNDREDS OF MILLIONS OF DOLLARS, YET EXPERTS INSIST THAT THE INFRASTRUCTURAL DAMAGE WAS NOTHING COMPARED TO WHAT A CONVENTIONAL WEAPONRY ATTACK. WOULD HAVE ENTAILED.

OFFICIALS ON THE SCENE, UNABLE TO REVEAL MANY DETAILS, COULD NEVERTHELESS TELL THE PUBLIC THAT THE ATTACKERS POSSESSED A METHOD OF INDUCING SEVER SACCULAR ANEURYSMS TO EVERYBODY WITHIN A FOUR BLOCK RADIUS, CAUSING INSTANTANEOUS DEATH. THE ONLY OTHER DIRECT DAMAGE NOTED BY INVESTIGATORS IS THE SHATTERING OF ALL GLASS WITHIN THAT SAME RADIUS, LEADING TO SPECULATION THAT SOME KIND OF HYPERSONIC MECHANISM LAY BEHIND THE GRUESOME ATTACK.

IN THE MIDST OF THE TRAGEDY, ONE SMALL KERNEL OF HOPE REMAINED. EMERGENCY RESPONDERS WERE

SHOCKED TO FIND A LONE SURVIVOR OF THE ATTACK, ROAMING ON THE EIGHTY-FIFTH FLOOR OF THE ARMITAGE BANK HEADQUARTERS: A GREY AND YELLOW HOUSECAT. WITH NO MICROCHIP OR TAGS IDENTIFYING ITS OWNER, IT'S HARD TO SAY EXACTLY WHO THE LITTLE TABBY IS OR WHAT IT WAS DOING THERE.

"HE'S A LITTLE MIRACLE," SAID POLICE CHIEF MICHELLE BRADSTONE. "LIKE THE TERROR ATTACK ITSELF, HIS PRESENCE IN THIS SITUATION MAKES LITTLE SENSE, BUT INSTEAD OF A MYSTERY OF HORROR AND DEATH, HE REPRESENTS A MYSTERY OF LIFE AND POSSIBILITY."

Forty-Two

The doorbell rang.

"What the fuck do you want?"

Rick Hathaway shambled down his apartment hallway, wearing a whiskey-soaked bathrobe and suffering through a terrible hangover. Things hadn't gone so well for him lately. His wife was still staying at her sisters. He was finally back on the job at NUCPA, but only provisionally. It would be another month before he was reinstated full-time. Until then, he only worked Wednesday through Friday.

It was a Sunday morning, and he had gotten trash drunk the night before. He hadn't even heard the news about the terror attack downtown. He certainly didn't know who would be at his door.

"I *said*," he yelled as he opened the door. "What the fuck do you—"

He silenced himself. It was Ben.

"Kid!" he said, smiling for the first time in weeks. He smiled around a smoldering cigarette – with Janette out of the house, there was no need to pretend he didn't smoke.

"We've got to talk," said Ben.

There was no mistaking the seriousness of his tone.

"Aww, Christ, kid. Aren't you a chipper bastard."

"Look at this," Ben said, handing Rick the newspaper outlining the events from the day before.

"Holy fucking hand grenade!" Hathaway said, the cigarette dropping from his mouth.

Ben reached down, plucked the cigarette from the carpet, and stubbed it out on a nearby ashtray.

"Oh my god!" Hathaway said, clearly in shock upon learning of all the destruction he had been unaware of.

"Have you got to the part about the cat yet?"

"The *cat?*"

Hathaway quickly scanned ahead.

"Oh my shittin' *Christ,* Ben! This is bad!"

Ben plopped down on the couch.

"You're telling me."

"We've got to tell Pettinger about this."

"She knows," said Ben. "She wants you to come into work tomorrow."

"But I'm still on… on…" Hathaway couldn't bring himself to say it.

"She pulled some strings. You're back on the job full-time now."

Hathaway, looking back down at the paper, shook his head.

"I don't know how much of a favor that's going to turn out to be, kid."

"I don't know either," Ben said, rubbing his temples. "But we know more about this cat than anybody else. So we get the job."

"Do you have any leads as to what they did with the thing?"

Ben shook his head.

"Someone on the local force gave him to a friend to take to a shelter, but it wasn't exactly the first detail on everybody's minds, with hundreds of bodies filling the streets. We can't even find the person who took him."

"So he's just… out there," Hathaway said with a shudder.

"Yeah," Ben said, a morose expression pulling at his face. "He's just out there." Ben went to Hathaway's cabinet, poured himself a drink. "Someone could be taking him home to live with them, as we speak."

Forty-Three

Leviticus managed to adjust to his life in the shelter as best he could. The young man who fed him every day was very nice, but he was only ever around for a brief chunk of time, and he had to divide his attention equally between every cat there. Though Leviticus and he had developed a bond, it was nothing like the bond Leviticus had known with his housemates. The cat could accept that, however. He hadn't really expected to be *happy*, just hoped he had a chance to escape.

The days passed.

One day, a family of three came in – a little boy accompanied by his two parents. When they walked through the doors to the smaller room where the cats were housed, Leviticus felt their approach as though they had set bells ringing with their entry. He got up, stretched himself out, and stood by the door of his cage, looking out at them eagerly.

Though they looked politely at all the cats, he could sense that they felt from the first what he himself had felt. The little boy's eyes spoke very plainly. After a brief consultation with each other, they shuffled out to take care of the appropriate paperwork. Leviticus had seen this process before, with other cats at the shelter, and he knew that soon they would come to put him into a little tote, and take him away.

As he watched the family filling out a form through the glass, a subtle movement in the background caught his eye. It looked like the tip of a cat tail whisking around beyond the table where they were seated. Looking attentively, Leviticus saw the spectral outline of a cat leap with feline deftness onto the table where his new family were seated. They didn't seem to notice the spirit of Leviticus's brother, but it could clearly see them – Leviticus's dead, unnamed brother was rubbing his head lovingly against the little boy's face.

A more clear endorsement of the family couldn't have been made. Leviticus put his hand to his cage door and meowed to his brother. The ghostly outline turned its head to look. Leviticus meowed again. Mistaking the caged cat's posture, the little boy waved excitedly to Leviticus. The ghostly brother, however, evaporated.

For a moment, Leviticus was downtrodden by his brother's disappearance, but the love already forming in the little boy's eyes and the warmth glowing in his own feline heart soon made up for any sense of loss he had at his brother's vanishing.

As the Redcliffe family took him out of the shelter and loaded him into their Auto-Beast, he looked up at the three happy faces smiling back at him, and he knew that he was finally going to belong. He knew, in that moment, that he had finally found his real family, and that he would do anything he could for these people.

He was, at long last, going home.

Forty-Four

Deinonychus was *miserable,* miserable beyond anything he had ever thought he could suffer and yet live through. He'd been trapped in this tiny cage for days now. He thought his cage at the NUCPA facility had been cramped, but he could see now that he was a fool. There, at least, he had had the clear air of the forest flowing through his bars. Here, he just heard the incessant mewling of his pathetic neighbors.

Crammed into a wall of cages, he heard them yammering on all around him – old cats, young cats, some even kittens. They wouldn't shut up! There was no escaping it.

If the ones on the left were asleep, the ones on his right were wide awake and hungry. The cat in the space above him sounded like he was practicing to be a certified tap dance instructor, from the metallic *'bong, boing, bong'* of his paws against the floor. If Deinonychus could be subjected to anything more demeaning than his present situation at the shelter, he was not imaginative enough to conceive of it.

They had given him a woolen 'toy' to play with, and he had promptly disemboweled it and strewn its fluff throughout his cage. The next toy was just a ruffled ball made of paper. He hated it.

Presently, as he was ruminating on the darkness of his plight, the door to their little chamber opened, and a young girl bounded in, followed by a rather dour-faced, shuffling woman. The little girl's excitement radiated off her as she bounced down the wall of cages, grinning at each cat in turn. Deinonychus couldn't stand to see so much vibrancy. What did that little girl have to be happy about, anyway?

*   *   *

The woman, evidently the small Namer's mother, didn't seem to appreciate her daughter's excitement, either.

"Calm the hell down, Ashley, or we won't get one. I don't want one anyway, but I was *hoping* you might shut up about it if I gave in."

"Oh, Mommy, Mommy, look at this little brown one!" Ashley said excitedly, poking her finger through the cage bars at a confused looking kitten.

"Not a kitten, Ashley," said her mother. "They'll go crazy and rip everything up. You have to get a grown-up kitty."

Preferably, she thought, one that was almost dead.

Ashley settled in front of Deinonychus's cage.

"*Oooh*, look at this one!" she cried. "He's *big!*"

Her mother, Jennifer Webber, thought about this for a moment. If the cat was big, maybe he didn't like to jump up on high things so much. Maybe he'd be a fatty and just sit around all day.

"Yeah, get that one, Ashley."

"*Oooh*, can I?"

Jennifer scanned the other cages, seeing only smaller, lither looking cats.

"Yeah, he looks good."

She leaned in and saw that he already had a nice-looking golden tag. So that would be one less thing to buy. Another item in this particular cat's favor.

"Definitely get this one," she said.

* * *

Deinonychus didn't like the woman, but the girl seemed okay. The pair went out of the room, and he could see them through the glass. He had the sense that they were negotiating for his release with the prison guard – a nice-enough girl who came in to feed them every day. During his internment at the shelter, he had seen this process happen before with the other cats.

As Deinonychus was placed into an even smaller box with cage bars over its front. Once sealed inside, he stared angrily at the cats trapped in the other bins as Ashley and Jennifer Webber bore him away.

Those prisoners were the last cats he saw for quite some time.

* * *

"Mommy, how do you say his name?" Ashley asked, looking through the holes in the top of the cat tote.

Jennifer scoffed.

"Dino-ickus," she said in the voice of authority. Lowering her voice to a mutter, she added:

"Stupidest name I've ever heard in my life."

November 1st, 2011 – March 12th, 2012

September 5th, 2012 – October 25th, 2012

September 14th – October 30th, 2013

-T.B.

Thank you for reading 'Through the Woods.' I hope you enjoyed it! If so, please consider leaving a review on **Amazon** or **Goodreads**. I am just a normal fellow who writes on my way to and from my day job, and whenever I can get away with it at home, so every good review helps.

If you liked what you read, and want to be notified the next time one of my strange adventures is released, please sign up for my mailing list here:

http://www.troyblackford.com/2013/08/author-updates-mailing-list-for-big.html

Thank you very much, and I hope you have a lot of fun with whatever you read next. Remember: be nice to your brothers and sisters!

About the Author

Troy Blackford is a 30 year-old writer living in the Twin Cities with his wife, infant son, and two cats.

His stories have appeared in places like Bewildering Stories, Roadside Fiction, Roar & Thunder, the Glass Coin, Rose Red Review, and Inkspill Magazine.

He has seven other publications available on Kindle and in Paperback.

You can find out more about him on his website: http://www.troyblackford.com

Made in the USA
Lexington, KY
17 September 2016